The Opposite of a Psychopath

charles tyler

The Opposite of a Psychopath

charles tyler

This is an IndieMosh book

brought to you by MoshPit Publishing
an imprint of Mosher's Business Support Pty Ltd

PO Box 4363
Penrith NSW 2750

indiemosh.com.au

Copyright © Charles Tyler 2021

First Edition

Part I of III

theoppositeofapsychopath.com | charlestyler.com.au

 A catalogue record for this
work is available from the
National Library of Australia

NATIONAL
LIBRARY
OF AUSTRALIA

https://www.nla.gov.au/collections

Title: The Opposite of a Psychopath

Author: Tyler, Charles

ISBNs: 978-1-922628-48-0 (paperback)
             978-1-922628-49-7 (ebook – epub)
             978-1-922628-50-3 (ebook – Kindle)

Subjects: FICTION / Literary; General; Psychological; Family Life /
             Marriage & Divorce.

Cover design and layout by Charles Tyler
Cover image by Charles Tyler

Gratitudes

Thank you, Jen, Jasmine, and Julianne for helping me believe I could, and Bernadette, and Leeann for helping me believe I should. Thank you, Andrea, Elise, Fiona, Glenda, Liz, and Jenny for your guidance and notes.

For Ivy and Lenny

find your lightwork

Part I
The Opposite of a Psychopath

MMXXI

Chapter 1

I t was a sentence which made no sense, but still punched a fist-sized hole straight through me. I could feel my eyes darting about her face, searching for signs of what she really meant, but she gave nothing away. She was expressionless and for the first time in a long time, her eyes were dry. There were no tears rolling down her cheeks and she exhibited no emotion to signify she was experiencing the same torment she'd just unleashed on me. She was motionless too, and like a statue staring into the distance, her coldness was as tangible as the marble she might have been sculpted from.

We'd just touched down in Tokyo after a gruelling nine-hour flight from Melbourne. Even though we were travelling to Greece in six-weeks' time, I'd organised this short trip wholly for her. She'd wanted to visit Japan for all of the nine years we'd been together, but until now, we hadn't made it happen. She never really explained why she was so infatuated with

Japan, but I suspected it had something to do with her friends telling her she would be worshipped over here; with her heart-shaped face, porcelain-white skin, jet-black hair, small nose, and big eyes a bit-too-far-apart, making her appear as one of their manga or anime characters.

We used to travel often, but our trips had become sporadic; unintentionally, and subconsciously demoted on our list of priorities during the past few years. We went to Indonesia twelve months ago and to New Zealand the year before that, but our recent annual holidays were a far cry from the fortnightly adventures we'd once shared.

I'd surprised her with this trip to Tokyo a month ago by inscribing the details of our flights onto her birthday card. We'd always bought each other 'experiences' as gifts and this year was no different, even if a weekender to Japan was slightly more extravagant than our usual entry tickets to exhibitions or theatre performances.

She'd woken early that morning, rising well before me, and was already in our study when I'd tapped her lightly on the shoulder with the corner of the enveloped card.

"Happy Birthday," I whispered.

"Thanks," she replied.

She'd cocked her head casually to acknowledge my presence but when she saw the envelope through the corner of her eye, she swivelled around fully to face me.

"Ooh, for me?" she asked, snatching the envelope out of my hand, and tearing it open.

I watched in breathless anticipation as her eyes flicked

from left to right, left to right, scanning my scribbles, and absorbing the granted wish within.

"I don't understand." She sounded surprised, but not in the way I'd hoped she'd be. Her eyes were lowered and neither her face nor voice showed any signs she was about to realise a life-long dream.

"What do you mean?" I asked, my voice rising along with my eyebrows. I moved beside her so I could read the card myself, hoping I hadn't made a mistake in what I'd written.

"I don't understand why you've organised another trip. You know we're going to Greece soon." Her tone was reproachful, as if telling me off for doing something stupid.

I inhaled slowly and forced a smile back onto my face.

"This is for *your* birthday. I haven't taken you away for *your* birthday since Paris eight years ago, and Greece is for *my* fortieth, so it doesn't really count. This is for you!"

I hoped my light-heartedness would help her mood, but it didn't.

"But we were in the UK back then and Paris was only an hour away; Tokyo is what, like nine or ten hours away?"

"Nine," I interjected, not wanting her to overstate the travel time to something it wasn't.

"Nine then. It's not the same thing as a one-hour hop to Paris, and I can't keep taking time off work. I don't have that much leave and if I use it all now, I won't be able to go back to Perth to visit my parents for Christmas."

I won't be going back to Perth? I thought *we* were going to Perth!

5

Her eyes rose to meet mine. Her tone had evolved from reproach to annoyance.

I kept smiling, but my cheeks ached with artificiality.

"I know, but you'll only need to take a few days as the other two days are on the weekend."

"It's too much. You shouldn't have."

Even though I'd wanted her to jump up from her chair and throw her arms around me to lavish me with kisses, I'd subconsciously suspected it wasn't going to happen. Her reaction and rebuttals only served to consolidate my view that I *should* have, and that I probably *should* have planned this trip much earlier than I did.

"I'm sorry, I thought I was doing a good thing."

My voice quivered as I relaxed the muscles in my face.

"You've always wanted to go to Japan, and I thought this would be a dream come true for you. I thought it could be like one of the weekend adventures we used to have when we were living in Bristol. We always said we should keep doing those types of trips when we got back to Melbourne, but we never did."

She shifted uneasily in her chair and kept looking at me blankly. There was nothing behind her eyes, no warmth, no thanks, no gratitude, and certainly no memory of our adventures in Bristol.

"I'm just so busy with work, and I'm not sure I'll be able to enjoy it. Besides, I may need to go to Tokyo anyway in the next week or two ..."

Her voice trailed off and her eyes darted back to the card.

She'd caught herself out in a lie by omission, having not mentioned her business trip in any of our conversations until then.

I stepped back, as if knocked off balance.

"Sorry; *what*?! You've never mentioned that!"

Her face softened, and so did her tone, to something almost apologetic.

"Well, it's not for certain, and I only just found out. It's for a conference and one of the guys at work thought it would be good for me to go with him."

She was lying, I was sure. But I had no proof.

"What guy?"

She looked up and her expression hardened into anger – or was it disdain?

"You don't know him; he's in charge of innovation and strategy."

"So, you get the opportunity of a lifetime, to go somewhere you've always wanted to go, and you didn't think to tell me?"

As I uttered the words, I knew I'd been sucked into a vortex I didn't want to be in. None of this was going to plan.

She jammed her foot into the carpet and swivelled her chair to face her desk.

"It's no big deal and there was nothing to tell. It was mentioned in passing and it may come to nothing."

"But it's not nothing as you're using it as an excuse as to why you don't want us to go together."

"I'm not."

I inhaled again and took another step back.

"Well, I wish I'd known, that's all. What do you want me to do? Do you want to wait and see what happens with your work conference or do you want me to cancel this trip now?"

It had taken less than a minute for me to run out of puff. If she didn't want to go, she didn't want to go, and it made no sense for me to try and convince her otherwise.

The energy I'd had to persuade her into activities I thought were good for us had diminished during the past few years, and I'd been coaching myself to walk away from situations that didn't make any sense to me.

She swivelled her chair around to face me again.

"Is it refundable?"

The hint of hope in her voice knocked me back another step, forcing me into the doorway of the study.

"No, but I've only booked the flights."

She turned back to her laptop.

"No, don't cancel it. I'll work it out. But you haven't organised the accommodation yet?"

It was as if she was asking the question of a colleague on her screen. All business.

"No, not yet, just the flights." My voice had fallen back to a whisper; my excitement and anticipation transmuted to regret. I was tired and drained of energy.

"Can I do the accommodation then?" She'd tilted her face towards me, as if she were asking for something as mundane as a glass of water.

"Sure, if you like."

I spun around and stepped out of the room as quickly as I could, extricating myself from a gravitational pull much stronger than I was.

Her spark of interest in sorting out our accommodation was my consolation prize, but I knew she wasn't doing it for me, or for us. Her expectations of hotel luxury had surpassed mine over time, and I knew she no longer enjoyed the cheap and cheerful digs that were part and parcel of our previous travels, despite my preference to spend more on food and experiences than on where we slept.

It was another small area of our lives where we'd once been the same but were now divergent.

On the night before our flight, she crept into our dining room where I was brushing up on some basic Japanese pleasantries, *kon-nee-chee-wah*, 'hello'; *sy-on-ara*, 'goodbye'; *ary-gatto*, 'thank you'. She looked worried and unwell, and much the same as she'd looked for way too long now.

"I don't want to go," she announced from the doorway.

"Go where?" I responded without paying much attention.

"I don't want to go tomorrow … to Tokyo."

What the fuck?!

This time it was me spinning around in my chair to face her, my thoughts chaotic.

I thought we'd been through all this. You've got the time off, you've organised the accommodation, and we leave in twenty-four hours. You've hounded me to go to Japan for

9

our whole relationship, and now that we're just about leave, you don't want to go?! Tokyo is the place that you've wanted to visit forever; and a place that I couldn't care less about. I'm doing this for you, not for me!

During our time together, we'd never raised our voices or sworn at each other in anger; and whilst I was tempted to break the rules, I wasn't going to start then. My gaze was fixed to hers and the stoic armour I'd worn throughout my whole life would have never betrayed my internal rant. Suppressing my true feelings and nullifying my expression were skills I'd been mastering for a long time.

"What's going on?" I asked, gesturing for her to come closer and to sit on my lap.

She looked as if she was going to be sick.

"You know …" she paused. "Well, you know how I don't deal well with jetlag … I don't feel up to putting myself through that awful feeling again. It just takes me too long to recover. I don't think I want to go."

I put my arm around her and drew her close.

"Jetlag? You don't want to go because of *jetlag*?"

"Yep, you know I can't handle it."

"Tokyo is in the same time zone as Melbourne and it's an overnight flight so we can get some sleep on the way and wake up ready to go. It's not the same twenty-four hours that normally causes your terrible jetlag. I do know how you suffer, which is why we haven't done a long haul since—" I scanned my memory— "since Italy five years ago. It's not that much further than Bali and you've been okay on those flights.

You'll be fine. You've been stressed with work and this will be a really good break for you; and for us. Besides, your conference was a non-starter in the end, and you've wanted to visit Tokyo for-ev-er. This is a dream of yours! You'll feel so much better for being there, but, if you're really not up to it tomorrow, then we won't go."

I wasn't sure who I was trying to convince more, and by the time I'd finished my spiel, she was crying. It seemed to be commonplace for her to cry these days, but something about those tears felt different.

I took a deep breath, not wanting to ask the question I knew I had to ask next. "What's *really* going on?"

She turned to stare at me and for the briefest of moments I thought she was going to tell me the truth. But then: "You're right. It will be fine. I just needed to get that out. I'll be fine. It will be good."

And that was it. She'd reeled off five lies in three seconds and as she finished, she jumped off my lap and scampered out of the dining room without a backwards glance.

For a split-second, I thought about chasing after her, but instead I shook my head in disbelief and turned my attention back to rehearsing Japanese pleasantries and to pretend that whatever had just happened, hadn't. It was a habit I wasn't proud of, but one I'd been practising for far too long.

She had a full day of work the next day whereas I had the day off to prepare and get ready. It was the perfect situation as I didn't need to deliberately avoid her and the possibility of

11

another request to cancel the trip. She'd half packed her bag before leaving for the office that morning and to my relief, completed the job when she returned home that evening. We ate our dinner in relative silence before clearing up, calling a taxi, and departing for the airport.

Our overnight flight had been as bad as she'd expected, and worse than I had hoped. In honesty, I'm not sure anyone ever gets a good night's sleep on a plane and we certainly hadn't. I'd donned my eye mask and pulled my blanket up to my neck whilst we were still on the tarmac in Melbourne. Ignoring the meal service, I pretended to sleep until the captain announced she was preparing to land. My theory was that pretend sleep would mimic the effects of real sleep, but the jury was still out on the benefits. I was committed to trying though, whereas she'd long since given up on the charade of closing her eyes, instead choosing to watch whatever was on her impossibly small TV screen. Not that any of it mattered, as the results for both of us were the same. We'd arrived in the cavernous and brightly lit Narita Airport tired and terse.

Thankfully, our disembarkation and progress through passport control were handled with admirable efficiency and did nothing to exacerbate our foul tempers. I was happy to ignore our moods and to trust in our regular post-long-haul-flight routine to fix us like it always had; a shower, a coffee, and an exploratory walk around a new city. They were our magical cures, and we were less than an hour away from all three.

We caught the N'EX train from the airport to Tokyo Central Station as the boutique accommodation she had chosen was adjacent to its concourse. We should have hailed a taxi as it would have been quicker and cheaper, but our lack of sleep had already affected our decision making.

We entered the hotel via a secret door in the corner of the station's enormous internal hall and waited in line at the front desk. As we were called forward, I handed over our passports knowing we were just minutes away from our resurrection, and the commencement of our new adventure.

"*Ohayou gozaimasu*, good morning, welcome!" The man behind the counter looked fresh and brand new. His hair was perfect, his face chiselled, and his shirt and black suit were flawlessly pressed without a single speck of dust or lint in sight. His lapel pin with two golden crossed keys informed us that this guy was at the very top of his game, a member of that exclusive global club for concierges, *Les Clefs d'Or*.

"*Kon-nee-chee-wah*, thanks for having us." I handed him our passports, looking, and feeling the opposite of his perfection.

"I see here you are staying with us for three nights."

"Yes, that's right."

He tapped away on his keyboard, his eyes scanning his screen for something that clearly wasn't there. My thoughts spiralled, panic rising.

Shit! Please, please have our reservation!

He breathed in slowly, his too-perfect jaw clenching in a slight show of embarrassment. "My apologies, sir, madam, our previous night's guests are still in your room and it will not be ready until 2:00pm."

I glanced at my phone and imitated his slow inhale. 10.09am.

Fuck me. Now what?

"Is there another room?"

"I am afraid not. We are fully booked this weekend as it is the start of summer holidays."

"Is there a place where we can have a shower and get cleaned up?"

"I am sorry, no. You are welcome to leave your bags with us, though. And to use our restaurant if you like? I am really sorry about the inconvenience."

I stepped back from the counter, pulling her gently with me.

"What do you want to do?" I strained to eliminate any sign of disappointment from my face or voice.

She shrugged with the enthusiasm of someone who'd forgotten to organise an early check-in and didn't want to be where she was.

"Do you want to kill four hours here or do you want to have a walk around?"

"I don't mind," was her similarly unenthusiastic reply.

I turned back to the concierge and checked our luggage in, pocketing a complimentary map from the countertop at the same time. The shower I was so desperate for was going to have to wait a little longer.

Mr. Perfect bowed as he handed me back our passports. *Les Clefs d'Or, my arse.* I bowed back, and he bowed again; causing me to again return serve. I wasn't sure how many bows were polite and how many were ridiculous, so I backed away and turned around with my best version of *ary-gatto, sy-on-ara.*

I led the way out of the hotel and into Tokyo proper for the first time since arriving. We'd spent the entire morning indoors and underground, and whilst I'd known we were travelling from our winter to their summer, the blast of the open air was completely unexpected. The heat of the day engulfed us like wildfire, and the air's heaviness was drenching and suffocating. I dared not look her way as she'd recently made it painfully clear that she hated the heat and more than that, humidity.

Our past travels had always been based on the slower pace of pedestrian exploration, and our plan for Tokyo was the same. We loved walking and we used our rambling as an opportunity to see the unseen and to experience a city's true grit. We'd done most of our previous travelling in cooler months and I hadn't realised she disliked the warmth so much until our recent trip to Bali.

Whilst there she'd become visibly uncomfortable, and once the temperature passed twenty-five degrees, she became irritable and impatient. She'd tried carrying a parasol and walking in the shade of buildings but in the end, she raised her white flag, refusing to leave our villa until after sunset.

I should have known that walking through Tokyo on a day like today after a night like our night was going to go badly. Just how badly, I was about to find out.

The area outside the hotel was a huge pedestrian plaza, maybe one-hundred metres long by one-hundred and fifty metres wide. It was mostly vacant except for two rectangles of perfectly manicured lawn, roped off to prevent people from trampling the grass. To the left and the right of us were boxy skyscrapers of varying heights, with two others in front of us, standing like sentinels guarding Gyoko-dori Avenue.

We checked our map for somewhere to start our impromptu exploration and found that the Imperial Palace Gardens were a short half a kilometre walk away.

"Let's try here," I said pointing to the green patch on the map. "Maybe it will be a traditional Japanese garden with trees and shade; cooler than here, anyway. And maybe there will be a café along the way."

"Sure," she replied, still looking as though she'd rather be anywhere than where she was.

My hopeful presumptions were wrong; there were no cafes along the way, and green on the map didn't mean green in real life. The gardens weren't *gardens*, at least not in the way we wanted them to be. There was no accessible lawn, very few trees, little shade, and no view of the Imperial Palace. There were no Japanese maples and no koi ponds, and the gardens completely lacked the cool, calm respite we were seeking. The industrial hum of the city surrounded us, and the sun's radiating heat from the gravel underfoot had become as intense as its rays from above.

We'd been out for less than half an hour and our clothes had already become pasted to us like wet rags. We'd dressed for a winter night flight and not for a summer day walking outdoors, and our jeans and long-sleeved tops were as out of place in this city as we were. Our enthusiasm for the Imperial Gardens had waned before it had waxed, and we'd fast reached our thresholds for discomfort.

"I can't do this anymore," she said, with resignation.

I wiped the sweat off my face with the palm of my hand, "Me neither. We need to get out of this heat."

We spun on our heels and retraced our steps. I assumed we were heading back to the hotel lobby but as we got closer, she spotted a five-storey cream coloured building to the south of where we were staying.

"There! Let's go there," she said pointing. "It looks like a mall."

Please be a mall!

A mall would provide solutions to our three most immediate problems; it would be air conditioned; it would have coffee; and best of all – it would have shops. Surely her love of shopping would temporarily distract her from our current discomfort.

We turned towards the gleaming block and as we approached the mall's curved faux-art-deco entrance our legs pumped a little faster in anticipation. The automatic glass sliding doors saw us coming and opened with perfect timing. Once inside, the relief was instant. We slowed to a stop, much in the same way an athlete slows down after they've passed the finish line.

As we enjoyed the mall's cooling embrace and surveyed our sanctuary for the remainder of the morning, I couldn't help but cringe at the irony of the past twelve hours. I thought I'd be doing a good thing whisking her away from our normal life to a place she'd always wanted to go; but it now seemed all I'd really done was make things worse.

We found a nondescript timber-slatted café which wouldn't have looked out of place in a Melbourne laneway, and with coffees in hand, ambled around the multiple levels of the mall with the expressed aim of killing as much time as possible. It was ghostly quiet, as though we had the entire building to ourselves. She drifted in and out of the exclusive boutiques, whereas I was content to glide past them. She loved high-end everything and enjoyed the experience of buying something expensive more than she enjoyed the item she was buying. She also had a talent for feigning interest in whatever wares were being spruiked, as well as a standard spiel for promising to be back. I watched her from a distance and wondered why she bothered wasting her energy with her repeat performance. It wasn't as though we were going to be back to see any of these people again.

After a few hours of silent and mindless meandering, we reached the topmost level of the mall and the end of the shopping precinct. Our refuge had cooled us down, but it had failed to dry us off and our icy damp clothes had become as intolerable as the heat and humidity that had made them that way earlier.

"What's that?" she asked pointing to a glass door in the distance.

"Not sure …" I started, before realising her question was rhetorical and she'd already walked off to find out.

I chased after her and as she pushed the door open, we were again confronted by the heat outside. She'd accidentally stumbled upon a rooftop terrace garden, and even though we weren't sure if it was public or private, we ventured outwards, embracing the feeling of warmth as vigorously as we'd tried to escape it earlier.

Like almost everything else we'd seen that morning, all in front of us appeared shiny and new. Triangular areas of grass were hedged by perfectly manicured bushes; decking was interlaced with paving, and paths seamlessly morphed into bench seats. It wasn't a large area and we saw all of it in a few minutes before finding a private alcove to take a seat in the same silence we'd become accustomed to.

As I sat with my eyes closed, absorbing the sun's rays to dry me off, she broke our quiet with that most clichéd of clichés.

"We need to talk."

I opened my eyes to look at her, but she was staring past me.

"I know we do," I replied, turning around to look at whatever had her transfixed, but could see nothing. "I've been waiting for this."

"You have?!" She sounded surprised, her eyes flicking to meet mine, before returning to their previous gaze over my shoulder.

"Yes."

I'm not sure why I responded in that way or why I'd chosen to use those words; they seemed to flow from me without conscious thought. I knew we needed to talk because we hadn't done so for way too long, at least not properly, and with no meaningful depth. I'd always thought we were the best of communicators, but now we seemed to be the worst, moving through the past year or two on cruise-control, coasting along day to day, playing nice with each other, and not doing anything to rock our boat.

I reacted instinctively as I'd done for of most of my life, shutting out what was going on before me, disappearing into the depths of my own mind. My brain was feverishly making connections, recalling, and analysing the details and timelines that had led me to this place, hearing four words no one ever wants to hear: *we need to talk.*

She spoke, breaking my train of thought and yanking me out of my subconscious. "I think I want to be on my own."

I found it an odd thing to say as she'd just had three hours to be on her own, and in actual fact, had already spent most of her morning that way.

"Okay, but can we check into the hotel first, get freshened up and then head out to do our own things?"

"No, I think that I want to be by *myself,*" she said, attempting to clarify, still looking past me.

Clearly, I wasn't getting something here. I tried again.

"Um, yep, that's what I mean." I leant forward to try to meet her gaze. "Let's check into the hotel, get cleaned up, have a shower and then you or I can head out."

She rocked back slightly, and as she did, she put her hands under her legs. "No, you don't understand. I think I want to *be* on my own!"

I put the brakes on my eyeballs rolling into my head. I couldn't understand why she was sending me away when we were so close to check in. I desperately needed a shower and needed to get changed into more climate-appropriate clothing.

"You mean right now?" I asked, trying to help her out.

"No, you still don't understand." Her eyes were still fixed on the view in the distance.

"No, no I don't."

"I want to live on my own!" she exclaimed.

Huh?

I suddenly lost sense of the connection between my body and where I was sitting. It was as though the concrete from the path below had risen through the soles of my feet and into my calves, fusing my shoes to the ground, preventing my legs from moving.

What the fuck?! Where was this coming from?!

I could feel a fire rising through my chest and into my neck, burning through my skin to the core within. My stomach was churning, and the void caused by her punching words remained just below my sternum. A golf ball-sized lump rose into my throat, corking anything that wanted to spew out. Her words evoked an instant, unrecognisable chaos within me.

Where did she want to go? Or, where did she want me to go? What was going on? If we just needed to talk, why was she starting with the end, rather than with the beginning?

I drew a deep breath and swallowed. "You're right, I don't understand."

It was the only truth I was brave enough to say out loud.

"Neither do I, but I think I want to live on my own; I don't know." She started rocking slowly backwards and forwards on her hands, shrinking into herself, possibly regretting what she'd just said.

"You think, but you don't know? I knew something was up and I knew we needed to talk but I really don't get what you're on about. Where is this this coming from." My eyes were locked onto hers, but she kept her gaze averted.

"It's just the way I've been feeling for a while."

"How long?" I asked, like it mattered.

"I don't know … a while."

If she wanted to shake me to my core, she'd succeeded. My mind was racing through my memories, and I started to feel like she'd set me up. She'd known something wasn't right the night before last when she told me that she didn't want to come here. She'd made up some cock and bull story about jetlag when she'd known it was something more. I knew she hadn't been herself and I hoped she didn't know what she was saying. I'd let it all go for too long and I'd let her reach the depths she was now plumbing. The past twelve hours had broken her, and it was my fault for pushing her to this brink.

"I just need some space," she continued, again snapping me out of my head and back into this unwelcome reality. Her voice remained quiet and calm, possibly in the hope that I would do the same. It worked. I spoke quietly:

"Okay; but needing space and living on your own are two very different things."

"I know, but it's just the way I've been feeling, and I don't know what it means." She glanced my way, a split second of eye contact before looking away again, obviously seeing something on my face she didn't like or expect.

"I don't know what I'm saying!" She sounded exasperated, as if she'd envisaged me having a different reaction.

She stood up and shook her head and walked off towards the doorway we'd only just come through.

I broke my imaginary shackles and got up as fast as I could, following her back into the icy mall.

As she led the way to the hotel, I stayed one step behind her. It was where I truly felt I belonged. The hot and humid air around me seemed thick with confusion and unknowing. My mouth was dry and my breathing shallow. I was sucked into another one of her vortexes; except this time, it felt physical. I could clearly see the back of her short black hair and the red bricks of our hotel, but everything else around us was a swirling blur of noise and colour.

My tunnel-vision nauseated me and for the first time in a long time, I had no idea what to think or say. My psychological comfort zone was being challenged like never before. Were we in the midst of a hypothetical conversation or was all of this real? Did she want her own space to get herself right so we could stay together or was this the start of our end?

They were questions I didn't want to ask for fear of the answers, so I did the only thing I knew how to do and remained silent.

I wished we were back in Melbourne, and not wasting time and money in a place neither of us wanted to be. The discomfort of this city was intensifying the tension between us and I wanted to be somewhere safe and normal, and where things made sense.

We arrived at our hotel within minutes and after several heartfelt apologies for sending us away, the concierge we'd met earlier checked us in and handed us our room key. We'd been awake for the best part of thirty hours and I was feeling the effects of sleep deprivation, dehydration, and the newly created feeling of impending doom.

The ride in the elevator took longer than it should have and the walk down the ridiculously long carpeted corridor felt like traversing the green mile. Room 108 was near its end; as she inserted the key and opened the door, a rush of cool air wafted over us. We entered quickly and closed the door behind us to preserve the temperature that had been thought-fully pre-set.

For a split second, I forgot all that had just happened.

"Wow, this is beautiful; you've outdone yourself."

She'd booked us into a junior suite of sorts with a small study area and a bathroom almost as big as the bedroom. It was all white and looked straight out of the pages of an interiors' magazine; furnished with expensive looking fittings and fixtures in silver, bronze, and metallic grey. The bed was a massive super-king, draped in the type of luxurious linen that promised to caress our skin and swallow us whole.

We dropped our bags and started to undress in our race to wash away the horror of everything that had just happened. Showering together was something we did on most days and even though the past twenty minutes had taken an unexpected turn, I still assumed we'd continue to do what we'd always done.

After removing her shoes and socks, she jumped backwards onto the bed, bouncing herself closer to the ivory velvet-covered headboard. She crossed her legs and picked up a magazine resting on the bedside table near her. "You go first, I'll wait."

"Are you sure?" My response was a reflex, an attempt to mask my disappointment.

"Yes, you go."

Fuck.

I shouldn't have been surprised but I was. Her recent declaration on the rooftop was spilling into her subsequent actions, and I hated that she was being consistent in this.

It had always been easy for me until now to discount what she said if her actions were contrary to her words, and her actions were usually contrary. It was obvious she was still processing our earlier conversation whereas I was desperately trying to pretend it had never happened.

25

I stepped into the oversized stone-tiled shower and adjusted the settings until I found one simulating a downpour of rain. I raised my eyes to the showerhead and let the multiple streams of water hit me square in the face. The fat droplets smashed into my forehead, bombarding me in the exact way I needed them to, cleansing my thoughts and washing away my morning. I scrubbed myself raw and as I moved out of the shower to dry myself off, I prayed that my day had been reset.

After she'd finished using the bathroom, we lay on the bed together in our clean and more suitable clothing, acclimatising to the comfort that had eluded us all morning. I was enjoying being horizontal and weightless, and more than anything, I was enjoying being cool.

Feeling rejuvenated, I rolled over to kiss her.

She received it without reciprocation, her narrowed eyes and pursing lips an unwelcome return to the reality I'd tried to ignore. I rolled back and held my breath to stifle my sigh.

For our entire time together, I'd known what to say and do in any situation, instinctively knowing how to best support her, but this was something new.

We'd always done everything together; it was how she wanted it. From the very start, she'd made me promise to stay by her side, regardless of what life threw at us.

"Promise to never leave me," she'd recite almost daily.

"I promise," was my rote-reply.

"Promise me that we'll always work through anything."

"I promise."

Did these promises still hold true? And if they did, did they apply to both of us, or just to her? Did she want me to leave to give her the space that she'd asked for this morning, or would she hate me for leaving her alone during a moment of crisis? Did she want me to stick around to continue the conversation we'd only just started, or would she eviscerate me for not listening to her demand to be alone?

I was stumped, genuinely at a loss, not knowing what she wanted me to do, but more than that, not wanting to ask her. My fear of her possible answers still outweighed the discomfort of not knowing.

It was a lose-lose situation and the only thing I could do was something. Anything was better than nothing.

I rocked myself off the bed to put my shoes on and to get ready to leave.

She propped herself up on her elbow. "Are you heading out?" The quizzical nature of her tone was neither pleased nor displeased and provided me with no insight into whether I'd made the right or wrong decision.

"Yep, I think so." I didn't look up and continued to tie my laces.

"Where?" she asked, raising herself to a seated position.

I stood up and faced her. "Into Shibuya I guess."

She sprung off the bed and made her way back into the bathroom, presumably to cry. She reserved bathrooms for most of her *secret* crying.

I picked up my phone and wallet from the dresser where

I'd dropped them earlier, and as I opened my mouth to say goodbye, she called out.

"Give me five minutes to get ready."

I raised my eyes to the ceiling and my whole body relaxed in relief, like one large uncoiling spring. We had the opportunity to start the day afresh.

This nightmare was over, and the holy trinity of a shower, coffee, and exploratory walk had worked its magic on her jetlag again, just like it always did.

I fell backward onto the bed as if falling backwards into a pool, immersing myself in waves of calm, comfort, and assurance. I would have raised my arms above my head and screamed 'YES!' if I were that sort of person, and if she wasn't within earshot. Surely, it was a sign that she didn't really want to be on her own; and more than that, she still wanted us to be together.

Chapter 2

We left the hotel via the same secret door we'd arrived through and navigated the brightly lit signboards and brushed aluminium ticket machines of Tokyo Central Station, boarding a red-M-Line heading west. The train wasn't as busy as I imagined, and even though all the hard-plastic seats were taken, we weren't crushed into the carriage like sardines.

The journey to Shibuya was blissfully civilised and more than that, it was unusually quiet. Our fellow commuters kept to themselves like introverted strangers, and even groups of families and friends refrained from unnecessary movement or conversation. Of the people I could see, none were eating or drinking, or talking on their phones or listening to music through headphones or earbuds. The peace and quiet was perfect, and it was still easy for us to comply.

Between the panics on her birthday and the night before last, she'd been interested enough in our holiday to Tokyo to have organised our itinerary for the entire trip. Mornings, afternoons, and evenings – she'd scheduled us to be going somewhere or doing something in each segment of each day.

I was happy to tag along to wherever she wanted to go as I knew she'd take us to all the cool places in Tokyo. She was an excellent researcher and had a knack for unearthing hidden gems through unconventional means. She'd once used a random cheap-eats blog as the basis for a week we did in Manhattan; and we experienced more *real life* during that holiday than any other before it. She'd lined up a succession of breakfasts, lunches, and dinners in cafés, bistros, and restaurants that tempted us off the beaten track and into the local NYC neighbourhoods. Her ideas fitted with our desire to walk everywhere and for us to experience life as the locals did. She called her itineraries must-maps, and she'd put one together for our few days in Tokyo.

We changed trains at Akasaka-Mitsuke using the metro's intuitive platform colour-coding and arrived in Shibuya three stops later. The train's air-conditioning had offered us a false sense of comfort and our return to the open air saw us once again smothered by the day's heat and humidity.

The first item on our must-map was the Shibuya Scramble Crossing, and as we walked towards it, she again broke our silence.

"This is the Times Square of Tokyo and one of the busiest pedestrian crossings in the world."

I looked up and around, hoping to be as awestruck as I

was when I first saw New York's Times Square, but I wasn't. It didn't seem as high or as imposing, or as crammed with screens and billboards as the Manhattan version, and the lights and colours didn't look anywhere near as vibrant.

"Maybe it will be better at night," I whispered to myself.

"Huh?" she replied, pointing to a vacant spot on the station's forecourt. "Let's stand over there to watch it; I want to see the crowds from a distance."

Regardless of its lacklustre appearance, the Shibuya Scramble Crossing was the busiest pedestrian crossing I'd seen. At each green signal, thousands of pedestrians crisscrossed the square in ten different directions across ten lanes of traffic, scurrying at various speeds to get to where they were going. Their movements reminded me of the insides of a perfectly engineered machine; with its thousands of well-oiled parts moving freely, without incident and without obstruction.

After watching the sequence repeating itself several times, she nodded her head my way to let me know it was time for us to cross the road to get to the other side and to experience the pandemonium for ourselves. We approached our starting position with hundreds of others and as the red lights turned green, I stepped off the gutter and into what felt like a swarm of angry bees. I was engulfed by people from every direction, stepping left, and right, backwards, and forwards, ducking, and weaving around them with my arms and hands flailing wherever there was space. Within seconds, I'd lost my course and couldn't be sure if I was still crossing the road or if I was heading back in the direction I'd come

31

from. Worse still, I couldn't see where she was or if we were going to end up in the same place.

Lagging behind the crowd, I stepped up onto the safety of what I hoped was the other side of the intersection and scanned through the crowds to see where she might be. There was no sight of her anywhere near me, but as I widened the search, I spotted her about fifty metres away, standing on the opposite corner to the one I was on. She gestured for me to join her, and as I waited for the pedestrian lights to change colour again, Shibuya's thinly veiled metaphor sent a shiver down my spine.

Just now, I'd been trying to avoid being bowled over by the hundreds of oncoming pedestrians, and I'd been doing the same with the barrage of thoughts and ideas about what she'd said to me earlier this morning. I was still confused by her statements about wanting to *live on her own* and I still wanted to know what she really meant. My mind was the scramble, and no matter how much I tried to ignore it, I couldn't help but feel I was going to end up somewhere different to where I'd intended to go.

"Coffee?" she asked, as I arrived by her side.

"Sounds good," I replied reflexively, still processing my mini epiphany and working out what I was supposed to do with it.

I didn't need another coffee, but I did need to stay comfortably by her side to do whatever it was she wanted to do next.

We walked away from the intersection, but she stopped us in a quiet space about one-hundred metres from where we'd started. "It's going to be a bit of a treasure hunt," she announced. "All the blogs have said this place has Tokyo's best coffee but that it's really hard to find. It's in the backstreets not far from here and apparently the café is located behind someone's house."

She showed me a screenshot of a map on her phone, and quickly swiped through a few photos to give me an idea of what we'd be looking for. Our target was Omotesando Koffee, a tiny minimalist cube of a café which looked more like a small shipping container than anything else.

She put the address into her phone, and we ventured forward, away from the crowds and away from the untidy chaos.

Residential Shibuya felt like residential anywhere; crisscrossed by narrow streets, narrower footpaths, and a baffling number of black overhead power cables. The area seemed rundown and was mostly made up of single and double-storey houses with the odd block of flats crammed in between them. Patches of unkempt greenery and an array of tropical vines gave the urban landscape a modicum of life.

As we were still close to Shibuya station and the *Times Square* retail district, I couldn't help but be surprised at the lack of gentrification.

"I imagine this will all be high-rises soon enough," I commented.

"Huh?" she replied, jolting herself to a stop just in time to avoid a lamppost. Her eyes lifted from her phone screen to glare at me for interrupting her concentration, and possibly to scold me for putting the lamppost in her way.

"Never mind."

We didn't expect our mission to be easy and it wasn't. There was no café at the listed address, nor in the place where her phone's blue dot converged with the red pin.

Regardless, we continued to zigzag our way across each of the nearby streets, hoping to find a sign or visual matching the images on the internet. As we crossed from one side of the road to the other, and back again, we spotted several other non-Japanese couples, most likely looking for the same place. Phones in hand, they too were walking in one direction before doubling back in the other. We nodded politely and smiled as we passed them, keeping our missions to ourselves. The café was supposed to be tiny, and she'd told me it could hold very few patrons. They were our competition, and we were now theirs.

The first hour of seeing the previously unseen and experiencing Tokyo's true grit was fun and enjoyable, as was the novelty of exploring a suburbia we would never have seen if we'd stuck to the main tourist attractions; however, by the sixty-first minute I'd lost interest in our quest and was hoping she had too.

We passed the same houses and same streets, and whilst we continued to wish to see something different in all the places we'd already been, we never did.

I reached for her hand to bring us to a standstill at a crossroad we'd previously walked through three times.

"Are you happy to keep looking?"

"Maybe it's closed," she replied. "Or maybe it doesn't exist anymore."

I crouched down and leant against a fence to take some pressure off my lower back, shielding my eyes from the sun to look up at her. "Let's try and find somewhere else close by. I'd still really like a coffee." I didn't, but after all the time we'd spent looking for one, I thought we may as well complete the task and reap the reward.

She stayed standing above me, swivelling her head around like a meerkat searching for something she'd missed. Her position above me supplied me with a sliver of shade, but not enough to provide any respite from the heat which was still radiating from every direction. As she lifted her phone closer to her face to check and recheck the address, a thatched panel in a residential timber fence across the road from us slid back, and two people walked out of a yard and onto the street. I tapped her on the calf and pointed; and as they moved out of the doorway and closed the panel behind them, we caught a glimpse of the café cube structure we'd been searching for. *The bastard was here all along!*

We crossed the street quickly and stepped through the doorway, sliding the panel shut behind us to protect its secret.

The premises were small, but not as small as the internet had led her to believe. There was space for two or three people in the cafe cube to our right, and maybe five or six others in the courtyard to our left; four of which were already taken by two couples we'd seen earlier. A tall maple stood at the rear of the property, casting a cooling shadow over the entire area. As I wondered whether the tree would still be called a *Japanese* maple, the scent of freshly ground coffee beans floated through my nostrils, activating the tastebuds on the back of my tongue.

I turned to face the café, jarred by how out of place it looked amongst everything around it. It was the embodiment of minimalist design; a cube within a cube occupying a section of the ground level of an old yellowish rendered two-storey house. The café area was a genuine cube: as high as it was wide and deep, and was lined in bright white plaster with black borders, as if to mimic the interior of a paper lantern. A second open cube was contained within the lantern cube, and in its centre was an elegantly dressed barista and all his tools and ingredients. He bowed to greet us and waved his hand at the coffee menu – a single A5-sized card sitting on top of the plywood bench separating us.

The menu detailed different coffee-making techniques, as well as descriptions of coffee beans of varying origins. Cold brews, slow drips, plunger, press, pour overs, and machine-made; Ethiopian, Guatemalan, Indonesian, Vietnamese, Colombian, Honduran and Ugandan, house blend, single origin or multiple, or a combination, blended in whatever ratio the coffee connoisseur might desire.

The menu was wasted on us as we were no experts, and our habits focussed on the basics.

"A house caffe latte, please," she requested, ordering for herself.

"Make that two, please."

We'd once made the mistake of ordering lattes in Italy and after being served two glasses of milk, we'd been conscious not to leave the word *caffe* out of our orders.

The elegant man clad head to toe in grey linen made our coffees one at a time and with the greatest of care. He took his craft seriously and didn't look like someone interested in small talk, particularly about how impossible his café was to find. We watched him intently, and without interruption, startled into momentary surprise when, as he finished pouring the warm milk into the syrup-like coffee with an artistic flourish, he then picked up the glass and unceremoniously poured its entire contents down the sink near the machine. He'd clearly seen something he didn't like the look of, even though we couldn't have cared less.

His second attempt passed his stringent quality assurance standards, and he presented his creation like a precious jewel, spinning the glass slowly to face her in the precise direction he wanted it received.

She accepted it with a 'thank you' rather than an 'ary-gatto' and stepped into the garden to drink it. I tracked her out of the cube with my eyes, hoping she'd take more time to drink her caffe latte than it took him to make.

He followed the same process for my coffee, although he didn't spin the glass with the same pomp he'd used to present hers. Perhaps there was a benefit to looking like a gorgeous character from an anime cartoon in Japan, after all.

I cupped my glass in both hands and bowed and
'arigato'd', before venturing out to join her. As I got closer, she
looked up, her gaze strangely hostile, as if I'd invaded her
privacy. She huffed, and marched past me to return to the cube.

What now?

I didn't react and did my best to pretend like nothing
weird happened, walking to the place she'd been standing. I
faced the fence and took my first sip of *Tokyo's best coffee*,
thankful no one could see my distorted facial expression as I
did. The brew was strong, and the tastes and flavours were far
too intense and complex for my simple palate. I could hazard
a guess it was *good* coffee as there was no bitterness or burnt
aftertaste, but it just wasn't to my liking. I wouldn't be coming
back for more.

After a minute or two and a few more forced sips, I
plucked up the courage to turn around to see where she was
and what she was doing.

She was behind the coffee machine with what looked like
a second coffee, in a cup rather than a glass. She was taking
photos of the barista and his surrounds, pacing backward and
forward beside the counter, holding her phone at odd angles,
trying to get that one single inimitable artistic shot.

I really hope you asked for his permission first.

I stepped back into the cube to put my half-empty glass
back on the counter. She saw me coming and put her phone
down to resume the glare she'd started a few minutes earlier.
I stopped dead, prepared to throw myself into reverse and
remedy whatever mistake I'd just made.

"Have you posted this on your socials?" she asked in a deeper-than-normal voice.

It seemed an odd request as she knew I didn't have a Japanese SIM card, and also knew I rarely used social media for anything.

"No," I replied, confused at her ongoing hostility.

"Well, don't," she commanded. "Don't include me in your posts whilst we're here and don't tag me in any of your photos."

I kept my face expressionless to hide my bewilderment. Her words made no sense. Was this an honest request or a deliberate attempt to unsettle me even further? I hated social media and only kept an account for my fledgling art gallery business. Why didn't she want anyone to know she was here? Hadn't she told her colleagues she was here; or maybe she hadn't told her boss? Perhaps she'd done something shifty and taken these few days off sick, rather than as planned leave?

There were so many possibilities for the intentions behind the words, and my brain couldn't help but descend back into its scrambled state, zipping through each one of them at warp speed. I was too taken aback to ask her what she meant, the only word spilling from my mouth was:

"Okay."

We were back on the mall's rooftop, her new commands whirling like razor blades in my mind.

Silent again after her brief outburst, she turned away to resume her photography and I turned back into the courtyard, my glass still clutched in my hand.

The four strangers seated there looked up at me from their seats with curiosity and mild confusion; or perhaps they were simply reflecting my own feelings. Like me, they were probably trying to work out the story of what was going on between us.

When she'd finished her second coffee, she thanked the barista, and came out to join me.

"Ready?" she asked, like nothing weird was going on.

I wasn't sure if our must-map itinerary still applied or if we were going to do something different. "Ready for what? Do you still want to go to the Meiji shrine?"

"Of course! Why not?" she replied, impatiently. "Don't *you*?"

I could feel the energy draining out of me onto the paving in the courtyard. I no longer cared about the shrine, Tokyo, or what was next on our itinerary. Right now, all I wanted to do was to go to back to the hotel, fall asleep and wake up from whatever perverse nightmare this was.

"Yes, I was just checking that you did."

I tipped the remainder of my cold coffee into a bush near the fence and delivered the empty glass back to the cube, I paid the barista with a bow, and returned to the courtyard in time for her to lead the way out through the same hidden sliding fence-door we'd used to arrive.

Two girls were standing on the same street corner we were on earlier, both with their phones in hand and looking as defeated as we had been before the magic door had slid open. I lingered in the doorway and stalled closing it until I'd made eye-contact with them and they'd been able to see what was hidden behind it.

"*Eccolo, eccolo!*" one of them yelled in an Italian accent whilst pointing our way.

I smiled, and left the door open for them, assuming that *eccolo* meant something like 'there it is' and feeling good that I was able to contribute to someone's happiness this afternoon.

We ambled through the laneways and eclectic shopfronts of Harajuku en route to the Meiji Jingu shrine, together but apart. We hadn't held hands for the entire day, and worse than that, the overly narrow footpaths were forcing us to walk in tandem or on different sides of the streets to stay out the way of vehicles. I could feel her stoniness had returned and that the distance between us was becoming even greater.

As she'd done in the mall earlier, she drifted in and out of the stores she was interested in without a sideways glance or gesture to let me know what she was doing or where she was going. After the third or fourth time, I stopped following her and stayed my course, preferring to observe from a distance.

She looked different to how'd I previously seen her, like a cat let outdoors for the first time, tentatively experiencing her unfamiliar environment with caution and bewilderment. She floated in and out of doorways, and I half expected to see her purr as she brushed her back past the architraves.

Something had shifted, but I couldn't work out what it was, only that before she'd always wanted me by her side, but now she didn't. She'd always told me she wanted us to experience things together, but now she'd become content to lose herself in herself, regardless of where she was. Fashion stores, sneaker stores, perfume stores, stores selling soap, jewellery, model planes, dreamcatchers, and kites; she visited them all and didn't once look my way to check in on me, or to see if I was still there. She left it to me to keep us visually tethered; mine was the responsibility to prevent either of us from losing sight of each other, or becoming estranged.

After an hour of wasted time, we arrived at our third must-map destination.

A giant 1500-year-old cypress torii gate stood at the entrance to a forest of soaring trees, an emerald-green woodland as incongruent in central Tokyo as the Omotesando Koffee cube had been in that old yellow house.

As we progressed inwards towards Meiji Jingu, the sights and sounds of industrial Tokyo disappeared behind us, drifting into the music of birdsong and the chirping of insects. The cloudless sky appeared as an overhead river, mirroring the meandering grey gravel path we were now crunching through.

After fifteen minutes in the cooler, fresher air, we reached a clearing in the trees, and at its edge, an oversized timber doorway. I'd enjoyed the peace of the walk but was still finding it difficult to be interested in our destination. My brain was pinging with the tumult of the past five hours and I was still no closer to understanding what was going on or why. She may have felt the same way as neither of us paused to admire the forest's clearing or the doorway's intricate carvings and decorations; instead, we proceeded straight through it, into the shrine's interior.

As the largest shrine in Tokyo, I'd expected to enter something enormous, dimly lit, and majestic, but instead, found myself back in the open air. The doorway was literally that – a doorway – and led to nothing more than a giant paved square, not too dissimilar to the plaza outside Tokyo Central Station; except without the grass or ropes.

I glanced her way to catch her attention and to let her know I was going to head directly to the square's centre. She indicated with a point of her finger that she was going to keep to its perimeter.

As I reached the middle of the square, I turned full circle to survey my surrounds, and to look for the shrine. On each side of the square were elongated buildings with pagoda-shaped roofs and ornate latticework hanging below their eaves. They were all constructed of the same deep brown timber and each side of the square looked indistinguishable from the next. One of the sides would have led to the main shrine building but as to which one it was, I wasn't really sure, and wasn't sure I cared.

My apathy and exhaustion were taking over, and I needed to find a way to snap myself out of it. I was in a special place and I wanted to force myself to tune in to whatever it had to offer.

I closed my eyes and took a deep breath through my nose, exhaled through my mouth, and took another, and another, and within half a minute, I felt a sense of calm trickle out of my lungs and through my chest and into my limbs. The surrounding forest and shrine buildings seemed to corral an atmosphere of serenity so tangible it felt like syrup, and despite the hundreds of people shuffling around me, it felt like I was on my own. Peace surrounded me and it was as if I'd entered a parallel reality where her words had not been spoken and everything was still okay. I closed my eyes tighter to gather in more of that feeling and inhaled the cool fresh air until my lungs stretched to their limit.

My breathing reminded me that I used to meditate regularly but hadn't for years, at least not intentionally. Meiji Jingu was letting me know that here and now was the opportune time to start again. The shrine's change in pace was exactly what I needed and was the perfect reprieve from today's escalating non-sense.

With my eyes still shut, I found it near impossible to believe I was still in the middle of Tokyo. The sounds of rustling leaves rose in my ears, dulling the sounds of footsteps and murmurs around me. Foreground noise was relegated to background noise and vice versa. The sensation was satisfying and dizzying, like the first few sips of good champagne on an empty stomach.

I opened my eyes to regain my balance and noticed two large trees on the edge of the square coming into focus: one vacant, and the other with thousands of small wooden signs hanging around its trunk.

The tree with the signs looked like a market stall, possibly selling inscriptions of inspirational quotes or prayers, or engravings of the temple buildings and the torii. I walked towards it, eager to investigate.

The signs were small plaques hung with thin rope and each one contained only text. They all looked unique, if hand-written in different-coloured inks and in different languages; red, green, blue, and black, Latin, Cyrillic, logographic, and abjad. They were mounted on long grey metal hooks, five or ten-deep.

The people around me seemed to be approaching the stall to hang plaques rather than take them away. Some were hanging the plaques in open space, others were hanging theirs behind existing plaques, as if to hide them; but no one was removing them and there was no one taking money or coordinating the activity.

To my left, several people were huddled over a series of trestle tables, handwriting messages onto the same little pieces of wood, and beyond them I saw a kiosk window where money was swapped for fresh blank plaques. My intrigue guided me towards a sign near the window.

Ema ¥500

Inscribe your wish and hang your ema on the wishing wall surrounding the sacred camphor tree. Our priests will pray for you and for your wish and your ema will be burned in a ceremony, freeing you from your wish, and your wish from you.

Cute. The tree was a wishing tree, and the plaques were wishing plaques, and here I was, wishing today never happened.

Normally I wouldn't believe in wishes or magic, but right now I really wanted to. Given everything that was going on, and the wishing tree standing right in front of me, I was more than willing to listen to Meiji Jingu and give it a go.

I stepped to the line in front of the kiosk window. When it was my turn, I instinctively asked for two of the little blank wooden plaques and handed the attendant ¥1000.

With my two ema in hand, I spied her on the other side of the grounds and made a beeline towards her.

"Have you seen the ema tree?"

"The what?" She sounded irritated.

"The ema tree. It's over there. The idea is that you write your wishes on a little wooden thing called an ema and then hang it on the wishing wall around its trunk. When the wall is full, they're collected and burned in a ceremony and the people making the wishes are set free. I bought us one each."

As I raced out my own version of what I'd just read on the sign, I heard my own voice and the ridiculousness of what I was saying.

"No, I don't think so," she replied dismissively, resuming her perimeter stroll.

I followed her and tried to hand her one of the plaques. "Go on. It's my little gift to you. Your wish will be your secret and you can keep it between you and this place."

I cupped her hand and put the ema into it.

"Why aren't you doing one?" Her fingers grasped the ema from my hand.

"I am. I mean, I will, if you will."

She snorted.

"I don't know."

"What's to know? Let's give it a go. I'll do mine over there." I pointed to a place far enough from the trestles and the tree so I couldn't possibly spy on what she was going to write.

She didn't offer a reply, but walked in the opposite direction to where I was pointing.

I did as I promised and wrote my wish with a green-inked pen from one of the tables I passed along the way.

Get me out of this.

And then, feeling a pang of guilt for being so demanding, I added *please* to the start and *thank-you* to the end and changed the word *me* to *us*.

Please get us out of this. Thank you.

I didn't know who I was writing the wish to, but I knew I needed their help. If there was any chance a piece of wood and some priests could magic away whatever this was, then I was all for believing it could work.

I walked to the camphor tree and hung my ema in the first vacant place I found, before making my way to the place I told her I'd be.

I kept my distance but kept my eyes fixed on her every movement. She was hunched over a trestle table furthest from me and seemed to be deep in thought, tapping her lip with her red pen and staring at the trees. Given her recent objection to the idea, she appeared to be taking it more seriously than she'd let on. The tip of her pen hovered above the ema for a minute or two before she started to write, as if she was struggling to find the right wish or the right words to fit her wish within the small surface area she had to work with.

After five or so minutes, she paused to read through what she'd written and made her way towards the tree. She took her time to read a few of the other ema before walking out of view to hang her own. Even if I wanted to, there was now no way of finding hers amongst the thousands of others.

She re-appeared a minute or two later and walked directly towards me. As she came nearer, I could see she had tears in her eyes.

I clasped her hand in mine and we walked away in silence, out of the shrine's doorway, out of the forest, and back into the hustle and bustle of Tokyo.

I was dying to know what she'd written but at the same time was grateful I didn't.

It was getting late, and with the sun setting, and cooling temperature, we made the quick decision to stroll the seven kilometres back to the hotel to see some more of Tokyo along the way.

It was a terrible decision as our route home was along busy main roads and through a concrete jungle. We found ourselves on the wrong sides of overpasses and underpasses and in places where we couldn't get to where we needed to be without retracing our steps. There were no restaurants or bars along the way and by the time we realised our error, we'd passed the point of no return. We kept our eyes open for vacant taxis, or metro stations, but none appeared where we needed them to be.

After a few hours, we passed the outskirts of the Imperial Palace Gardens and ventured into the home straight of the intimidatingly wide Gyoko-dori Avenue. We'd been walking together – I hoped amicably enough – in our own separate worlds, but she again waited until the eleventh hour to break our silence.

"You know how I've always found other women attractive?" She was looking ahead, and her tone was matter-of-fact.

"Yes." No surprise there; she'd always loved fashion, fashion models, and glossy magazines.

"Well, I'm not sure what that means." She kept walking, as if she was talking to herself.

"What do you mean you don't know what that means?"

"I just don't know what it means, that's all." She sounded annoyed that I hadn't heard her the first time.

"Are you saying that you're *attracted* to women now?" I turned around to look at her.

"Yes, I always have been." She flicked her eyes to meet mine.

I stopped abruptly and stood to face her.

"But are you saying that you want to *be* with wom …?" My voice cracked as I choked on a lack of air in my lungs, the result of not taking a breath before starting my question.

"No, that's not what I'm saying. I just don't know what it means, that's all."

Then why the fuck did you bring it up?

It had been a long day, and after no sleep I could feel I was about to lose patience with her riddles.

I want to be alone; I want to come with you.

Let's get coffee, but don't post it on your socials.

I'm attracted to women; I don't know what it means.

Three of these conversations in one day when we hadn't any of these conversations in the past three years was more than enough for me. She was wearing me down with these obscure comments and I just wished she'd say what she needed to say, or not say anything at all.

I resumed walking towards the hotel which was now in view. I didn't reach for her hand and she didn't grasp mine. She spoke again.

"Hypothetically, what would you do if you had a fantasy or a curiosity that I wasn't in to or that I couldn't satisfy?"

I could feel the back of my neck bristle. Was this a continuation of her previous statement?

Please stop talking. If you're as tired as I am, you have no idea what you're saying. You just need to be quiet now, get home, go to sleep and we'll pick this up in the morning.

My pace quickened. Time to knock this on the head. "Well, I don't and I'm perfectly happy with what I have."

It was my truth, but I hadn't answered her question.

"But say you did? What would you do about it?" Her

50

tone sounded genuinely curious, even though she had to have known exactly what my answer would be.

"What do you mean? I wouldn't do anything about it!" My voice was rising, and my steps quickened further. The hotel was so close now, but she still wasn't done with me.

"So, you're telling me that you would completely ignore your urges, and the pursuit of experiences you're curious about just because you're with me? Are you really telling me that if I couldn't give you want you wanted, that you would live your life unhappily ever after?"

Snap.

I kicked my heel into the ground to stop walking and threw my head back to stare at the night sky in frustration. "Yep, that's exactly what I'm saying. Don't you feel the same way?" My response was clipped and did little to mask my feelings.

"No, I think that's an awful way to live."

I was taken aback by the disgusted look in her eyes.

Snap. Snap.

My mind swirled as her words crashed into one another, my jaw dropping in pure disbelief. Going by her definition, I'd just spent the past six years of my life *living an awful life*. I'd dropped everything to care for her and to support her with whatever she needed, and had lived *unhappily* with the hope things would get better, and now she was talking about being unhappy with the fact that she couldn't *fuck* whomever she wanted?

My anger was stirring, but the angel on my shoulder wanted to rescue us from her line of questioning and to find a way out of the conversation. "I'm not sure if you're being serious; but isn't marriage forever? Isn't that what marriage is all about; to be happy and satisfied with the one that you're with, and to work through anything?"

She ignored my questions as though she hadn't heard them and resumed her journey across the plaza towards the hotel's main entrance.

"Okay, but say it was something like S&M; and I didn't want to do it; wouldn't it be okay for you to experience it elsewhere to get it out of your syst—?"

"No," I growled.

Why was she chipping away at me like this? What was it about my answers she didn't understand?

Our conversation seemed to be moving away from the hypothetical and perilously toward the personal. It was apparent that she had an itch she wanted to scratch but she wasn't being clear about what it was. Did *she* want to experiment with women, or S&M, or both?

I could feel the heat rising into my neck again, frustrated at her lack of clarity. Every word out of her mouth was a new mystery, calculated to confuse: I no longer had the capacity, or the inclination to solve. In our whole time together, she'd never mentioned any of this, and now she was dropping it all on me at once, bombshell after bombshell, all whilst on holiday, in a place I didn't want to be.

A pressure was building in my forehead, and the stoic armour I'd worn all my life threatened to come loose.

"But, imagine for a moment you did. What would you do?"

Snap. Snap. Snap.

"Why the fuck would someone get married if they wanted to do everything they wanted to do without concern for their partner? To be married … to be with someone is to sacrifice being with other people! Why don't you get that? A promise is a promise and throwing away an entire marriage for a few moments of pleasure is a fucking stupid idea."

Shit!

The golf ball-sized lump in my throat had saved me from myself earlier, but this time the damage was done. I'd said what I needed to say, and I couldn't swallow it back.

She didn't react or respond and instead walked at twice her normal speed through the hotel doors and to the elevator, her finger stabbing at the up-arrow button at least ten times.

I hoped that this being the first time I'd ever raised my voice and sworn directly at her, she'd be shocked into a reaction, but she didn't say anything.

She power-walked down the hall and entered our room, going directly to her luggage. She picked it up and threw it on the bed. "I want to go home." Her eyes were glassy, and she was angry unlike I'd ever seen her. Shocked, I fell back on logic.

"What? Now? It's 8:00pm; there won't be any flights to Melbourne tonight!"

"Yep. I don't care, I don't want to be here," She swiped at the tears in her eyes with her wrists and clenched fists, pushing past me and storming into the bathroom.

I followed her in, only to catch her hateful scowl in the

mirror's reflection. "We're only here for two more days; besides, we don't have changeable flights and we'll need to buy new ones if you want to go home early."

She snatched her toiletries from the shower and vanity and stuffed them into her wet pack with unnecessary force.

"I don't care. I just don't want to be here." Her face was red, and her voice shrill. Her teeth were clenched, and her tight jaw was limiting her vocabulary to just those few words.

I stepped back from the bathroom doorway and sat on the bed, my head throbbing as my frontal lobe worked overtime to find some logic or reason to what was going on.

What had I missed? Why was this happening?

The fragile house of cards she'd started constructing this morning was clearly falling down and nothing I did would keep it from doing so. Where had I gone wrong?

I fell backward onto the mattress and mentally flipped through the storyboard of our day until we were back on the rooftop garden of the mall.

Alone.

On her own.

By herself.

Click.

Maybe there was a compromise.

"Why don't we stay here and why don't you just do your own thing for the next couple of days? Spend the days on your own. You do your thing and I'll do mine. Isn't your brother here racing cars somewhere? Why don't you get out of Tokyo and go visit him?"

The bathroom went quiet.

A few seconds later her head appeared sideways through the door. "What will you do?"

"Don't worry about me. I'll be fine."

Her face softened and the blood from her face drained into her neck.

She retreated back to the bathroom, and for the first time today, it seemed I'd said what she'd needed me to.

Chapter 3

Our second morning in Tokyo was as delightful and luxurious as the previous one had been miserable and uncomfortable. We'd slept on our respective edges in the same bed and had risen early to make the most of our included breakfast and to fuel up for our days ahead.

The hotel's dining room was as opulent as any other we'd seen, let alone dined in. The space was sectioned off into smaller private alcoves by heavy glass dividers and was furnished with silvery-grey velvet seats and rounded tables with thick white linen tablecloths. Each tabletop was adorned with a full set of patinaed silverware, fine bone china, and crystal glassware, and the food selection at the buffet was diverse as it was plentiful.

Her good night's sleep and the indulgence of our perfectly prepared eggs Benedict appeared to have put her in a better mood, and after she'd gulped down her first glass of pink grapefruit juice, she cracked a smile and even made time for small talk.

"Beautiful space, isn't it?"

"Much nicer than the plane yesterday."

"Look at this knife; it's lovely but isn't as heavy as it looks."

"I wonder if the coffee here is any good."

"Are you looking forward to today?"

She'd called her brother shortly after my desperate circuit-breaking suggestion she spend the day without me and had arranged to meet him at a racetrack in Ebisu.

After she'd confirmed her plans and bought her tickets, I considered my own options of hanging around Tokyo for a second day or doing a day trip of my own. I checked a map of Japan to see what was nearby and decided to visit Kyoto; not just to see the city, but to fulfil my childhood dream of riding on a bullet train to get there.

I'd wanted to experience a Shinkansen ever since I first heard about them as a five-year-old, but my request to have a ride added to our must-map for this trip had been summarily dismissed. 'There are just too many things to see and do in Tokyo itself, and we're not going to have time to do a tenth of it,' she'd told me. 'We'll leave it to next time, just like we've always done with places we've wanted to revisit.'

I didn't push my request as Tokyo was for *her*, and also because her rationale was valid. During all our previous travels, we'd deliberately left out at least one major place, landmark, or attraction as something to do when we returned. The Colosseum in Rome, Le Marais in Paris, Coney Island in New York City, Mayfair in London; they were all places we'd omitted for another time; and riding the bullet train in Japan was an addition to our ever-growing list of things we hadn't yet followed up on.

After we'd finished breakfast and brushed our teeth back in the hotel room, I walked her to her train's platform to make sure she got to where she needed to be and to give her every possible second to change her mind about heading to Ebisu without me.

There was nothing about today I wanted, nor was I excited about, except maybe the train trip, and the idea of us spending time apart so we could improve our time together seemed counterintuitive to the point of stupidity. We were already good at not talking about the things we needed to talk about and going our separate ways to ensure we wouldn't have to talk about the herd of elephants in our room was ludicrous.

She didn't seem to feel the same way and left me at the platform gate with a "See ya," without ever glancing back.

"Have a great day," I said with a wave, knowing full well she couldn't see nor hear me.

Feeling nauseous and with the void beneath my sternum reopening, I navigated my way back through Tokyo Central Station's malls and halls to find the Tokaido Shinkansen office.

I'd bought my train ticket to Kyoto last night, but after clicking *pay now*, the confirmation text on the webpage politely informed me I needed to visit their office to pick up the tickets in person. It was an infuriating process, but after the hellish day I'd already been through, it hardly registered as something worth getting upset about.

After a few laps of the central parts of the station, I found the Tokaido office with a queue of people forming outside its shuttered doors. Through the gaps in the metal screen, I could see staff in bright yellow uniforms shuffling papers and busily preparing their counters and workstations for the day ahead. At a few minutes to 9:00am, a man dressed in a blue suit approached the entry door. He paid no attention to the gathering crowd eager to get in; his eyes instead fixed on his wristwatch. He waited until he saw what he needed to see, and after what felt like more than a few minutes, he turned a key to raise the shutters and unlock the front door.

My wait in line was brief, and when I was called forward, I *konichiwa'd* and showed the woman behind the counter the confirmation email on my phone. She replied with some words in Japanese I didn't recognise and turned around to a table behind her. She flipped through a bunch of alphabetised envelopes and located the one with my name on it. Rather than hand it to me, she opened the flap and extracted two printed tickets. She looked me up and down and studied my face with her stare.

"Engrish?" she asked.

"Yes please," I replied with an involuntary smile.

She held one of the tickets above the counter and

pointed to it with her free hand. "Use this one to go to Kyoto, carriage nine."

She shuffled the tickets and pointed to the second one, "Use this one to go from Kyoto to Tokyo, carriage eight."

She put the tickets back in the envelope and presented it to me with two hands and a slight bow.

I received it in the same way and bowed back with my best version of '*domo arigato*'.

I had twenty-five minutes before my train's departure but rather than loiter around stores I wasn't interested in and think about things I didn't want to think about, I chose to make my way to the platform early to locate the boarding area for my carriage.

Thankfully I did, as it took me twenty of those minutes to locate the platform I needed to be on, as the information on the Shinkansen departure screens was more complicated than I'd anticipated. There were no trains departing at 9.30am terminating in Kyoto and after repeatedly jogging between platforms, and checking timetables, I was able to deduce that I needed to board the train bound for Hiroshima which would stop in Kyoto along the way.

With a sense of relief, and five minutes to spare, I found the sleek bullet train resting at the platform with its doors open. Its huge, elongated nose and small driver's windscreen made it look more like a luxury yacht than a train and gave it the appearance of moving fast whilst it was standing still. It was enormous and seemed unnaturally tall for a train, towering above me at almost double my height, three and a half metres or even more.

I walked halfway down the train's length and boarded carriage eight, navigating the narrow aisle to my allocated seat, not realising until it was too late that I'd mindlessly used the details on my return ticket rather than my outbound one. A man sitting in *my* seat informed me of my mistake, and after making my way to the next carriage, I found another man looking overly comfortable in my seat. He was settled-in and had his newspaper splayed across the opened tray-table.

I stopped next to him and triple checked the details on my ticket, not wanting to appear an idiot twice in two minutes. He didn't look up to see why I'd stopped so I tapped him on the shoulder to get his attention and to draw his eyes to my ticket.

He examined it quickly and mumbled something unintelligible. I still felt a bit panicked that I might again have the wrong carriage, or even the wrong train, and I really didn't fancy the idea of not being able to find the right seat. Standing up for the next two and a half hours to go somewhere I wasn't supposed to go held no appeal, and I'd sooner disembark this train than put myself through another day of torture.

Without making eye contact, the man folded his newspaper, lifted the tray-table, and stood up with a huff. He took his bag off the overhead luggage rails and stomped off into the carriage behind us.

"Thanks mister," I whispered under my breath, bewildered

that he hadn't checked his own ticket to compare its details to mine before leaving.

Maybe he didn't have a ticket; or maybe he had an unreserved ticket and was trying his luck to get a seat, hoping with only a few minutes to go, he was about to get his wish. Either way, it didn't matter and was no longer my problem.

I took my pre-warmed seat and sank into it, feeling much heavier than I was. In the distance I could hear the dull thud of the train doors closing, and the whirr of the air-conditioning getting louder. I closed my eyes and breathed, hoping to feel some of the syrupy serenity that was in abundance yesterday at Meiji Jingu.

All of this was really happening.

She'd left me to do her thing, and I was left alone to do mine, even though I had no idea what exactly mine was.

I did some quick arithmetic in my head and worked out it had been eight years since I'd done anything on my own; eight years since she'd joined me in Bristol and turned my world inside out.

I couldn't remember the last time I'd thought about my life *Before Her*, but the memories of those years were now flooding back to me, filling the void she'd left today, flashing up like projections onto the back of my closed eyelids.

Eleven. We'd met at work eleven years earlier when she needed my help with a marketing project she was working on. My heart had skipped a beat when she materialised at my desk unannounced. Tall, with big eyes and flawless skin. Her voice was deeper than I expected and had a cheeky seriousness to it. She wore a blazer and had a pen stuck through her weirdly tied ponytail. She seemed a bit offbeat and I immediately found her attractive.

She lived in Brisbane and I lived in Melbourne; we worked on her project and whilst we did, we chatted intermittently about life and love. She was in a long-term relationship and I was enjoying the freedom of not being in one. She was twenty-three years old and had been with her boyfriend for about three years, eagerly waiting for him to pop the big question; desperate for the commitment, and for an engagement ring. She'd felt she'd already put in the years and that she deserved her happily ever after.

I, on the other hand, was five years older than her and had never liked the idea of marriage. I couldn't understand her rush to get hitched, but I never quizzed her about it. It was her business, after all. After a few months of working together, her project ended and we had no reason to stay in contact, but we did.

Ten. A year later, I was expatriated to Bristol to do the same job I'd being doing in Australia, managing call centres and customer service operations. I didn't know anyone in the UK and even though I'd been an off-the-chart introvert all my life, I found the isolation from friends and family almost too much to bear. I distracted myself with my work and spent most of my time in the office, sixteen hours a day, six days per week.

I lost three months of my life living that way before I discovered Bristol had an international airport and cheap fares to mainland Europe on most weekends. Pisa return, £30, Venice, £45, Paris, £50, Barcelona, £60, Prague, £70. I'd not made much time for travelling prior to arriving in the UK, and the opportunity to see Europe from close by was too good to resist. For the rest of my time in Bristol, I travelled somewhere new and exciting, each and every month; and I loved every solo minute of it.

Nine. A year after I'd decamped to Bristol, she split up with her boyfriend and sent me a flirty text. Our text exchanges led to regular emails and phone calls and culminated with me flying to Brisbane for our first date. We were smitten with each other and even though living on opposite sides of the globe was an inconvenient way for us to start our relationship, we were committed to each other and to giving it a go.

Eight. After a year of doing the long-distance thing and her flipflopping on her decision about which one of us needed to move countries to be with the other, she chose to move to Bristol. I wangled a job for her with our marketing department, and she moved into my life at home, at work, and on my monthly travels. We only had six months together in the UK before my expat assignment ended and we were both asked to return to Australia.

When we did, she asked me to make her another promise.

"Promise me we'll always travel together. Promise me we'll never be one of those couples who travel separately."

Fuck. So, what happened to change things?

As the train rolled soundlessly from the station, I opened my eyes and extracted my phone from my pocket. After confirming my train ticket last night, I'd cobbled together my own must-map for Kyoto by using as many of the internet's *Top 10 things to do* lists I could find, but I still wasn't convinced I could fit it all in. I scanned through my itinerary with revolving feelings of dread, anticipation, and apathy.

It was the same tripartite of feelings I'd had nine years ago at the Carnivale di Venezia. Amongst all the colour, joy, and energy of Italy's world-famous festival, I'd been frustratingly numb and unable to enjoy it. I'd just returned to Bristol after our first date and our first two weeks together and left Australia not knowing when I was going to see her again. Even though logic told me I would, I was in a type of catatonia which I couldn't shake, and it ended up ruining about three months of my life.

Not today.

If I was going to get any enjoyment out of today, I needed to pretend like it was ten years ago, *Before Her,* and I was off on one of my monthly solo adventures to Europe. If I wanted to, I could take a break from my normal life and just let today be different; to do the things I wanted to do, in the way I wanted to do them. Rather than rush around to see as many things on a must-map as possible, I could stroll the streets. Rather than take photos I'd never look at again, I could just experience the sights in person, in random order as I passed them along the way. Today, I could pick and choose.

65

I decided that the only thing I really wanted to do was walk along the Philosopher's Path; a two-kilometre trail along the banks of a canal I'd not previously heard of. It was famed for its Sakura, and whilst there'd be no cherry blossoms for me at this time of year, I still liked the way it looked on the internet as well as the idea of its name. If there was any place I was going to be able to work out what was going on with her – with *us* – it would be somewhere with a name like that.

I shut my eyes again and breathed in my new choice. If I wanted to *waste* my entire day at the Philosopher's Path, I would, and I wouldn't feel guilty about it or beat myself up over it.

The day was now mine and would be of my own making. Today would be unique in its own way, unlike yesterday and unlike the succession of nine years of days before it. Today would be the opposite of my normal days and along with it, I would be the opposite of me.

A shiver ran through my neck and electrified my spine.

It was the best idea I'd had in years.

Following the first few metropolitan stops through the west of Tokyo, the train gathered speed with what felt like limitless power. It was as though a huge hand pressed into my lower back, pushing me forward faster than my body could comprehend. Digital screens at each end of the carriage told us how fast we were travelling, and I breathed out a quiet 'yay' when our maximum speed of 285 kph was reached, not that it ever *felt* that fast. The pressurised carriages and dearth of foreground scenery provided few points of reference for our velocity. Mount Fuji seemed to be the only view outside the window to signal we were moving at all.

After two hours and twenty minutes, the bullet train braked slowly into Kyoto Station and ground to a gentle halt. It had been a journey smoother than any other, and if I'd been blindfolded, I would have guessed my trip had been taken in a plane rather than a train.

I stepped down onto the platform as if in slow motion and kept myself in first gear to make my way to the exit. Every fibre of me wanted to rush through the crowds to start my adventure, but I'd chosen to force today to be different, to experience life on a deliberate go-slow.

Today, I would be rushed past by the rest of the world; cursed at for walking too slowly, and nudged out of the way by less patient souls. My opposite was on carriage nine destined for Hiroshima and if I still wanted to be him when I returned later that evening, I was sure I'd be able to find him.

The plaza outside Kyoto Station looked similar to the one outside Shibuya Station, but with a tenth of the people. It was another wide-open paved space with few trees and a bus-station at its front. Shopping centres and office buildings surrounded it on all sides, and it even had its own scramble of six zebra crossings near its entry: a big bright white X in a box.

The Philosopher's Path was about eight kilometres north-east of Kyoto Station and even though the opposite of me should have wanted to catch a taxi, I still wanted to experience Kyoto by foot.

My new 'non-must-map' plan was simple; walk east for a bit and then turn left and head north. If I was lucky, I'd bump into some interesting things along the way, but if I wasn't, it wouldn't matter. Today was as much about the journey as it was the destination.

How very clichéd!

My eastward trek began on the overly decorative footpaths of Shiokoji-dori, and within fifteen minutes I was out of the central business district and halfway across the Kamo River. The waterway was mostly dry except for a small stream near one of its banks and a couple of large ponds pocking its weed-covered riverbed, and whilst it wasn't the most attractive waterway, it appeared to serve a purpose as the dividing line between Kyoto's CBD and its suburbs.

The city's high-rises were behind me now, and in front of me, on the other side of the bridge were smaller house-like buildings, and beyond them, rolling green hills.

From my vantage point on the Shiokoji-dori bridge, I could now see that the hills weren't just to the east, but to the north and south as well, making it feel as though Kyoto may have been built in the centre of a giant crater, possibly within the caldera of an extinct volcano. I couldn't be sure if either were true, but without a Japanese SIM card or a Wi-Fi network connection, my geological inquiry was going to have to wait until later.

The area on the other side of the river was nothing like I expected and made me wish I'd chosen another way to get to the Philosopher's Path. It was derelict and dangerous, and the further I walked down Shiokoji-dori, the worse it got.

The road had narrowed to just one lane and the two-way traffic was jostling for position along with any pedestrians crazy enough to have walked this far, pedestrians like me. With the sounds of horns blaring from every direction, I needed a quick escape. I stepped into the doorway of a boarded-up building to take stock and reconsider my options.

I could turn around and walk back into the safety I'd come from, potentially wasting an hour having got nowhere; or I could keep pushing forward with the hope Shiokoji-dori would get better and that the road I turned into to head north would be less hazardous.

I peered out of the doorway to see if I could locate the next major intersection, but with cars and trucks hurtling past me in both directions, I couldn't see much past the front of my face.

I took a deep breath of the exhaust laden air to steel myself and stepped back onto the street with faux-courage and real determination to continue my journey.

The Philosopher's Path better be worth it.

By the time I'd reached a sign saying 'Higashiyamagojo' my decision to ignore my must-map felt like a stupid one. Apart from some fancy footpaths, and a climate change-affected river, I was yet to see anything interesting, and whilst I didn't yet feel like I was totally wasting my time, I did feel like I was wasting the opportunity to see more beautiful parts of Kyoto.

The remainder of Shiokoji-dori felt like a death trap and my new pathway north along Higashioji-dori Avenue had led me to a massive junction of countless roads, and what looked like a freeway underpass.

Everything was so ugly, and the heat of the sun combined with the heat of cars and trucks only served to exaggerate my falling spirits. I wasn't sure I could tolerate another five or six kilometres of the same hell without some sort of reprieve, or something to make this trip worth it.

Without any sense for what lay ahead of me, I crossed the junction and arrived at a narrow alley with a bunch of arrowed signs all pointing in the same north-easterly direction. All were in Japanese except one –

This Way
Sannen-zaka
Ninen-zaka

Even though my must-map was still firmly in my pocket, I recognised the place names from every *Top 10* list I'd read through last night.

Sannen-zaka and Ninen-zaka were districts of Old Kyoto, and apparently were both famed for their traditional architecture, lack of overhead powerlines, pedestrian-only pathways, and the cheery legends of their slippery stone steps; slip and fall in Sannen-zaka and you'd die within three years. Do the same in Ninen-zaka and die in two. I had no interest in slipping, or falling, or dying, but after an hour on the ground in Kyoto, I was happy to deviate away from the Philosopher's Path if it meant seeing something more stimulating than the boring concrete and bitumen I'd unwillingly surrounded myself with.

Without wasting another moment, I pointed myself in the direction of the arrows and walked up the inclined alley towards whichever *zaka* was first. The signs said nothing about the steepness of the road and the burning sensation in my quads suggested I may have been climbing one of the hills I'd seen earlier from the river bridge.

After another half a kilometre of sidestepping traffic through more of Kyoto's dreary back streets, I arrived at the top of the Sannen-zaka steps, and to what looked like a portal to a different world.

The view in front of me was a picture-perfect postcard of Kyoto one hundred or one thousand years ago and stepping into Sannen-zaka felt like stepping back in time. The narrow descending pathway was lined with traditional timber shophouses, lantern-like streetlamps, and weeping cherry trees, and even though I was physically here, none of it felt real. The buildings looked like two-dimensional cut-outs, as if they were propped up from behind with nothing but fresh air, but regardless of Sannen-zaka's resemblance to a movie set for Old Kyoto, I was still happy to have made the detour. Beauty was on display everywhere and even though I was presented with photo opportunities at every turn, I kept my phone in my pocket. Rather than take photos of things I'd never look at again, I reminded myself, I was just going to experience them in the present.

I wanted to absorb the tradition and history of my surrounds, but as I walked further down the path, the more I realised Sannen-zaka for what it was; a tourist trap and commercial hotspot.

Busloads of people were decanting into Sannen-zaka's tiny alleys and laneways and tour guides with different coloured umbrellas acted as muster points, leading their charges directly to one of the many *'authentic'* artisan studios.

I stepped out of the way to watch the consumers consume. Westerners hired patterned kimonos and silk obi to dress as geisha and have their photos taken near burled cherry trees or in shophouse doorways, with some even donning wigs and having their makeup done to complete their look. I held my breath as their wooden geta slipped on the smooth stone paving and winced as they slipped and fell on their wrists and arses whilst trying to perfect their poses for the perfect shot. I prayed they weren't hurt – or worse still, superstitious.

Tourist magnet or not, Sannen-zaka's beauty was beyond compare, and its splendour more than compensated for my less-than-ideal experience of getting there and served to reset my day. The past hour and a half faded to nothing and Sannen-zaka left me feeling rejuvenated to restart my journey towards the Philosopher's Path with renewed vigour.

Beyond Sannen-zaka and the connected district of Ninen-zaka, a series of dead-end roads forced me off my route towards the Philosopher's Path and delivered me to the outskirts of Maruyama Park. I didn't recall the park appearing on any of the Top 10 lists, but as I'd been on my feet for about two hours, it didn't really matter.

I searched for lawn to have a quick lie down, but like the parks in Tokyo, there was none around; it was all just gravel and pebbles.

I found a vacant bench on the park's outer perimeter and tilted my face towards the sun. The air felt cooler than it had been for the past hour, but the humidity had intensified.

With my eyes focussed upwards, I could now see why. Storm clouds of colossal proportions were metamorphosising overhead. They appeared as if in time lapse, and as I stared at them mesmerised, big round waterdrops began falling from the sky.

The deluge was quick and powerful, and it sent the crowds in front of me scattering in search of shelter. I stayed rooted to my bench, embracing the cleansing feeling of the warm water hitting my face, much like I'd done in our hotel room's shower.

Within minutes, the fast-moving clouds dissipated, and the sun re-emerged along with the blue sky, the change reminiscent of a scene from a biblical movie. A warm breeze followed the sun's rays, wafting over the park like a huge fan to dry me off as quickly as I'd got wet.

My reaction – or lack of reaction – to the rain took me by surprise. If today had been yesterday, I would have grabbed her hand and run for cover with the others; but because today was today, I reacted differently. Perhaps my decisions on the train to do things differently and to be my opposite were seeping into my subconscious, or maybe it was because I was on my own and was starting to enjoy it.

Once the bullet train had departed Tokyo, I'd consciously relegated the happenings of yesterday to the back of my mind. I batted away my memories of the mall rooftop, the café, and the walk home last night like baseballs, making perfect connection with each one, sending them out of sight over an imaginary fence. I'd shot down most of my incoming ideas about what was going on with her and between us, as I wasn't going to let them ruin my day as they had done yesterday. I was still a long way from being okay with whatever it was that was going on with her and between us, but Kyoto was providing the perfect distraction.

I rose from my rapidly drying concrete bench and checked the wetness of my clothes by patting myself down, and easing the fabric away from my skin. My shirt was no damper than it had been before the rain and no more uncomfortable. My rest stop in Maruyama Park had topped up my energy and increased my excitement about what the rest of my day had in store.

I didn't need to wait long for my next wow-moment, as the road out of the park lead me directly to the fluorescent-orange Heian-Jingu Shrine Torii Gate, and into the Heian Shrine.

Whilst my day in Kyoto had started off with all the ugly, it was now blossoming into all the beautiful.

The Heian Shrine square stole my breath; an open area of about one hundred metres by one hundred metres, covered entirely in small white pebbles. Several areas had been neatly raked into geometric patterns, making the shrine square appear as a gigantic Japanese Zen garden.

Like Meiji Jingu in Tokyo, the square was surrounded by timber buildings, but unlike Meiji Jingu, the buildings were vibrantly painted the same bright orange as the torii and were capped with emerald-green roofs. All the structures looked recently refreshed and whilst they were spectacular to look at it, it was what appeared beyond them that really piqued my excitement.

Surrounding the shrine buildings on three sides were treetops of varying heights and widths, their branches swaying in the breeze, beckoning me forward. I clasped my hands together in a prayer-like fashion to my lips. *Please be a Japanese garden.*

From my central position in the square, I turned clockwise on my heel, narrowing my eyes to locate a possible entry or exit for the secret garden. I spied two that looked promising and made my way to the one on my left.

In the shadows of the pagoda-shaped eaves, a ticket window came into focus, as did a young woman sitting behind it.

I approached her quickly and pointed to the door, with a two-word question, "Garden entry?"

"Hai, yes."

"One, please," I asked, holding my right index finger in the air.

"Six hundlet," she replied, tearing a perforated ticket out of her book.

I swapped my cash for the ticket and bowed twice in my excitement. "Arigato, arigato,"

Once through the entry door, a pebbled-pathway snaked its way through lush greenery towards the banks of a lily-filled lake.

Along the path were stone carvings to admire, timber-bridges to cross, and smaller koi ponds to stare into. The leaves from spindly old trees provided the greenest of canopies and an umbrella of cooling shade. The shrine gardens felt like an enchanted forest; everything I imagined and had hoped for in an authentic Japanese garden was there. They were an incarnation of peace and order.

I took my time to stroll through the manicured shrubs, bushes, and trees from one side of the shrine to the other, and when I arrived at the exit, I felt an odd reluctance to leave. I milled around for a few moments, before choosing to do the most un-Japanese thing I could; I was going to walk back in the direction from which I came.

Going the *wrong* way meant that I could see most of the disapproving looks on the faces coming towards me, but none of them mattered. Rather than rushing around to see as many things as possible, I was enjoying being exactly where I was.

I walked the paths three times in each direction before I was satisfied and ready to continue towards the Philosopher's Path.

I exited the gardens on the opposite side to which I entered, and as I strolled out of the shrine square and down the home-straight of Reisen-dori, a screeching sound that had sounded far away was slowly becoming nearer and louder. I hadn't paid much attention to it earlier, but as I was getting closer to its source; it was becoming impossible to ignore. The high-pitched noises were similar to metal scraping on metal, like a train turning on curved tracks, except it was endless and there was no train.

Stepping towards the cherry trees near the entrance to the Philosopher's Path, I covered my ears as the screeching hit full volume.

The racket appeared to be emanating from thousands of poorly camouflaged cicadas adhering to the trees lining the path. Nothing like the delicate lime-green cicadas I'd once seen in Melbourne, these were big and dark, about three centimetres long with black and brown laced wings, a curious hybrid of moth and bee. Regardless of how close I got to them, they held their positions, and continued to flex their tymbal muscles at an almost deafening frequency.

It wasn't the start to the Philosopher's Path I'd anticipated, but as it had taken me three and a half hours to get here, nothing was going to stop me from walking to its end.

From the top of the tiny Nyakuoji Bridge, I took a moment to tune into the view ahead whilst trying to tune out the cacophony. The Philosopher's Path was in fact two parallel paths, both of them on the left bank of the canal, narrow and straight, and separated by a suspended metal cable.

The path on the far left was covered in smooth bitumen and looked more like a bicycle lane without the markings, whereas the path closer to the canal looked like a thin row of square steppingstones. The paths had clearly been built in different eras, a contrast between the old and the new, the traditional and the modern. The canal itself looked like a stone-sided stormwater drain; no more than two metres wide and two metres high; although the clear dark water rapidly flowing through it today would have only been thirty or forty centimetres deep.

With several deep breaths and my chin held purposefully high, I commenced my philosophical stroll on the smoother Philosopher's Path, drinking in my surroundings with undivided attention.

Despite the chorus of cicadas, the path was incredibly peaceful. The cherry trees lining the sides of the canal reflected the sunlight and made everything appear green, giving me the feeling of being deep within a rainforest. With few other people out walking or cycling, the space around me felt like it was mine, not just physically, but psychologically as well.

During my first one hundred metres on the path, I recognised the return of the conscious awareness of my surroundings I'd felt yesterday at Meiji Jingu. I'd sensed it earlier in Sannen-zaka, and again in the Heian Shrine gardens, but until now I hadn't been able to put a name to it, nor its cause.

It was mindfulness.

When did I stop being mindful, and why did I stop?

It used to be who I was, and how I lived my life.

How did I become so distracted, and when did I stop being me?

When did I stop *breathing* and when did I start taking my life and experiences for granted?

My questions persisted for a few seconds before my attention was diverted to the many shops and houses along the path which were now coming into view. I hadn't expected the Philosopher's Path to be a residential area, but the further I progressed, the more obvious it became.

At about the one-kilometre mark, the vibrant colour of a small French-looking café stopped me in my tracks. Its fire-engine-red window frames and awnings contrasted against grey concrete walls, and its open bay-window drew me in to investigate further. Two tables with checked tablecloths stood guard at its entrance, both facing outwards towards the path and the canal.

How very Champs-Élysées!

I waved at the man inside to get his attention and pointed to one of the tables to let him know I was going to take a seat. He was out within seconds with an English version of their drinks-menu.

"Our kitchen closed so drinks only, okay?" He had his pen and pad at the ready.

It was almost 4:00pm, two hours since I'd last sat down in Maruyama Park. It didn't matter there was no food, as I was just grateful to have a rest. "Yes, thank you, arigato."

I traced my finger over the menu thinking I might like a coffee to keep me going but before I opened my mouth, I remembered two things; I'd never had an enjoyable coffee at a *French* café, and the second was what I'd pledged earlier today.

Sooo, what would the opposite of me like to drink this afternoon?

"I'll have a beer, please," I said, pointing to one near the top of the list.

"Certainly, thank you." The man bowed, and hurried away, returning almost instantly with a bottle and a glass. He levered the metal cap off the bottle with an opener holstered at the front of his apron and poured half its contents into the glass before disappearing again into the darkness of the café.

I moved the glass to the side of the table and picked up the cold condensation-covered bottle to search its label for the memory of when I'd last had a beer. If it had been some time during the past few months, I couldn't recall when.

I took a long, drawn-out sip from the bottle, and rested it back onto the table, a shiver running through my neck and out through my shoulders.

The cicadas were still incessant with their mating calls, and whilst their shrieking didn't seem as loud as when I first arrived, it still felt as though they could shatter glass.

I could feel their vibrations on my skin, and deep within my organs, and I could feel them fracturing the armour I'd been wearing throughout this journey. The glistening sunlight bounced off the leaves and branches overhead and, in a sensation that felt almost physical, pierced my forehead to illuminate memories I'd been ignoring, suppressing, and squashing.

I couldn't tell if it was the effect of the shrines, the gardens, or walking along this path; or if it was just because of the alcohol in the beer, but Kyoto was forcing my guard down and was loosening me up to start facing my reality. This city was pushing me to face a demon that had her hands on my throat since long before I'd contemplated buying the airplane tickets to Tokyo for her birthday.

I'd done my best to fight her off, and shut her out, but like the shrieking of the cicadas, she too was becoming too intense to ignore.

Three, three, three, and it seemed to be happening again.

For the three years before we'd got together, she'd told me that she'd been unhappy. Unhappy in work, family, love, and life. In the year after we'd met, she'd been open and honest with me about her search for a new career, her topsy-turvy relationship with her mother, her toxic relationship with her boyfriend, and her diagnosis with bipolar disorder. She'd told me about her manic behaviour at job interviews, how she'd wanted to change her surname, how her ex had refused to marry her, and how she hated taking her prescribed lithium. She blamed her illness on everyone and everything around her and had made me believe she was a healthy person in an unhealthy environment, By the time we got together, all that changed and her symptoms simply – miraculously – disappeared. She was the happiest and healthiest she'd ever been, she said, and she convinced me I was the reason why.

For the three years after we got together, we lived a fun and exciting life of travel and adventure. She moved from Brisbane to Melbourne and then from Melbourne to Bristol to be with me. We travelled Europe together, got engaged in Florence, and returned to Australia to create our 'forever home' in Melbourne. All through those years, she showed no signs of any mental illness and was a picture of health and happiness. The world was our oyster and on the third anniversary of our first date, we got married.

Three months after our wedding, she collapsed on our bathroom floor. It was the start of a full-blown nervous breakdown. Her incapacitation forced her to quit her job, and without noticing, we withdrew from our lives as we'd known them. She was diagnosed with depression and for the next three years was in and out of psychologist and psychiatrist offices. She was counselled and she was drugged, and we kept all of it to ourselves, hiding the painful reality of our lives from our friends and family.

After those three years, she said she'd had enough of being sick and decided she was well again. Despite my protestations, she abandoned her medication and counselling and set about creating a new life. She re-entered the workforce, and swapped jobs three times in a year before landing her 'dream job' at a digital agency, a place where she told me she'd found her new happiness. She'd been there for the past two years and during that time had put all her time and effort into her renewed career, and I'd continued to support her with whatever she needed.

Based on a pattern I was beginning to recognise, she was again coming to the end of a three-year cycle. Maybe I was on the lookout for it, but it seemed to me the signs during the past few months and especially the past few days indicated her mental health was again deteriorating and she was headed for another breakdown.

Why does this keep happening?

Is it another bout of depression, or – worse – bipolar again?

When will all of this be over and when will I have my wife back?

I finished the now warm beer in the bottle with a single swig and moved it to the side of the table.

"Would you like anything else?" The waiter emerged from nowhere and shocked me back to the present. He was holding another copy of drinks menu. "We will close soon."

I put my hand on my heart to press the adrenalin back into it.

"No thank you," I replied, handing him ¥700. "Domo arigato."

I finished the beer in the glass with an elongated sip and stood up feeling more lightheaded than I should have. I stretched myself out, ready to move on to finish the other half of the Philosopher's Path and the other half of my hypothesis.

I'll give you until the end of the path to think about this, and when you turn around to walk back, you'll put it out of your mind. You've had a good day and I won't let you ruin it with thoughts of her.

83

There was no doubting that during the past three months, she'd become increasingly withdrawn, at least from me. She'd stopped doing most of the things that were good for her, and by extension, good for us. She wasn't eating well and had stopped exercising; she was working more, partying more, drinking more, and spending much less time at home with me and our dog.

In essence, I'd been holding on, white-knuckled, hoping for better days (like I always had) and had been ignoring her behaviour (like I'd always done), not wanting to make a big deal of an illness she didn't have any control over. I couldn't see the point in making her feel worse than she already was, but until now, I'd failed to consider that by not saying anything, I'd inadvertently accepted everything she'd thrown at me. The net result was that she stopped communicating with me and was doing whatever she wanted to do with no regard for me or our relationship.

Looking back, I realised I'd spent two-thirds of our relationship bent out of shape, compensating for her behaviour with my unqualified support. 'I'm fine!' she'd say, repeatedly, but it was abundantly clear to me now that she wasn't *fine* and hadn't been for a really long time.

My dilemma was I *wanted* her to be as healthy as she thought she was, but I couldn't try to convince her she wasn't. Any attempt to confront her about her behaviour might lead her to accuse me of undermining her, or worse still, gaslighting. She'd told me she'd already had that experience in her life. Her ex-boyfriend had controlled her every move for almost five years, and this had made me hypersensitive to saying or doing anything that could ever be construed as controlling.

I still had all the memories of how happy she was during our first three years together and was still hoping for a rebound to those moments. My wish for this holiday to Japan wasn't just to give her something she'd always wanted; it was to travel back in time, to revisit the happiness we'd shared at the start of our relationship, if only for a few days. I thought that by granting her a wish, that she would be happy, and by extension, so would I.

Whatever I'd been doing until now wasn't working, and I needed a new strategy and plan of action. *Who was it who'd said doing the same thing again and expecting a different result was insanity?*

I knew I couldn't tell her what I was thinking, but I could use her words and actions during this trip to convince her that there was a problem *we* needed help with. Then, when we got home, she might get back into counselling, and maybe we could try couples' counselling.

Next, I needed to divert her from considering living on her own until after our holiday to Greece. Maybe the holiday in itself would give us the chance to heal. Five years between holidays was too long and we needed a proper break from our lives to give our relationship the best chance at surviving ...

As I finished my plan of action, I arrived at another stone arched bridge and the end of the Philosopher's Path. I'd walked the second kilometre without knowing I had; without seeing the scenery or hearing the cicadas.

The path was complete, and so too was my philosophising.

I stepped onto the bridge at the end of the path and looked back down the straight line of the canal. The waterway's stone-lined sides and trees on either bank led to the same single vanishing point in the distance. It was another vista without end, another metaphor sending a shiver down my spine.

Perspective; it's all about perspective.

She didn't really want to be on her own, she just needed more support to work it through.

I stepped off the bridge to start my return journey, paying attention to two young boys creeping out from under it. Both were staring into the darkness of the running water, and each had a tree branch in their hand. The boys were transfixed by the shadow under the bridge and had become completely still. From my vantage point, the scene looked like a picture from a fairy tale book, with the boys seeking out treasure or trolls.

They hadn't seen me, so I tiptoed back to the edge of the bridge to peer over their shoulders and to get a glimpse of what had them spellbound.

Just below the surface was a school of catfish-sized carp; their large grey-brown bodies flexing in snake-like motions to keep themselves stationary in the fast-moving current.

The fish must have come into view at the same time for all of us, as the boys thrashed their branches into the water with all their might. Their sequential squeals and screams temporarily drowned out the cicadas and as they splashed around in shallows, I craned my neck to check on the success of their fishing expedition. They'd missed, and the carp had scattered, hopefully dispersing to somewhere safer.

Well done fishies, well done.

The two-kilometre walk back along the Philosopher's Path was the perfect start to the end of my day. I'd put a cork in my three-three-three hypothesis at my turnaround point and had re-assigned yesterday's events to the back of mind. By doing so, I recognised a new feeling, and one I hadn't had all day. I was hungry.

I hadn't eaten since breakfast and was starting to feel the effects of using energy I didn't have. Fatigue was gripping my legs like a vice and I knew I needed to fuel up before the train trip back to Tokyo.

Even though I'd promised myself not to look at it, I pulled my phone out of my pocket and consulted my must-map. I'd researched a dining precinct not far from the train station, and it made sense that I find it before heading back.

Within an hour and a half, I arrived at my destination of Pontocho Alley, a narrow strip of restaurants parallel to the Kamo River. The alley was filled with what looked like hundreds of two-storey buildings lining the sides of its one-metre-wide lane, forming a tunnel of dimly lit eateries with little, if any, signage to suggest what they served.

'Normal me' would have completed a circuit of the alley before making a dining decision, but today's opposite-of-me walked into the first restaurant I clapped eyes on.

My random choice was a tiny nine-seat restaurant-bar, with just one spare stool available near the cash register. Before I'd closed the belled door, the chef shouted, "Irasshaimase!" into the air, and gestured with an upward facing palm for me to take a seat at the counter. He dropped a crumpled and stained paper menu in front of me and as I ran my eyes over its English translations, I could scarcely stop my salivation.

I hadn't thought much about Japanese cuisine for this trip other than wanting to eat sushi at Tokyo's Tsukiji Fish Market, but what I'd failed to consider until now was Japan's other famous export.

By sheer chance, I'd stumbled exhausted and famished into a teppanyaki bar dedicated to wagyu beef.

Jackpot!

The menu contained nine variations of the same thing, sliced wagyu steak with one of nine different flavoured sauces. There was no option for how diners wanted their beef cooked and no options for starters or desserts; however, miso soup and steamed rice were offered as complementary accompaniments to the marbled delicacy.

From my elevated position at the counter, I could see the grill and hotplates sizzling with several steaks of equivalent size.

Less than a minute after I'd ordered mine, the chef whisked one off the grill, put it on a wooden block, sliced it into slivers, and plonked the feast in front of me.

I snapped my bamboo chopsticks apart and wasted no time getting the first piece into my mouth. It melted on my tongue like beef-flavoured butter and before it had completely dissolved, I was already considering ordering a second serve.

The meal was the perfect end to the perfect day, and even though the whole trip had been thrust upon me against my will in the worst possible circumstances, I wouldn't have wanted today to be any other way.

I'd walked ugly areas, beautiful areas, temples, gardens, and the way of the philosophers. I'd been rained on, dried off, deafened, and opened up, and I knew in my heart of hearts that I wouldn't have experienced half of it in the way I had if I'd been here with her.

I'd done things today in my way at my pace and apart from the morning's false start, it had felt unexpectedly good.

I boarded my return train to Tokyo with ten minutes to spare and again sank into my allocated seat. I felt even heavier than I did this morning, but at the same time I felt a whole lot lighter. With a huge smile of my face, I closed my eyes and became consumed by wave after wave of almost visceral contentment, reminding me of my first time in Madrid, nine and a half years ago.

I'd landed in the warmth of Spain after suffering through my first UK winter, and like I'd done today, I'd made a conscious decision to stroll rather than rush. The 23-degree temperature thawed my bones and enticed me to visit parks and gardens rather than galleries and museums, and I'd chosen to *waste* most of my time in Parque del Oeste and Parque de El Retiro. It was whilst lying under the flowering chestnut trees in the latter, that I'd been overcome with the same feeling of contentment I now felt in the train to Tokyo. The overgrown grass had made an ideal mattress, and the drummers on the Alfonso XII Monument had provided the perfect soundtrack. I remembered wanting to be nowhere else nor wanting for anything more than what I had in that moment.

It wasn't a morbid thought, but I remember thinking that if I was to die then and there, then I would have been content.

It was a time when she was still in her previous relationship and I was enjoying the freedom of not being in one, focussing on my own journey to a place of comfort within myself …

I was well on my way to happiness, so what exactly happened?

I opened my eyes as the train doors closed, feeling strangely optimistic. I'd been through this sort of thing before and arrived at similar feelings of contentment. Why not this time? I felt confident that no matter what happened next, everything was going to be okay.

As the train departed Kyoto station, I shut my eyes again and welcomed another feeling move through me, unfamiliar in recent times. It was the feeling of hope.

Chapter 4

She'd arrived at the hotel before I did and was reading in bed when I gently opened the door. The room was dark except for the dim glow of her bedside lamp, and with my eyes still adjusting from the bright lights in the hall, I could barely see she was there at all. Her half-illuminated face tilted in my direction, but if she was smiling to greet me, it was obstructed by the darkness and the top edge of her magazine.

"Hey," I whispered, tentatively closing the door behind me.

"Hey," she replied at full voice, flicking to the next page.

I sat at the desk chair in the study area and swivelled it to face her; I wanted to know everything about her day. Did she enjoy it? Was it worth it? Was she as content and hopeful as I was? Was her time away from me what she needed to get us back on track? Was this solitary activity, a one-off, or was it something she wanted to do more of? What did she tell her brother about why I wasn't there? Had she missed me?

I bent over to unlace my shoes but kept my head up trying to make eye contact.

"How was your day? How was Ebisu; and how was it seeing your brother?"

"It was good." She didn't look up. "It was nice to see him."

"So, you had a good day out?"

She licked her finger and turned the page. "Yeah, it was fun."

"Did you see much of Ebisu, or just the racetrack?"

She flipped the page again, and then again, and sighed. "Just the track, but we went to a bar afterwards."

My shoes off, I sat back in the chair, waiting in silence for her to look at me, and possibly ask a question about my day, but neither was forthcoming.

"Did you have dinner?"

Her eyes met mine, flickering with impatience. "We snacked at the bar; there were a group of us, mostly from the track. We did flights of whisky and I bought some small bottles to take home with me."

Her clipped answers seemed angry, but I couldn't be sure if it was intentional, or if she was just tired.

"I didn't know you liked whisky."

"Yep, I've been getting into it recently."

In our nine years together, I'd only ever seen her have a Scotch once, with her father and it was only because it was his seventieth birthday. She loved her gin and vodka-based cocktails, but like me didn't have the palate for brown spirits, at least she'd never said as much until now. I wasn't sure why she'd bring up whisky as a highlight, but she seemed to be making it clear she didn't really want to talk about her day, let alone mine.

I stood up from my seat and went into the bathroom to have a quick shower and to finish getting ready for bed. I could feel her lowered mood pulling me down from my Kyoto-high and I was keen to preserve it for a little bit longer before I was brought crashing back to earth.

I slid into bed next to her, and as I did, she put her reading glasses and magazine onto the floor and switched off her lamp. I turned onto my right side to face her, hoping for the resumption of our nightly peck on the lips to say goodnight, but she rolled away from me to face the window.

"Sweet dreams," I whispered.

"I hope so," she replied.

I woke at 8:00am and got ready to leave the hotel by 8:30am. My mind had raced all night and even though it was the second night in this bed, I hadn't got much sleep. No matter: I was keen to get out and about and to make the most of my last day in Tokyo.

Our original must-map plan had been to wake early for the 5:00am Tsukiji Fish Market sales, but with our previous day's trips and prior night's lack of conversation throwing discussion of our itinerary out the window, I hadn't bothered to set my alarm.

I gathered my wallet and phone from the desk and poked

my head into the bathroom where she was brushing her teeth. "I'll see you later."

She turned to face me and with a mouth full of toothpaste asked, "Where are you going?"

"I'm heading to the fish market."

She spat into the sink and turned the tap on. "Why? Won't the sales be over?"

What the fuck do you care? You didn't give a shit about what I did yesterday, so why does today matter?

"I guess so, but I still want to check it out and maybe grab some breakfast whilst there."

"What, sushi for breakfast?!" she asked, poking her tongue out like she was about to retch.

I smiled at her in the mirror's reflection and withdrew back to the bedroom. "Yep, why not?"

I opened the door to leave, but she raced out of the bathroom and picked up her shoes. "Give me a minute, I want to come."

I let go of the door handle and again fell backwards onto the bed, this time into a swamp of déjà vu. I'd ridden her waves of ups and downs, dis-ease, and non-sense for six years, it seemed, and whilst I'd naively hoped it was at its end, yesterday's enlightenment in Kyoto, and now, today's antics, had shown me it was just getting started again.

I'd promised to stick by her through thick and thin, and I would, but I was tired of her pulling my strings and wanted a little something in return. I wanted her to be well again, happy again, and consistent again. Most of all, I wanted her actions to match her words and, perversely, would have been happier if she'd wanted to do as we'd done yesterday and just spent the day apart.

We caught a taxi to the markets and after browsing the aisles of fresh food, dried food, and kitchen utensils, my stomach started grumbling for the breakfast I'd been craving. The sushi stalls were on the market perimeter and I was keen to get to them before they closed or sold out of this morning's catch.

I reached out to touch her elbow to stop us near a fruit stall. "I'm going to head to the outer area to grab some sashimi. I know you don't like seafood so if you want to leave or do you own thing, we can catch up later to pack and check out."

She looked miffed, as if she had no idea what I was talking about. "No, I want to try some too."

I rolled my eyes. "What are you talking about? You hate the smell of fish, let alone the taste!"

"Yeah, but we're here now and I can't leave without giving it a go. Besides, I'm sure it will be different here."

"Are you sure?" I sounded like a parent asking their toddler if they were telling the truth.

"Yep, come on, before I change my mind."

We exited the inner market and stopped at the first sushi stall we came to. It looked like a caravan without wheels and had six stainless steel stools facing its serving window. We perched at the two on the left side and used their pictured menu to point out our orders to a man behind the glass. I chose a combination of tuna and salmon, and she asked for a platter of salmon only.

The sashimi was sliced with the sharpest of knives and presented to us on a bed of iceberg lettuce. The serves were more generous than we were used to in Melbourne, and we could have easily shared one plate between the two of us. Each of the twelve slivers were thick and firm, and each was too big to eat in one bite.

I turned to her with a blissed-out smile, and just in time to see her lever her first slice of salmon into her mouth. She'd doused it in a mix of tamari and wasabi and by the look on her face, she wasn't enjoying it. Her eyes filled with tears and she threw her head back as if swallowing pills, skolling the whole portion in one go. She took a moment to dry her eyes with a napkin, before pushing her plate towards me. "More for you, I think."

It was just another thing on this trip which made no sense. It was admirable she was willing to give it a go, but why didn't she just try mine first instead of ordering her own? What was she trying to prove, and who was she trying to prove it to? Maybe her tastes were changing, and she'd thought she'd test it out like she'd done with the whisky flights last night; or maybe it was just that she needed to give it a go to know for sure that it was something she still didn't like.

I finished my platter and half of hers and even though the sashimi had felt light going in, its oiliness was starting to sit heavy. I slid off my stool and stretched out my chest. "I'm going to walk back to the hotel, but you can catch a taxi if you like."

I wasn't bothered if she joined me or not, but I wanted to give her an opening to get out of the mistake she'd made by coming here, as well as another opportunity for her to be on her own before we headed home.

"No, it's okay. I'll walk back with you."

I turned away so she couldn't see my confusion. What was happening here?

Her contradictions were the perfect opportunity to raise the idea of counselling, but I'd made the decision during my sleepless night to wait until we'd returned to Melbourne. I didn't want to blindside her on the last day of *her* holiday with a plan I knew she wouldn't be keen on. I wanted us to be at home for the conversation, so she'd have her own space to mull it over. Better that I should bide my time for about a week; until we were back in our normal routine, and she'd recovered from her *jetlag*.

We walked back to the hotel via Ginza, Yurakucho, and Yakitori Alley, and spent our last few hours in the hotel room, resting, packing, and getting ready to leave.

We self-served our check out and caught the N'EX train to Narita Airport, and within a few hours, were boarded, buckled in, and blanketed up on the tarmac ready for take-off.

As the plane's engine roared to life and catapulted us forward, I had a chance to think about her three-days' worth of confusing words and actions. The mall, the café, the ema, her riddles, her demand to leave early, her attitude towards me last night, and her contradictions today. I felt a cold shock running through me, as if someone had tipped a bucket of ice water over my head. This was a trip we should have never done and was going to be one to remember for all the wrong reasons.

If things had been bad before, they now felt at breaking point. The already cracked glass of our relationship, held together by sheer unrealistic positivity on my part, was fracturing further, the spiderwebs of cracks continuing to deepen. I had to consider the possibility that there might be no way to fix it. No going back.

Fuck you, Tokyo.

Chapter 5

Our arrival through Melbourne Airport was quick and easy, and as neither of us had checked luggage, we breezed through passport control and customs, and entered the front door of our house within an hour of disembarking the plane.

She dropped her bag by our bed and raced to the bathroom, turning on the shower taps as soon as she got there.

Sure, by all means, you go first ...

I dropped onto our bed with an almost audible thud, my body behaving as a deadweight. It felt like I hadn't slept for days, and now I was thinking about it, I probably hadn't. Last night had provided no respite, as the flight attendants deliberately left the cabin lights on so they could chat, making my pretence of sleep all the more impossible.

Even though I was going to wait a week to ask her to restart counselling, I'd spent my sleepless hours imagining what that conversation was going to look like. I'd run through too many scenarios to count over the past two nights, but all of them had ended in the same way, with her crying at me in frustration. I was yet to come up with the best way to start the conversation without it all blowing up in my face and hoped that some rest and normality during the next seven days would help me articulate the right words and approach.

"Are you still there?" The sound of the shower had just stopped, and she was calling out to me from the bathroom.

"Yep, I'm here," I replied from my horizontal position.

"I think I'm going to go to work today."

I sat up as if punched in the stomach. "What?! Are you serious? Don't you have the day off?"

"Yes, but I don't want to waste time here if I don't have to, and if I go in, I won't need to take another annual leave day."

She emerged from the bathroom in a towel and had a look of determination on her face.

"Are you sure? Aren't you *jetlagged*?"

"No, I'm fine. I slept on the plane and will be fine." She put her earrings in and went back into the bathroom. My mind boggled: she *slept* on the plane?

"Are you right to drive?" I stammered, still coming to grips with this unfamiliar situation.

The sound of her hairdryer filled the void between us.

"Yep, I'll be fine."

A few minutes later, she appeared fully dressed and ready to go, walking towards me as if she was already late for something. "I'll see you later and I'll unpack when I get home tonight." She extracted her laptop out of her bag dropped by the bed earlier, and rushed past me into the hall, and out of our front door. There was no kiss, and no goodbye, and the house shook as she closed the door behind her, perfectly punctuating her exit.

Fucking hell. What is going on?!

I slumped back onto the bed and rolled onto my right side. It felt like a situation where I needed to open my lungs in a primal scream, but there was nothing in me to let out. I felt heavy and deadened, anaesthetised by her words and abrupt exit, but they were feelings I was well accustomed to.

I hadn't shed tears since I was sixteen, and I couldn't remember the last time I yelled or lost control.

I grew up in a household where the opposite was the norm, with my father regularly yelling or stampeding. His mood swings were erratic and volatile, and I'd spent my childhood doing my best to keep out of his way. He had a fiery temper and an even worse rage, and my overriding fear in life was that I'd inherit his less savoury traits.

As soon as I was old enough to recognise I had choice and freewill, I maintained constant vigilance over myself, identifying and analysing characteristics and impulses which looked like his. I taught myself to evaluate my thoughts and feelings, and to stifle my instincts and reflexes before they converted into words or behaviour I'd later regret. It seemed I'd become so successful at it, that there was no longer any internal emotional fires which needed extinguishing.

I rolled onto my back and returned to my imagined

conversations, running through them again and again to find a better introduction and the best possible words and tone to get her to give counselling another go. I could use this morning's rush to get to work as a conversation starter, or the way she was towards me in the café, or our argument walking back from Meiji Jingu, or our conversation in the mall, but she'd just say there was nothing out of the ordinary about any of it. She'd tell me she'd acted reasonably, and I wouldn't be able to argue with her, as calling her unreasonable still wasn't an option. Trying to explain to her that she wasn't behaving normally, without undermining her remained the predicament I couldn't yet see through.

She'd rushed out the door like she was escaping something, like she had someone to see or something to do. She didn't need to go to work today, and she didn't need to worry about her annual leave day. It was a story and a smokescreen for whatever was really going on, and we desperately needed professional help to work out what it was.

I was playing a game of pretend chess and she already had me at check. My next move had to be made now as she'd been clearly working me towards checkmate for three days. The counselling conversation couldn't wait a week, I decided; we were already at crisis point and I had to confront it today, whether I was ready or not.

I bolted upright, trying to jolt myself from lethargy. There was lots to do today, and I had no choice but to get it done on my own. I needed to unpack, shower, eat, shop, and visit my parents to pick up the dog.

By 6:30pm, my anxiety was reaching its limits, with my breathing becoming shallow and ineffective to reflect it. The front door had just opened and closed, and the dog was barking to herald her return from work. I had no idea where the next half an hour would go and wanted at the same time to get started, and to delay the conversation for as long as possible.

"Hey," I shouted, to let her know I was upstairs in our living room.

She didn't reply, but instead I could hear her shoes on our staircase, stepping on each slowly one by one, rather than her usually quicker two by two.

That's not right! I'd normally get a fifteen-minute grace period, where she'd change out of her work clothes, take off her makeup, and potter about before joining me.

Her footsteps didn't pause near our study, and became louder with each second, louder and louder until she was casually standing in front of me with her hands in her pockets.

I looked up at her and lost the connection between my brain and my mouth.

"Hey, how was your day? You must be tired; I've made us dinner, just let me know when you'd like it, and I'll warm it up." My words flowed out of me at random. They resembled nothing of what I had planned to say.

Her eyes were glistening, but I couldn't tell if she'd been crying or was about to. The rest of her face was expressionless, and she looked like the same stone statue I'd first encountered on the rooftop in Tokyo. Her eyes locked onto mine, as if she was steeling herself to say something. She drew a long and purposeful breath to speak.

"I think I'm going to stay at my brother's apartment for the next few days."

There. It was out. Her words dissolved my anxiety, replacing it with pure panic, and not a little defensiveness. It was as though someone had snuck into our living room with a clapper board and had yelled, 'take two', rewinding the clock by three days to continue a conversation she hadn't got right the first time.

Worse than that, none of my countless imagined scenarios had started with her saying what she'd just said; in fact, none of my scenarios started with her saying anything at all. I was meant to be the driver here.

I fossicked around on the couch to find the remote control to mute the TV, and to buy myself another two or three seconds to invent a response I hadn't yet rehearsed.

"What's going on?" The severity of my tone caught me off guard. I hadn't intended to be harsh, but my voice exposed the annoyance I was keen to keep hidden.

"I already told you, when we were away, remember? I want to be on my own." She matched her tone to mine, seemingly irritated I wasn't keeping up.

"Yes, that was a conversation you started three days ago which you haven't brought up again."

"Yes, and nothing has changed. I still want to be on my own."

"But you haven't said why, and you haven't told me what I've done to make you want to be on your own."

"I don't know why, and you haven't done anything; it's just something I need to do."

I bit my lip to prevent myself from responding too quickly and to give me a moment to process something else that had been bothering me since our first morning in Tokyo. There was something else at play at here; an intangible but increasingly strong undercurrent of ill feeling, that until now, I hadn't been able to identify.

For the past few days, and possibly even longer, she'd lost all sense of her usual kindness and compassion. She was showing no empathy, speaking to me like I didn't matter to her in the least. She was acting like we weren't a couple, and as if we weren't married. She was treating me like an inconvenience, an obstruction she needed to get out of her way.

We'd based our entire marriage on the motto of *always being kind*, and at some point, during the past three days, or three months, or three years, she'd stopped being kind. Her words, her tone, her expression, and even in the way she was standing above me with her hands in her pockets clearly demonstrated her contempt for me, and for us. She was telling me what she was wanted to do as if she didn't need to consider anyone but herself.

To her this situation wasn't important; to me, it was. I'd spent six years of our relationship caring for her, and supporting her, and I wasn't going to give up on her now.

I gestured to the cushion next to me. "Please sit down."

She stepped towards the couch and sat on the cushion next to the one I had my hand on.

I turned to my right to face her. "Look, I know you're going through some stuff, but running away and leaving isn't going to help. We've been here before, and—"

She scowled. "We've never been here before; I've never asked you for space before."

"You're right, you haven't, but you're not asking for space—"

"Yes, I am!" she fired back. Her cheeks were red and tears were welling in her eyes.

I closed my eyes to block these signs of distress; it was the only way to stay focussed. "Have you thought that maybe we're not as on top of your depression as we'd hoped; and that—" She cut me off again.

"I've told you already, I'm not sick and I don't think I ever have been. I'm absolutely fine, and this is just something I've wanted to do for a while."

"You keep saying that, but you haven't once said anything to me about it until three days ago. Remember me? Your husband? We used to be good communicators and you haven't communicated with me; you haven't discussed the way you've been feeling, so excuse me if all of this is coming as a bit of a shock."

I'd done my best to regain control of my tone, but emotion was again sneaking into it. "I want you to be well, I really do, but I don't think you leaving is the best thing for you, or for us. I promised we'd work through anything and I want us to work through this together. Don't you?"

She was sitting on her hands again and rocked back

slightly in her seat. I'd not seen the posture before Tokyo, but she was doing it again, appearing to shrink into herself. Her now-dry eyes stayed fixed onto mine but their icy-blue still showed an absence of warmth or care.

"Yes, but—" I cut her off before she recited the same lines she'd probably been practising all day.

"So, let's work through this together. I agree we need to do something different but living apart can't be the answer. Can we please try something different? Can you please start counselling again?"

"I don't want to, and how is that different from the last time—?"

"And we can do couples counselling together too. Or you can do you own sessions, and I will too. We can both see the same person or different people, whatever you like; whatever it takes."

She pulled her right knee to her chest and rocked back; she might as well have crossed her arms in defiance. "I don't think counselling will help."

I put my knee on the couch and turned my body to face her fully. "But it will!"

She looked confused, as if I didn't know what I was talking about. "You don't think you need counselling; you're just saying you'll go to get me to go."

"It doesn't matter what I think; this is about what we need to do for *us*." The emotion in my voice was escalating, and I could hear my own desperation.

"I don't know." She shook her head.

"What's to know? We just need to give it a go. Let's make a deal; let's do as many sessions as we can fit in before Greece, and then—"

She held up a hand, cutting me off.

"That's another thing; I really don't want to go to Greece. It's not the right time, but you should still go, without me."

Fuck me. Now she's cancelling my fortieth birthday present and a trip we've had planned for over a year!

"I'm not going to Greece without you; but as I was saying—"

She interrupted again.

"You should though, it's for your fortieth and you should still go."

I pretended not to hear her.

"I don't want to go without you, but if we do the counselling and the counsellors think it's a bad idea for us to go on a three-week holiday together, then we won't, okay? Can we give this a go first? Can you give us a few weeks to try and work this out; please?" My desperation had dwindled to unashamed begging. I knew I had no Plan B, and no idea what my next move would be if she refused.

She paused and turned her head towards the TV. "Look, I don't think it's going to help, and I don't think I'm going to change my mind. I've wanted to be on my own for a while, but I'll give your counselling idea a go on one condition."

"Sure! What is it?"

"If they support my decision to have some time on my own, then you'll be okay with it."

"Yes, yes, absolutely; but I want you to be open-minded about Greece, too. We haven't had a decent holiday in five years, and we need to get away; we need a break from all this; okay?"

She got up from the couch and walked off, stomping down the stairs and into our bedroom below.

So, that's a yes then? Did she nod?

I was out of breath, and my head was spinning. It was as though she'd held my face under water for the past few minutes, and I had no real idea what I'd said or what I'd agreed to; I just needed to get some air back into my lungs.

I slouched deeper into the couch and tilted my head back to stare at the ceiling. Exhaustion was crawling over me like spiders, paralysing my muscles and my feelings about what was going on. My skin seemed to be burning with an internal heat but the rest of me was cold and confused.

I had no idea what was happening in her head, and she was yet to give me a reason for wanting to leave. How were we supposed to solve the problem if I didn't know what it was?

Throughout our relationship, I'd promised her I'd never leave her, and also promised her we'd always work through anything. Now, I was holding to that: regardless of what she was now saying.

This was just another test of the strength of our relationship. She wasn't going anywhere until we'd exhausted all our options to prevent that from happening.

I promised her I wouldn't give up, and I wasn't going to break that promise.

Chapter 6

It had taken two weeks of gentle reminders and follow-ups, but we were finally seated in front of a counsellor for our first ever couples' counselling session.

We were in one of several consulting suites in a grand old Victorian terrace in inner Melbourne; a clinic referred to her by our family doctor. The space was bright and white and was filled with a jumble of furnishings from multiple decades. The blue carpet was old and needed replacing, and the two huge windows behind us looked painted shut. A dark, heavy looking banker's desk sat to our left, its top obscured by files, and piles of paper; and a white laminate bookshelf sat opposite it, filled with a greater number of knickknacks than requisite psychology books. Various artworks hung on the remaining walls, with the one above the cast iron fireplace we faced, looking as though it had been knocked askew by a small earthquake.

We sat in a triangle formation in the middle of the room, with the counsellor sitting in front of us on a high-backed leather chair, and us positioned next to each other on patterned polyester seats from the nineteen-eighties.

"So, why are you two here?"

Our counsellor looked seventy years old but was probably closer to sixty. She was tall, slim, and had wiry blonde hair; and at first glance, she reminded me of my primary school librarian. There was nothing about her question and demeanour that suggested she was anything but clinical in her approach, but I guess it was the approach we were paying her for, rather than compassion.

The two of them had met in a one-on-one session earlier in the week, but this was the first time with the three of us together. I had no idea what had already been said and what hadn't, so I let the silence draw out until it became uncomfortable, and until the counsellor nodded my way to encourage me to answer.

"Well—" I started, "Well, you both already met in your session on Monday, and I'm here because I want to work through whatever we need to work through with the help of a professional who can give us the tools we need to get us back on track. I assume you know we're going through some relationship stuff, and I think we need help to navigate it."

My answer wasn't enough, and the counsellor kept her eyes fixed on mine, silently urging me to continue.

"Well, we've battled through her bipolar and depression for a number of years now—" The counsellor raised a hand, so I stopped.

"Let me stop you there. I've been told that there never

really was any depression, or bipolar, and that it was all most likely a misdiagnosis."

"Maybe, but I guess that's for you to decide, not me. I'm just going on what previous psychologists and psychiatrists have said, and—"

She interrupted me again, lifting her pen into her opening mouth to try to disguise her surprise.

"Can you just run that by me again? It wasn't just general practitioners doing the diagnoses. It was by psychologists and psychiatrists?"

"Yes, of course."

I wasn't really surprised. Her question – and shock – only seemed to validate the necessity of us doing counselling together. I expected I'd need to fill in blanks and correct distortions and thought it might be less confronting with a professional third party in the room.

"Yes. She was diagnosed and was treated for bipolar before we met; over nine years ago. She was on lithium at the time. She was well for three years and was then diagnosed with depression six years ago. Things felt like they were getting better about three years after that, but they clearly haven't, and now she wants to live on her own. Anyway, none of that really matters; the reason we're here is to work through whatever we need to work through to stay together." I paused, momentarily running out of steam, before continuing, encouraged by the counsellor's silence.

"We used to have a great life of travel and adventure and everything slowed down after we got married. We have a trip to Greece planned in four weeks' time and I'd really like us to get away from it all, and leave all this behind, and just enjoy each other's company for a few weeks to see if we can reconnect and get back on track."

The counsellor scribbled a few notes onto her notepad and then set it on her knee. "I agree; I couldn't agree more. I've already said to her that if you can't make your relationship work on holiday, then you're going to struggle to be able to do it here."

What the fuck?! Why did she keep that from me?

The session ended after another forty-five minutes of fact-checking and telling me what I already knew but delivered us nothing in terms of solutions or new things we should try working on.

She'd stayed silent and stared at the blue carpet for most of the session and didn't once acknowledge that she'd been dishonest or had omitted details which could have been important or helpful.

I still couldn't imagine what the two of them had talked about two days earlier but based on our discussions during the past fifty-minutes, it didn't seem to be related to us, or to Tokyo, or to her wanting to live on her own.

I walked out of the clinic with my jaw clenched in silence, equal parts livid we'd wasted an hour, and grateful we had. I unlocked the car and we both fell in, slamming the big heavy doors a little harder than we ordinarily would have. Before I put my seatbelt on, I swivelled to face her.

"What was all that about?"

She ignored my question and stared blankly at the space between the windscreen and a tree trunk in front of us.

"I want to change counsellors," she said flatly. I was silent. She continued:

"I don't like her; I didn't like her on Monday, and I still don't like her now."

"Why? Because she agrees with me about Greece?" I couldn't help but smirk as I put the key into the ignition and roared the engine to life.

"No, I don't like that she doesn't understand what's going on."

I put the car in reverse and backed it onto the road.

"She's not the only one. I don't think anyone understands what's going on, especially me."

Arguing about changing counsellors was bait I couldn't afford to nibble at. For her to take our couples counselling seriously, she needed to trust the person we were working with, as well as the process we were going through. If she didn't, she was not only going to dismiss everything they had to say, but she was also going to reject going to Greece and refuse to stick around at home. She was playing this game better than I was and had checked my king again. There was only one thing I could say to stop her from packing her bags when we got home.

"Fine, work it out; change counsellors, and let me know when our next session is. I don't mind who we see, so long as we see someone."

As I drove us home, the possibility of worse to come between us spun me into a spiral of pessimism and hopelessness. Her declaration in Japan and her attitude towards me during the past two weeks might not be about her wanting a temporary break; it might actually be about her wanting to be on her own *permanently*. If this counselling didn't work, and if the trip to Greece didn't work, then we were possibly heading towards our end. The idea of us splitting up and divorcing was as unfathomable to me as teleportation or time travel.

She'd not yet *said* we were heading that way, but she never said what she was thinking. She'd always presented her thoughts and feelings as problems needing solving, and I'd been our delegated problem solver.

My rolodex of memories flipped furiously as I tried to work out when this pattern had started, and *why* it had started. Was it three years ago when she was recovering from her breakdown; or was it before that, when she got sick? Or could it have been when we returned from the UK and needed somewhere to live; or was she like this whilst we were doing the long-distance thing?

No, no, no, and no. She'd started her posing of life's problems as riddles even before our first date. She was the quiz master, and I was her contestant, and it had been this way from the very start.

She'd drip-feed me her cues and clues and would leave it to me to puzzle it out and present back to her with a unified picture. She'd never given me the puzzle box or a picture of what it was I was trying to piece together, as it was a part of my job to fill in the blanks whilst deciphering what she was thinking and feeling. My job was to deduce what was going on.

She'd given me her hints in Japan, but I wasn't piecing it together in the way she expected me to. She was still too vague, and her messages too coded for me to make sense of them, or maybe the emerging picture was too incomprehensible to continue.

This was a puzzle I didn't want to complete, not unless we were going to remain together at the end of it. This time I wasn't going to follow her lead, and I wasn't going to give her an easy way out.

Did she want us to stay together, or was she already gone? Were we fighting this together or was I the only one in the ring?

I squeezed my eyes tight to shut down my thoughts. This was a line of inquiry I didn't want to investigate any further.

With a week to go before our flights to Athens, we were back at the psychology clinic for our third couples session. She'd organised a new counsellor and this was our second time seeing her together.

She liked this new one better, and had seen her twice on her own, but I didn't like her at all, and had felt she didn't like me either.

Counsellor Two was in her fifties, but psychology seemed to be a new career for her. She behaved like a recent graduate, referring to theoretical tools and tricks from books rather than from her own experience and expertise. She had wild brown hair and a badly hidden streak of misandry. She'd fumbled her way through our first session and had used activities that didn't match our conversations. During that meeting, she'd thrown a set of value cards onto the floor and had asked both of us to pick the three or four values that resonated with us the most. There were no duplicates in the deck and the inevitable outcome of the activity was that we'd each have differing value sets. It was as though she was working with us towards the predetermined outcome of breaking up, and her methods were biased towards getting us there. She'd put my nose out of joint by mentioning the possibility of a trial separation had been explored at their very first session together, but I was still unsure as to whose suggestion it actually was.

This was our last hour of counselling together before our holiday and the final opportunity for us to plead our cases before judgement was made.

"So, where are both of you at?" The frizzy-haired counsellor wasted no time in getting stuck into it.

"I still don't want to go. I want to use the time to be on my own, and to figure things out."

"And you?" The counsellor switched her dispassionate gaze my way.

"Well, I don't think your suggestion that we take a break is a good one. I'm not sure what it will achieve, nor what we're supposed to do whilst we're *on* the break. We're not fifteen years old, and I think we should be working through things together, not apart. As for Greece, I think we should go for the very same reasons. We'll have none of the distractions we have here, and it will be three weeks of time dedicated to us. I still think that if we can't make our relationship work over there, then we're going to have trouble making it work here. I want us to go and give it a shot."

"So, you're still at an impasse."

No, you Muppet. What exactly are we paying you for?

"I don't think so."

I wanted to get in first with my last-ditch plan before they both ganged up on me to make me forego the holiday I'd been waiting for.

I turned away from the counsellor to face my wife directly. "What if we do Greece like we did Ebisu and Kyoto? What if we have separate holidays together? You do your thing, and I'll do mine. We can have breakfast together each morning, or not, and we can even get separate rooms in the hotels and separate seats on the plane. You can still use the time to be on your own, and to figure things out, just without the distractions of work and our normal life. We'll connect when you want to and won't when you don't."

Her face turned red. "That's a stupid idea. Why would we do that, and what would be the point?"

"Well, my hope is that you'll actually want to spend some time with me by choice; and that you may remember the way we used to be and how we could be again."

The counsellor looked like she was trying to suppress a smile, and I could have sworn I saw a tear in the corner of her eye. Perhaps, she was hearing my anguish and desperation but perhaps she could also hear my logic and reason. "Sounds like a win-win to me," she said, looking at us one by one.

She shrugged – was it agreement, or resignation?

"Okay, but I like my normal life, and I don't need a distraction. I'm not getting us separate rooms. We'll just have to manage as best we can, but know that I'm going to do my own thing and you can do whatever you want. I still don't want to go, but if it's the only way out of this, I'll go."

Out of this?

It wasn't the exact response I wanted but I was going to take it.

The drive home was another quiet one; I felt that neither of us had won. I should have been happy as she'd finally agreed to the holiday, but her reluctance and clear indication she was doing it under sufferance bothered me, as did the ominous words she used: 'the only way out of this'. But at least there was hope. My entire strategy for the past five weeks had a singular focus, to make sure we got to Greece together. For me, our holiday was the key to rekindling our relationship and without it, we'd have no chance.

In the quiet of the car, I reflected on whether I'd been too stubborn and blinkered in my pragmatic approach to the problem solving of our relationship. Step one was supposed to lead to step two, which would lead us to step three, but I was no longer sure it was going to happen that way.

Was my aim to save the holiday or save our relationship?

Until now, I'd considered both as two parts of the same whole, but I was no longer certain of my own motivations. I'd booked and paid for all our flights and ferry rides more than nine months ago, and she'd booked, but not yet paid for all our accommodation as her gift for my birthday. I hadn't wanted to acknowledge it, but there was a small part of me that wanted her to see it through, and to give me what she'd promised. I'd done my bit and I wanted her to do hers.

My stubbornness about my plan had been met with her own towards hers. She'd spent the past five weeks pushing me to my limits; her late nights getting later and her couldn't-care-less attitude becoming worse. She behaved as if she were already single again, doing as she pleased without an ounce of consideration for me or for our relationship. In fact, she'd done everything in her power to get me to call off the trip, and to ask her to leave, but I'd absorbed it all. I'd ridden her waves of mental illness before, and I knew I could do it again. I'd seen how her depression altered her behaviour, and I could see it again now.

She was not herself, and I wanted her back.

I clung to my hope that I'd find her again in our joint passion of travel; in the rich history of Athens, the romance of Santorini, and the relaxation of Naxos; however, if I couldn't, she'd still get her time alone, and at least I'd get my birthday present.

Chapter 7

For the first two weeks of our holiday, we slept in the same bed each night and had breakfast together most mornings, but beyond that, she kept me to my agreement and did her own thing.

She'd wake at sunrise and start her days with a run, two things she'd not done before. Like me, she wasn't a morning person, but unlike me, she didn't like running. She'd told me on our first date that she had thicker than normal blood and that if her heart rate rose, she'd be prone to fainting. It wasn't normal first-date conversation, but we were forced to speak about it after she'd scared me senseless by passing out just before dinner. She blamed it on the rush of the day and on her elevated heart rate and told me she usually managed it with blood-thinners; and maybe that's what she was doing now.

After our hotel breakfast each morning, she'd bid me farewell to head off into the city. She didn't tell me where she was going, nor what her plans were, and I never probed deeper than she wanted me to. My fear of giving her a reason to flip out and want to return home early was greater than my curiosity, however she did sometimes make small talk in the evening to tell me what she'd done, and what she'd enjoyed about her day.

In Athens, she spent most of her time in the upmarket shopping district of Kolonaki, whereas I spent most of mine exploring the archaeological and historical sites around the Acropolis. During the evenings, she'd drink cocktails by the hotel pool whilst I traipsed around Lycabettus Hill, the Panathenaic Stadium, and the Temple of Olympian Zeus. I never visited the pool bar and she never saw the Parthenon up close. I bought us both Greek SIM cards, and we'd keep in occasional contact via text and would meet for lunch or dinner if we were ever in the same place at the same time.

As I'd done in Kyoto, I kept things slow, seeking out and wandering the paths of philosophers. I sat on Areopagus Hill and in the Ancient Agora and contemplated the nature of my knowledge, reality, and existence. I rationalised the plight of my relationship, and at the same time, ignored the severity of its dysfunction. I knew there was little I could do to bring us back together except give her space and wait for her to be ready to do so.

My strolls in the footsteps of Socrates, Plato, and Aristotle rekindled my interest in reading, and once we left Athens for Santorini, I spent most of my second week doing just that.

I didn't read fiction for pleasure and was far more interested in reading anything and everything about human behaviour and what made people tick. I'd always loved learning new theories and new perspectives, but at some point during the past nine years, I'd stopped seeking them out. I wasn't sure when or why, or what had led to me being content with all I knew at the time, but our present circumstances had reignited my craving for new knowledge. I felt primed, and on the precipice of learning something transformational, something to rock my world and change my life, both prospects to be hastened by the current direction of my marriage.

My primary focus, unsurprisingly, was relationship psychology. I wanted to better understand how we'd got to where we were and what we needed to do to get us back on track. I read articles and watched videos and was continually reminded of the things I thought I already knew but had unintentionally forgotten.

We'd often said to each other that we needed to grow together or else we'd grow apart; but I realised that after our first year together we hadn't done anything proactive to ensure we remained on the same path. We'd failed to discuss how we were growing, and changing, and whether what we wanted or needed was something different; something that we hadn't wanted or needed previously. The way we'd started our relationship was the way we continued to live it, or at least it was the way that I was; still living by the promises she'd made me make, even though she hadn't asked me to make them for years. I was still living by the idea that she didn't like whisky, and that she wasn't interested in getting up at sunrise to run, when clearly, she did, and clearly, she was.

Through my reading and learning, I discovered I'd been subconsciously treading on eggshells around her for the past six years. Her bipolar and depression caused me to continually guess, and second-guess what it was she needed from me. I imagined our life as a game of tennis; she was the one perpetually serving, and I the one receiving.

Put simply, our relationship revolved around her moods and what I thought she needed from me to be to best support her. If I thought she needed a hug, I hugged her; if I thought she needed to be alone, I left her alone. If she wanted to be cheered, then I did my best; and if she wanted to whinge and complain, I listened and provided solutions. She never told me what she wanted or needed though, and I'd repeatedly used her depression as the reason why.

My mantra was straightforward. As her husband and friend, I supported her the best way I knew how. If I'd ever prioritised what I needed or wanted, then I would have stopped doing that long ago. Leaving her was never an option; marriage was for life and I wouldn't have asked her to marry me, if I wasn't certain we'd see it through. I was committed to her through sickness and health, and the fact she was considering leaving me was beyond my understanding. I was positive I'd done everything right, and I wanted a return to our better days. She was all I knew, and all I wanted to know, and whilst I had a moment of equanimity in Kyoto, I couldn't imagine being without her.

We'd arrived by ferry to the Greek island of Naxos for the third and final leg of our Grecian holiday. It was late

September, and the temperature was cooling off and the wind picking up.

A car had picked us up from the port and dropped us off at a villa in what felt like the middle of nowhere. It wasn't the accommodation she'd booked, and due to the island commencing their closure for the low season, the hotel manager had taken the liberty of arranging for us to stay at an upgraded honeymoon villa, five kilometres out of town. It was stunning accommodation; one of only nine self-contained houses, each with its own sauna and pool.

They were perfect residences for loved-up couples who wanted a private escape, however, for us, it was an unwelcome opposite of what we'd been expecting. Without shops, cafes, or archaeological sites to easily escape to each day, Naxos was going to provide us with a whole new challenge to navigate; the challenge of being alone together.

I could only smile at the irony of how our three-week getaway was to end. She'd treated me as more or less invisible since Japan and if there was a turning point for our relationship in our road ahead, I still wasn't able to see it by the time we got to Naxos. We'd been existing in parallel realities, on different sides of the same coin, sharing the same space but without connection.

She'd successfully avoided talking to me for the past two weeks and during the next week, it was going to be impossible not to. Our lack of communication was the cause of us heading to nowhere, so the cure had to be an obvious one. If I didn't say something this week, then I could be confident that nothing would be said.

After we'd unpacked our bags and checked out our new surroundings, we both lay on the bed staring at the chalk-coloured ceiling. Our villa was newish but was constructed to look old, like it was a cave, or carved out of rock. There were no visible corners or edges and the floor seamlessly morphed into the walls and into the ceiling.

Everything was the same colour white, like a cell in a psychiatric hospital, stark and sparse, but with a little less padding on the walls.

Five days here was going to seem like five years.

My head was full of unsaid thoughts and my internal monologues were swirling, and I could feel my nervous energy transforming into nausea.

I cleared my throat with no idea of what to say or how to start, but knowing I had to. I kept my focus on the ceiling and blurted out the first thing that came to mind.

"Sooo, why aren't you attracted to me anymore?"

Okay, that's a start; not a great start, but it's a start.

Her breathing stopped and she became completely still. It was a presumptive statement on my part, as she'd never said as much, but I could guess from the past few months that if she was still attracted to me, she was no longer showing it.

With the seconds ticking by, she let go of her breath and sighed. "I don't know; I really don't know why." She sounded genuinely sorry, even though she hadn't used the word. She knew her answer was going to cut me, but I was the one who'd handed her the blade.

Fuck.

It wasn't the response my subconscious was aiming for, and was a hole-in-one I didn't want to hit; I wanted the bunker or the water or the rough, but not the cup. I wanted her to dispute my question and call me an idiot.

She'd used to describe me as the most attractive person she'd ever seen; not just met; but seen. With all the models and actors on the planet, I never believed her, but as ridiculous as it sounded, it had been nice to hear.

Hearing the opposite sucked the air out of me and turned me inside out, but I fought to stay calm; now that we'd started a conversation, I couldn't back off. I clutched at a fragment of conversation in Japan to continue.

"Does it have anything to do with what you told you told me in Tokyo? About being attracted to women?"

I turned my head to face her, catching a glimpse of a tear seeping from her left eye down her cheek and disappearing under her ear. Her skin was bright red, and her forehead looked sweaty, like she was using all her energy to hold herself together.

"I don't know." Her voice had fallen to a whisper.

My swirling thoughts slowed. I swallowed down the nausea, leaving my mouth dry. A veil of calm and numbness wafted over me.

How do we overcome this? Attraction can't be forced; it's either there or not, and if it's not, what are we going to do? Surely, we can ride it out. There have been times when I haven't been attracted to you, and it's changed back. We just need to wait. Time cures everything, doesn't it?

Before I could voice my thoughts, she continued, "I don't know what's going on, but it's been like this for a while, maybe a year or two—"

"A year or two?! You've been keeping this to yourself for a *year or two?* Why haven't you spoken to me about it? Why haven't you shared what you've been thinking?" My voice rose, my thoughts racing again.

"I was trying to work it out. I can't explain it. You're the perfect husband and I know there isn't anyone else out there like you. You're one of the most important people in my life and I never want to lose you."

No one else like me?

Don't want to lose me?

One of?

Why was she saying these things?

Had she been thinking about finding someone else?

Had she been thinking about losing me from her life?

I rolled my head back to face the ceiling, a flight of butterflies in my stomach.

"But, whatever happens, I never want to lose our friendship, it's just too important to me."

Fuck me! Is this really happening? Is this how we end? In isolation on Naxos with five days to go, and her wanting us to be *friends?*

The butterflies pushed into my throat.

I'd not kept in contact with any of my exes and admired people who did. I'd always viewed breakups as final and had never wanted to drag something old into the new. I saw keeping in contact with exes as being tied to them, and never truly letting go. I liked my past to be in the past and wasn't sure I'd ever be able to change the way I thought about it. Not for anyone, not even for her. I thought she knew that about me. Had she forgotten the rule, or was she hoping she was different?

I cleared my throat and swallowed an involuntary need to tell her what she wanted to hear. I had to be honest.

"Um, I'm not sure what we're talking about, but hypothetically, there will be no friendship if there is no us. If we break up, I'll be gone. You know I haven't kept in contact with any of my exes. A breakup is a breakup, and over is over. If we ever broke up, I'd probably move overseas, and we wouldn't be in each other's lives. We'd probably never speak again."

Through my peripheral vision, I could see she'd turned onto her side to face me, her face redder than before, and her tear-filled eyes wide open with disbelief.

She opened her mouth to reply but didn't say anything.

I remained focussed on the ceiling, fused to the mattress. My skin was overheating, and my forehead was throbbing as it did when I was angry; except I wasn't. The butterflies were dying and decaying within me, and my numbness had returned. I felt fatigued, as if someone had pulled the plug to drain me of my energy reserves.

I needed to sleep.

My whole body jerked as she put her right arm across my chest, tucking her hand into my armpit. She curled into a foetal position, burying her face into my bicep, throwing her leg over my hips, and grasping me tight. She hadn't touched me in months, let alone hold me the way she was now.

Within moments of her embrace, she lost all control and sobbed into my arm. Her cries were muffled but her anguish was palpable. It was as though she'd heard someone close to her had just died or been diagnosed with a terminal disease.

We lay in that position until she was drained of tears and until her convulsions slowed to sporadic twitches, relaxing into a deep, sleep-like state.

I lay motionless – and emotionless – hovering above my own body, looking down on two people I didn't know, and who quite obviously didn't know each other.

How had it come to this?

Come to what?

She hasn't said anything.

She hasn't broken up with you.

She's just crying because you're being a stubborn dick.

I was numb, soaking wet, and needed to get up.

I needed to get out.

"I'm going for a walk."

I levered her arm and leg off me and with what felt like a seamless movement, I pivoted off the bed, grabbed my shoes and walked out the door, down the driveway and towards the road.

I perched on the gutter at the front of the villa complex and put my shoes on, swivelling my head right towards the town we came from earlier, and left towards the island's unknown. She didn't follow me out, and I wasn't sure I wanted her to.

Which way?

Known or unknown?

Go left.

I got up and jogged the first one hundred metres. The unnamed strip of bitumen carved through what looked like the rocky outcrop of a hill. Tufts of weeds and thistles sprung from dirt saturated with plastic rubbish, and brick buildings which had no right to be there, clung to the hillsides like monuments to the past. None were finished; all were just shells with no fixtures, fittings, windows, or doors.

Real estate signs spruiking luxury inclusions and a millionaire's lifestyle, still stood at the front of each one, but they too were weathered, broken, and falling apart to be convincing.

This was the derelict and rundown area of Naxos, a remnant of a better time, a boom time, but now just a memorial for what could have been.

How very apt.

After half an hour of walking, the grey-blue of the Aegean Sea emerged in front of me like an oasis. The choppy waters appeared at the end of a narrow cobbled street dividing tightly packed shops, bars, cafes, and motorbike hire stalls; a whitewashed and stuccoed version of any main street in Bali, except everything was shuttered and closed.

I hadn't seen anyone else on my walk, no people, no cars, and no animals. I'd had the road to myself, and this part of the island to myself. I was alone and felt like the last person on earth, and the apocalyptic landscape created the perfect backdrop.

I walked directly to the sand and sat down, folding my arms on my knees, and putting my chin on my right elbow. It was windier than earlier, and the sea looked as angry as the grey cloud-filled sky above it.

I was still numb from whatever had happened at the villa.

If it was cold, I couldn't feel it. If my legs hurt from the walk, I couldn't feel them. I felt strangely as though I had accompanied myself here as my chaperone. I knew I was still me, but I couldn't feel myself in my body. I'd separated from myself and I wanted to be back together.

I stared at the ocean wanting to feel the breeze on my face, or the sand underneath me, but the sensations kept their distance, and kept me wanting.

I needed to stay here until I could feel again, until I felt whole again.

The island of Paros emerged in front of me on the horizon, even though it had been there the whole time.

I wonder if I could swim there.

Paros was the island we were supposed to visit for the last leg of this holiday. We'd spoken about Paros or Folegandros in depth, but I don't remember ever us talking about Naxos.

Why were we here?

What was the attraction?

My blood ran cold at the thought of *that* word, snapping me back to a unified reality. I was myself again.

The wind was icy, and the sand was grainy, and I needed to get back to the villa or risk hypothermia.

After my return, we both pretended the conversation had never happened. I didn't bring it up again and neither did she, but from the time I walked back into the villa, the dynamic between us seemed to change, somehow for the better.

I hoped it was regret for what she'd said and that she was having second thoughts about wanting to be on her own. Nine years was a lot of life to throw away for a fleeting change of thought, and something she wasn't yet sure about.

For the next four days, she spent more time with me, not because she had to, because she didn't; but because she *wanted* to. Each time I tried to give her some time and space, she impinged on mine. No sooner would I leave to do my own thing, she'd send me a text asking where I was and if she could join me.

She wanted us to see the old town together and was even happy to walk the five kilometres to the Apollo Temple in the heat at midday. She was making an effort, and for the first time in years, was doing things she probably didn't like doing, just so we could be together.

We strolled the Naxian beaches together, sat on the sand

together, ate together, and explored together. It felt like a return to our old days and a possible cleaning of the slate, even if there were still no overt signs of attraction.

I felt a familiar comfort in her actively choosing me as a companion in her holiday and was happy to take what was on offer. The aim of our counselling had been to get us on this holiday, with the aim for us to decompress and reconnect. It felt like we were progressing in that direction. Were things finally going to plan?

At the very least she was friendly again, and friendship was something we could use to relaunch our relationship, just like we had back at our very start.

Chapter 8

Our flight home to Melbourne was as unadventurous and uncomfortable as the one we'd taken to Athens three weeks earlier. Our holiday together/apart, had transformed into one together/together and my hope was building for whatever stage or phase was next. Regardless of the first two weeks in Athens and Santorini, and the first two hours in Naxos, I'd had a wonderful time and the weeks away felt more like months. I felt refreshed and energised and after our past four days, I trusted she felt the same way.

Once she'd dried off and got dressed after her post-flight shower, she started transferring clothes and shoes from her suitcase into her carryall. It seemed as though she was dividing her clean clothes from the ones needing washing, but something about her method wasn't making sense.

"What are you up to?"

"Packing."

"I can see that; but what for?"

"I need to be on my own. We gave the holiday a go, and now we need to give this a go. I'm going to stay at my brother's."

The coldness of her words again punched a fist-sized hole straight through me.

What the actual fuck?!

"Are you *serious*?"

She looked up from her suitcase and her hostile gaze informed me she was.

"For how long?"

"I don't know, maybe a week or two."

Her packing was becoming less orderly and more frantic as she spoke.

I sat on the bed completely numb with the shock of it. It was as though her words were tranquillisers and my ability to feel any reaction to them was snatched from me.

I still wanted her to stay; but I no longer knew why.

Her emotional rollercoaster was making me sick, but I'd been on it for so long, that I was now scared of getting off it and onto solid ground. The past couple of months had been hard work, but nothing compared to the arduous work of the past six years.

Maybe I need a break too. And then I paused.

Why was I still fighting so hard, and what was I fighting for? More of the same?

Was this some sort of Stockholm Syndrome?

"*Are* you coming back?"

I'd meant to ask *when* she was coming back but my fatigue gave rise to that most Freudian of slips.

"What sort of question is that? Of course, I'm coming back! I just need some time on my own."

She was lying. I could feel it at the base of my sternum. She was being a coward and was taking minor steps towards a major exit without saying so.

It had been about nine weeks since she first said she wanted to leave, and now I knew that she hadn't budged from her original position. Despite placating me by agreeing to go to counselling and to Greece, she'd just been biding her time until both were over, and I'd run out of solutions to our problems. No matter what I'd tried, nothing would have worked. I should have known.

She'd been stubborn from the start of our relationship and had always got what she wanted, and once she'd uttered her words on the rooftop in Tokyo, it was most likely a fait accompli in her mind. She'd never truly entertained the idea of *not* leaving to be on her own. I was the only one who thought she'd change her mind. But I still couldn't give up asking in desperation:

"Can you please explain what's going on? Can you tell me what I've done?"

"You haven't done anything; I just need to go."

She threw her bag over her shoulder and walked past me and out into the corridor. I didn't get up to follow her out as there was no point, and the sound of the door thudding against its frame proved it.

It had taken her a little over two months, but in the blink of an eye, she was gone.

Breathe, just breathe. You've ridden this out before, and you'll ride it out again. Her depression is obviously worse that you thought, and you've misread the situation. You made a mistake these past years by staying out of her way and not confronting the little things as they happened. You left her alone to do her thing, and now she's doing just that.

I got up from our bed and dragged myself towards the bathroom.

A shower would help, just like it always did.

I turned the taps on full, and stepped in. The water was lukewarm and showed no further signs of heating up. She'd used most of the hot water in the tank and it would take hours to get to the temperature I wanted.

Just deal with it.

There was so much to do today, and I needed to get started, as none of it was going to happen by itself.

The list: unpack my luggage, walk to the shops, do grocery shopping, visit my parents, pick up the dog, clean the house, do the laundry, cook dinner, put the suitcases away, check in on the gallery, organise catch ups with friends, clear my emails, air the house, walk the dog, vacuum, mop, dust, get petrol, and visit my sister.

I needed to wash away the thirty-hour transit and bring myself back to life. I needed to have breakfast and refuel for the day ahead.

When was the last time I'd eaten or drank anything? It

must have been on the plane; surely, I'd had something to eat and drink on the plane?

Today was a new day and tomorrow would be too. She wasn't gone, she was just gone for now. It could be a good thing, I could get everything sorted in my own way without having to worry about her. I'd get everything ready for her return.

But *why* did she leave? What had I done to deserve this? What did she mean when she said I 'hadn't done anything'? Who leaves someone if they haven't done anything wrong? Who leaves someone who has done everything for them; and who has supported them through thick and thin? Who does that?

I thought we were good in Naxos. Romantic beach walks, exploring new places like we used to do in Europe. It had felt like the old us.

The treadmill of my thoughts continued: *I'm sure she has her reasons, but she's just not yet able to articulate them, just like me. I don't always know how to express myself and sometimes I just need to let things percolate until I work them out; but I wouldn't haven't left until I had worked them out. Actually, I wouldn't have left at all.*

I wonder if she's found someone else. She could have been cheating on me for days, weeks, or years, and I would never have known. Is that why she didn't want me to post on my socials in Tokyo? I trusted her from our first date, and I still do; I never thought I'd have a reason not to.

Bread, milk, cheese, and eggs. I needed to remember to get bread, milk, cheese, and eggs.

I'm sure we were good in Naxos. She had her outburst, and it was over. What's she been holding on to all this time?

I wonder how I'll remember Greece. It was such a cool place, circumstances notwithstanding. Athens looked so run down though, so many beautiful buildings in states of disrepair, but so many people working to keep the city clean. Old people though, people who probably didn't have enough money to retire on, forced by the government to work on into their seventies and eighties for their pension, sweeping streets, and collecting rubbish in the early hours of the morning, whilst everyone else was sleeping.

The Acropolis though. That was everything I imagined it to be and more, even if I didn't imagine it to be covered in scaffolding. At least I know what the marbles are and why Greece wants the UK to return them. I think they should. And how interesting that the Greeks themselves are removing all the ancient structures to put them into their own museums so that they aren't lost to time. I wonder how much of the Parthenon is real and how much of it is fake? I really liked the way the Acropolis Museum displayed the friezes and metopes, such a clever way of preserving art and history whilst exhibiting them in a modern way.

Santorini was a stupid place for us to go. Oia is quite possibly the most romantic place on earth at sunset and it felt like a honeymooner's paradise. We must have been the only two people on the whole island not holding hands or kissing as the sun dipped over the horizon. I liked the clapping though. I wonder who thought up the idea to clap at sunset to get the sun to reappear for a second setting? I'd return though, just for the walk along the caldera ridge. What a place! Picture-perfect, photogenic beyond measure. I reckon it's impossible to take a bad shot in Santorini, and I'll probably regret not taking enough. The whitewashed walls and the azure blue domes were on a million postcards, but I still can't believe they were real and not made-up. It was beautiful but was still a stupid place for us to go; it didn't suit us at all. Santorini was a romantic bridge too far for us.

I wonder if normal people rant in their heads like this?

Naxos though, that was more for us. It had a great rural feel, but I'm not sure I'd go back, as I'd probably like to see some other islands before I did. So windy, and I wonder if it will be forever tarnished by our moment in the villa with her sobbing. What was that about and what she was going through? Was she saying her goodbyes? Was that why it was so easy for her to leave this morning? Had she already made up her mind? Surely not, the rest of the trip had been so good. Naxos Town was stunning, just like Venice with hills and without the canals. Narrow alleyways weaving through shops and houses with the odd square or piazza thrown in for good measure. I wonder if any of the other islands have a Venetian influence? Something to research later.

I hope my car battery is okay. Three weeks is a long time for a car to sit there without being switched on. I guess I'll just have to deal with it if I have to.

Smoke alarm battery. I need to get one of those too. I think I heard it beeping earlier.

I wonder where all this is going. She said what she had to say in Tokyo, and we did our couples counselling, and we obviously need some more. I got her to Greece, and we had our separate holidays together, and spent some quality time with each other at the end. I thought we were in a good place but we're obviously not, or maybe this is just all a part of the usual process we seem to go through every three years.

The attraction thing she mentioned is a worry though. What exactly am I supposed to do with that? How does someone who was so attracted to you stop being so? And how do you make it come back? I'm worryingly sure you can't; someone is either attracted to you, or they simply are not. But if she was, and now isn't, then surely it can go back the other way. It's a smart move on her part though; because if she isn't attracted to me anymore, or at least says she isn't, then she knows there is nothing I can do about it. I wonder if her non-attraction to me has anything to do with her being attracted to women now. If she's discovering she's gay or bisexual, then that's also something I can't do anything about. If she wants to be with women; I am not a woman, ergo, she won't want to be with me. Intriguing.

It will be sad if she goes though. Quite apart from anything else, I'll miss her choice of holiday accommodation! I certainly didn't feel worthy of those boutique suites in Santorini. They felt far too luxe, and I'm not sure I had the sensory capacity to appreciate the décor in the way it should have been appreciated. A shame. I reckon that was just the state I was in, and if there was to be a next time, it would be different.

I got the holiday and my fortieth birthday present, at least she saw that through. I wonder how much it cost her. More or less than the flights and transfers? I guess none of it really matters as it's all done now.

Where will she park her car at her brother's apartment? I'm sure he has more than one car and city apartments rarely come with more than two car spaces. Did she even take her car? Maybe it's still on the street.

How long exactly is this going to last? A few days? I reckon it will be at least a week, otherwise what's the point? Do I call her, or am I supposed to leave her alone? She didn't tell me the rules for what she is doing, but let's face it, she has no idea. I'll touch base by text a couple of times per day to keep connected and to let her know I'm still here and thinking about her and am looking forward to working it all out.

And her suitcase from Greece, what am I supposed to do with that? I don't particularly want it sitting around waiting for her to get back. Too much of a reminder. I guess I'll need to sort that out too.

Why did I get so excited about her flirty text nine years ago? I was in Bristol and I was happy. I had it all, a fantastic job, lots of money, and travel at my fingertips. Sure, I didn't have anyone to share it with, but I didn't want anyone to share it with. I was happy and content, or at least I thought I was. But I did, and here we are.

And now? Let's wait and see. It's all a part of the process. Done.

I turned the taps off and stepped out of the shower to dry off. I was hungry and it was time for breakfast.

Chapter 9

" So, how can I help you?"

My counsellor's consulting room was slick and shiny and quite the opposite of the old-world clinic I'd visited with her for our couple's therapy. It was on the fourth floor of a new low-rise office building in the CBD, overlooking a busy intersection and train station.

His desk was in a corner of the room and faced a wall, but he didn't sit at it. Instead, he took his place in a chair facing the windows, deliberately positioning me between him and the more attractive view outside.

He was dressed in a dark blue suit and wore a light blue shirt without a tie. His silver cufflinks caught the sunlight whenever he moved his hands, temporarily blinding me with each gesture. He was immaculately presented and looked more like a stockbroker or a lawyer than he did a psychologist. His short black hair and cleanly shaven face didn't reveal his age, and whilst he was big for his height, he wasn't overweight. In addition to his appearance, everything else about his demeanour suggested he wanted us to get down to business.

It had been four weeks since we'd got back from Greece, and about a week since she called me to tell me we were over. In truth, she didn't actually call me to tell me we were over but when I pushed her for a resolution, she capitulated. I'd become fed up with her stalling tactics and her not being honest about what she was doing, why she was doing it, or what she was planning to do next.

I'd done my best to leave her alone and to give her the time and space she needed. I'd sent her check-in texts every few days and she'd responded to each, sometimes immediately, and sometimes after hours.

Up until her call, I refrained from asking her for timeframes or answers. I knew that pressure would only push her to do something she might not necessarily want to do, but at the same time, I was becoming more impatient for some clarity.

For the past three months, I'd existed in a place where nothing was happening and where nothing could happen, and I was tired. I didn't know if I was supposed to keep trying or if I was supposed to get over her. I wasn't sleeping well, and my days had been blurring into an indefinite continuum, punctuated only by night.

I'd kept our estrangement to myself and had refrained from sharing the details of it with friends or family. I didn't want to make our situation public until I knew what was going on, and I didn't want the people we knew to judge her negatively for what she was doing to me. None of them were aware of her bipolar or her depression, so none had the background needed for context, and I wasn't yet ready to share a story that wasn't fully mine to share.

Her call had started with the normal pleasantries about how we were and what we'd been doing, but I'd had a feeling of dread as soon as the phone had rung. Without knowing how, I knew it was her before picking it up, and I knew it would be our day of reckoning; when all would be revealed – and resolved – one way or the other.

My ability to control my situation had been dismantled, and I couldn't see how reconciliation was possible, even if we both desired it. The protective film I'd used to hold the smashed glass of our relationship together had peeled away and the shards were now rubble on the floor. I'd come to the realisation that repairing our relationship to its former state was impossible and that if we were to continue to be together, then we'd need new rules and parameters. It would almost need to be a new marriage to each other, as if we hadn't started – and ended – the previous one.

During the call, she'd mentioned she was planning to stay where she was for a bit longer; that she was still trying to work things out. I asked her what that meant for us and she danced around the question. So, still, not wanting to provide me with any answers.

It was the old pattern. She was trying to creep out of the back door whilst she distracted me at the front, and just as she'd done since Tokyo, she wanted me to fill in the blanks and solve the problem for her. I knew it was my fault she took this tack, as it was what I'd always done, but knowing it didn't make it any easier to deal with it.

So I pushed her.

"So, what exactly are you doing?" My tone was calm but laced with irritation.

She started crying, fumbling her way around the big question as she'd always done. "We're having a break, and we're working things out."

"*We* are not doing anything. I want to know what *you* are doing. Tell me what *you* are doing; I want to hear what *you* are doing."

"Well, we—," she started again.

"No!" I almost shouted, cutting her off. "Not *we*. What are *you* doing? This is all about *you* and what *you* want. Just tell me what *you're* doing. I want to hear *you* say the words".

She started crying, increasingly incoherently.

"This is so hard for me."

I imagined her leaning on her brother's kitchen bench, phone to her ear, and tears and snot freely flowing from her face and into the kitchen sink. But this time I was unmoved. It was as if someone had flipped a switch in me, and I no longer felt the urge to back off.

It seemed that the more emotional she was, the less emotional I became. It was as though there was only one bucket of feeling for both of us, and she'd taken all of it for herself. I was subconsciously balancing out her yin with my yang, even though I could clearly see my lack of emotion wasn't being helpful.

"And how about me? How do you think it feels to be me, with you calling the shots for the past few months? Just be honest. For once, please be honest. Just tell me what you're doing."

I'd opened the door for her to say what she needed to say, and if she didn't walk through it, she wasn't ever going to.

"We're bre—I mean, I'm breaking up with y—"

I couldn't let her finish. "Why?"

The harshness of my voice caught me off guard, my defences skyrocketing like huge plates of protective armour, barricading me behind an impenetrable sphere. I should have let it all out, matching her sobbing and wailing with tears of my own, my voice cracking when I asked my question; but instead, I felt nothing. There was no rush of sadness, and no other discernible emotion to show me that the life I knew had come to an end. Her five words had confirmed the obvious, serving to provide me with a tiny sense of relief, like the last puff of air leaving an already deflated balloon.

"I, I, I don't know," she stuttered through her stifled wails.

"Riiight. You're breaking up with me and ruining our marriage, but you don't know why. Brilliant, just brilliant. How about your stuff? When do you want to come and get that?"

"I don't know."

"Fine, I guess I'll talk to you later to work out the details."

My coldness sent a shockwave of guilt through me. I cared for this woman: why was I talking to her like this?

It wasn't the way I'd envisioned our end, mainly because I'd never envisioned an end. Being a forty-year-old divorcé was never a part of my life plan, but here I was, separated from my wife and sitting in a counsellor's office, seeking help in my first solo counselling session.

I cleared my throat to answer his question.

"It's the classic story. Boy meets girl, girl has a mental illness, boy supports girl to get well, girl leaves boy."

The counsellor's face remained unmoved. He didn't look particularly amused by my flippancy, but said nothing, instead jotting something down on his pad.

"Seriously though, it's a long story. I don't want to dwell on it as I'm here to get on with things from now on. She had bipolar when we met, and we had nine years together of ups and mostly downs. She was diagnosed with depression six years ago and we both hoped she'd beaten it; but we were obviously wrong.

"I'm here to learn the tools to help me through my divorce and so that a process that should only take six months doesn't take me two years.

"I'm also a bit worried for my own mental health. Ever since she first told me she was thinking of leaving, and maybe before that, I've felt like my personality has split and I've become two people. It's as though I'm not going through any of this in real life and that I'm caring for myself as I would another. I don't seem to be able to feel any of it directly, but I *can* feel empathy for myself from the outside, like I'm standing beside myself to guide the way. I really don't want to develop D.I.D. – you know, dissociative identity disorder. I'm familiar with how these things can start and want to resolve it before it becomes an issue.

"I was overly cold to her on the phone when she called to tell me were done. I didn't recognise myself and whilst I'm angry at her, I don't want to be that person."

His eyes were down as he was reading something. "I see from your doctor's notes that you've studied psychology."

"Yes, that was a long time ago but I'm here because I know I can't counsel myself. But a part of what I was just saying, is that when she told me that we were over, I asked myself, what would be the first bit of advice I'd give a friend in the same situation? My answer was, get help, get yourself into counselling."

He jotted some notes in his pad and drew what looked like circles or arrows joining to something he wrote earlier. "Why do you think you feel like your personality has split?"

Despite what I'd just said to him, it seemed he was going to try to have me counsel myself anyway.

"My best guess is that it's a defence mechanism. That my mind is protecting itself, and that it's a coping mechanism to help make sense of something which currently doesn't."

"And your coldness on the phone?"

"Probably a similar thing; acting in a way contrary to type – my opposite – to make it easier for me to see it as over."

He rested his notepad on his lap and gave me a slight smile. "You have nothing to worry about. The fact that you are fully aware of what your psyche is doing is proof. You know it's a defence mechanism and it will normalise over time. You don't need to stress about it, and you don't need to feel guilty about it. Tell me, what is your overarching feeling towards your separation?"

I didn't need to think about my answer to his question, as I'd been feeling it on and off for seven days.

"I don't want to sound heartless, or like I'm coping with this better than I am, because I'm not, but my overarching feeling has been relief."

"That's not heartless at all. If you'd said anything else, I would have asked you why. Caring for someone with mental health issues is stressful work, and whilst there may be a sense of loss when that goes away, relief is usually not too far away. Guilt normally follows too, but that's normal. There's nothing to feel guilty about."

His smile dissipated, and his face took on a stern expression, as if he'd just given me an order.

"Do you have any children?"

"No; it was one of the things that brought us together. Neither of us ever wanted to have them."

I knew what his next question would be, as it was the question everyone always asked next; I had my rote reply ready.

"Why?"

"It's something I've never wanted; it's just not in me,

like I was born without the gene for procreation; and she was the same."

My answer was usually enough to stop further inquisition and I hoped it would be here too.

"What did her bipolar or depression look like to you?"

"I never really saw her bipolar as it was there before we got together, but her depression looked like any depression, I guess. It started with her collapsing, and losing her memory, then quitting work, and spending a lot of time in bed, like she had a really bad flu. I can't remember how long that lasted, but not long after, she became a shadow of her former self."

"How do you mean?"

"Well, it was like she wasn't there. She looked similar, but her soul had disappeared; there was nothing behind her eyes. We interacted, and we did things together and with friends, but she wasn't *herself* anymore."

"So, what did that mean for you."

"How do you mean?"

"How did her depression affect *you*?"

"It didn't. Well, I guess I've never thought about it. I just did what I had to do …"

"And what was that?" He was biting the end of his pen and staring keenly at me, but I still wasn't sure what he was asking.

"I supported her, and I looked after her and I gave her what she needed."

"And not to sound like a typical counsellor, but how did that make you *feel*?"

"I'm not sure I felt anything, really. I just did what any husband would do. Just got on with it, but now she's left, I feel really let down. Like I was trying, and she wasn't."

"Not every husband would do what you've done. Nine years is a long time to be surrounded by mental illness and to ride someone else's ups and downs. What do you do for a living?"

It was a strange non-sequitur; just when it felt like we'd achieved some depth, he was retreating us back to the shallows.

"I used to work in corporate, mainly back-office operations and then human resources. I threw it all in five years ago and opened an art gallery for aspiring and emerging artists, and I also do some management consulting on the side."

"And that pays your bills? I wouldn't think there was much money in art right now."

"No, there isn't, and I know very little about art. I never studied it, but I've always liked it. I wanted to be an artist when I was finishing high school, but the commercial art gallerists I spoke with put me off. They asked the same questions every time. Where have you exhibited before? How much did you sell? For how much? And so on. How exactly are you supposed to answer those questions if you've never exhibited before and are just starting out? So, I put it all away and went to uni and started a 'normal' career. I never forgot my experience though, and when I quit the workforce, I thought I'd start a gallery where I never asked those three questions of anyone."

"Very noble, and does your consulting provide you with money to live?"

153

I couldn't tell if he was being patronising, or if he was worried about me not being able to pay him for his sessions. I tried not to sound defensive.

"The consulting provides me with pocket money. I invested in property when I was younger and have enough to keep me going. It isn't a lot, and it may not last forever, but it's enough for now."

He scribbled more notes and looked over my shoulder and out of the window.

"You need to get a job."

Huh? Where was I? Was I here to receive relationship advice or career advice? Had my doctor referred me to a career counsellor instead of someone who could help me get over my failed marriage? Is that why he looked so business-like and professional?

"Um, that's an interesting thought, but something I really don't want to do. I hate the nine to five and more than that, I hate the commute. I wanted to get out of the work-force before I was in it."

He switched his gaze back to me. "It's your choice, but you really need some structure in your life. You need a routine; to get up at a certain time, go to work, do something for x-hours a day, and come home; even if it's part time, and even if it's something that isn't in your field of expertise. Do something you'll enjoy, something that isn't nine to five, something without a commute; work in a shop, or a café near your house. It doesn't have to be in an office, and it doesn't have to be high stress."

I sat back in my chair. "I've never thought about work like that. As a form of de-stressing."

"It's not forever, it's just for now. This is about what you need right now, and it will help. Routine helps, as does getting out of the house. Distracting yourself whilst you heal is not a bad thing. You don't need to deal with your breakup for every waking moment of the day: give yourself permission to *not* think about it! You need to try different things. What do you like doing; what are the things that make you happy?"

Good question. I knew I didn't like the drudgery of corporate work, which was why I got out, but I didn't necessarily like the gallery business either. I wouldn't say I *enjoyed* it, and I wouldn't say it made me happy.

So, what does makes me happy?

I smiled and opened my mouth to respond. It was a simple enough question with a simple enough answer. But at first, I could only draw a complete blank.

My rolodex of memories flipped again, this time searching for the card with my *likes* on it. It had to be in here somewhere.

I pursed my lips and tried again to speak; only to realise that it wasn't the words I was looking for, it was the response.

I looked around the room for clues for what I liked and what made me happy, hoping the answers would present themselves on the walls, or the ceiling, or on his desk.

I shifted uncomfortably in my seat, knowing my silence

had become unnecessarily long. The man opposite me pinned me down with his stare, relentless in his quest for an answer. He seemed to have all the time in the world.

My smile fell away and my mouth dried out. My temperature was rising, and I could feel myself becoming flustered. I needed to say something to break this deadlock. *Anything.*

We all have likes and dislikes, so what is that I like?

I opened my mouth again. "The arts, good coffee, eating out, and walking my dog!"

"You need to keep doing those."

After another forty-five minutes of telling my story, I walked away from his office perplexed, and as if in a trance. How could I have not known what made me happy? How was it I didn't have a thousand answers, let alone just *one* good one? Eating out, and walking my dog aren't *likes*, they're just things normal people do.

With my counsellor's advice to *try different things* echoing in my ears, I walked past the train station I'd used to get here and to a bar next door to it, something I'd never done on my own in my own hometown.

I ordered a beer, just like I did in Kyoto and looked out to the river.

Likes and happiness. What do I like and what makes me happy?

Did I not know, or didn't I have any? I'd spent so long

trying to make her happy, so had I forgone my own happiness in the pursuit of hers; possibly projecting hers as my own?

They were thoughts I'd not had before, let alone considered, but my counsellor's simple question had put me on a new philosopher's path.

Throughout our relationship, we'd done the things she wanted to do, and rarely did the things she didn't. We ate at her favourite restaurants and cafés and we primarily spent time with her friends and colleagues. I'd accompany her to fashion shows, cocktail parties, and other soirees full of bloggers and wannabe socialites, and I'd disliked every minute of it. I despised those events and the people they attracted, but as she loved them, I'd sucked it up and kept a smile on my face. I didn't feel animosity towards her for doing what she wanted to do, as making her happy was what I wanted to do above all else.

Could it be possible that up until now, my own happiness only existed as a product of hers? That her happiness equated with my own, and even if I was unhappy doing the things that made her happy, I became happy simply because she was?

I sat back in my seat, still staring at the river with my trance deepening.

Was this real or was I making it all up?

How have I never seen this before?

I hadn't actively thought about my own happiness for the past ten years, not since the time I'd struggled during my first few months in Bristol. I couldn't remember my thoughts at the time nor what made them change, but I did remember what I'd discovered at approximately the same time they did.

Bristol International Airport.

I'd turned my unhappiness in the UK to happiness by travelling; by getting out of town, and by exploring new European cities every month; and I'd loved every minute of it. Before my soon-to-be ex-wife sent me her flirty text, I was travelling the world, one weekend at a time.

I was the most content I'd ever been, and that contentment provided a good foundation for my happiness. I'd loved experiencing new cities in my own time and at my own pace, without must-maps, and without having to *compromise*. Maybe it was why I'd enjoyed Kyoto and Athens so much despite the circumstances. They were echoes of my former life, and a reminder of what I used to enjoy.

Promise that we'll always travel together. Promise that we'll never be one of those couples who travel separately.

Fucker.

I'd willingly given up my happiness from our first days together, without thought, and without question, and now I knew this, I could easily go back; back to doing the things I liked before meeting her.

It had taken a couple of hours and a glass of cold beer, but I finally had a genuine answer to my counsellor's question. Travel. Solo travel was what I liked doing and what made me happy, and I needn't waste any more time thinking about it.

By the time I got home, my newfound happiness about travel had dissipated and my anger and despair about the way she'd upped and left had taken its place.

Her suitcase from Greece was still against a wall in our bedroom, and even though I'd somehow avoided noticing it during the past few weeks, it was now all I could see. It was a lightning-rod for my memories of the past week, month, year, and decade.

Whilst studying my psychology degree about twenty years ago, I'd discovered I had an overdeveloped sense of introspection, where my gut reaction to any situation was to look inwards; to work out what I'd done to cause it. I blamed myself for everything, taking responsibility and accountability for things that went wrong, whilst conversely handing over credit for when things went right.

What had I done wrong? What could I have done differently? What other words could I have used? Was my timing bad? Was it important enough to say? Was it my mistake? How did I contribute to it?

This was my incessant internal dialogue, and it had been on repeat since I was a child.

She still hadn't provided me with a reason for why we were splitting up and not knowing was corroding my brain like acid. I liked *knowing*, and I liked closure. Without these two things, I wasn't sure how I'd move on. How could I learn from my mistakes if I didn't know what they were? How could I stop this whole horrible mess from happening again?

I made myself a cup of chamomile tea and sat on the couch.

A flashback of her standing above me with her hands in her pockets flitted across my eyes, but I winced it away, not wanting to relive the feeling of that day, nor the waste of time between then and now.

I stared at the ceiling and thought about her phone call from a week ago. She'd ended our relationship in the same way she'd started it, by phone. A text to start it, and a call nine years and three days later to end it. I'd felt no differently after the call to how I'd felt before it, but since then, my irritation had been simmering.

I played the call over and over in my head. How had she thought it was appropriate to end our marriage in that way? Sure, I'd pushed her, but she should have hung up when she knew what she was going to do and should have come over and done it face to face. At what point in our relationship had she become so heartless to do me the simple courtesy of breaking up with me in person? And how was it fair to do so without providing me a reason?

It seemed she'd forgotten I was a part of the relationship too, and that my life would be affected as much as hers by what she was doing. She knew I liked closure, so why was she leaving me up in the air? What had I done to be punished in this way? I hadn't cheated, I hadn't been coercive, controlling, or violent, and I hadn't done anything wrong.

I'd given her everything she wanted, so why didn't she want me? I'd ridden her ups and downs and had cared for her for years, but none of it was enough; it was never *enough*.

I'd given her a good life in Bristol and in Melbourne; I'd supported her when she was off work, helped her with her business, financed her home, her car, and her lifestyle, and she'd taken it all without so much as a thank you.

I wondered if, perhaps, it wasn't my fault at all. Maybe it was her fault, and maybe there was nothing more I could have done or said. Maybe she was cheating, which was why she wouldn't elaborate on her reasons for going. Maybe she'd strung me along for as long as she thought she needed me, and when she didn't anymore, she kicked me to the curb.

She told me she didn't have depression anymore and had recovered, but her actions weren't the actions of a well person; she was still depressed, and maybe she still had bipolar. She hadn't taken the experts advice and hadn't looked after herself. I'd been doing all the heavy lifting and had been nursing her back to health and now I wasn't going to reap any of the benefits of it. I'd done all the hard work, only for her to find someone else to enjoy it with.

She'd betrayed me in the worst possible way.

Was any of our relationship real, or did it just exist in a haze of mental illness? Had she given us a chance to work it out, or had she just pulled my strings like a marionette for as long as I can remember?

Had I been an active participant in my own life, or was I just an innocent bystander caught up in her havoc?

Did she do the same thing to her ex-boyfriend before I'd come onto the scene? If she did, it was no wonder he didn't want to marry her.

How long had she known that she was going to call it quits before saying something? Did she ever want our relationship to work out? Was the time between Tokyo and Greece just for her amusement? Were her late-night work meetings secret rendezvouses for her affairs? Was she already fucking that female colleague of hers from Shanghai? Were her trips to Canberra for work, or just dirty weeknights away? Were the shoes she supposedly bought me a year ago really two sizes too large, or were they for the married French guy who lived down the road? What about the vintage watch she said she was paying off at a jeweller for my birthday? She never gave it to me, so was that even for me, or was it all just another story? What about her bipolar and depression? Was any of it real, or just a ruse to get a couple of years off work? What about her housemate in Brisbane after she left her boyfriend? Was she sleeping with him? And her housemate in Melbourne before she came to Bristol; what about him? Was she a pathological liar? Had our whole relationship been based on lies, or just most of it? Was any of it was real? Did she ever love me, and why did she marry me? And why did I stay with her? How could I have lived like this and for so long? Why did I do this to *myself*?

My mind was a cesspool, my thoughts spiralling towards the depths of hell and I felt powerless to stop it. As fast and furious as the questions popped into my mind, so too did the frustrating realisation that I was probably never going to get answers to any of them.

My ruminations were poison, and I was the only one suffering from their effect.

How did I allow this to happen? None of this was part of my plan. Marriage is a serious commitment and I was sure she was the one.

How did I get this so wrong?

I knew the statistics but believed they didn't apply to us. Ours wasn't supposed to be the one-in-two marriages that would end in divorce. It was meant to be the one-in-two that lasted the distance.

How can I ever trust my judgement again?

My memories of our relationship were rotting. I knew I was trapped in my head and my mind was working overtime, to no productive end. I needed another counselling session, but the next one was still four weeks away.

Without dialogue, and without answers I was going to disappear into a black hole. On the one hand, I didn't want to face the unwelcome possibility: that she wasn't kind and caring, but cold and calculating; that she never involved me in her thoughts because she didn't *want* me to know; that I was her subordinate and had been for our whole relationship.

And on the other, I didn't want to cast her as a villain, and me as her victim, because I knew that wasn't the complete truth either. No matter what story I invented, the one fact I knew, was that I had let this all happen, and in the end, I had no one to blame but myself.

Even if she'd conned me into thinking we were on a journey together. Even if she'd been deceiving me into believing she still loved me.

I could be angry at myself, but what use would that do? It had happened and there was nothing I could do to change it.

I needed to get away.

I needed to escape from her, from here, and from me. I needed to travel to somewhere I liked, somewhere where I could leave my thoughts behind and be happy.

Chapter 10

We'd been to Bali together three times previously, but I hadn't been here on my own. Prior to meeting her, I'd not been interested in visiting the island due to its reputation as a party hotspot full of drunken twenty-somethings getting up to mischief and causing trouble. News articles and reality show advertisements did nothing to change my opinion, and made Bali look like the antithesis of a relaxing holiday. Prior to us meeting, she hadn't been keen on Bali either and we'd agreed not to include it on our holiday list – that was until her travel agent convinced her to give it a try for our honeymoon.

We'd tasted affordable villa luxury twice before in Thailand and desired something similar for a week's getaway after our wedding. We'd originally planned to return to Hua Hin for a third time but were put off by the nine-hour flight and the three-hour drive to get there.

We couldn't afford Bora Bora or the Maldives, so she enlisted the help of an agent to find us something to meet our criteria; a self-contained private pool villa somewhere warm and not too far away, near a beach and out of the hustle and bustle, and which didn't cost the earth.

Seminyak in Bali was the only destination to tick all the boxes, and it would do so at half the price of Hua Hin, and in half the travel time.

We treated our honeymoon as reconnaissance to see if we could enjoy Bali from the privacy of our own villa; and we did. During our second and third stays, we fell in love with the island, and spoke about plans of leasing a house for six months each year, splitting our time between Seminyak and Melbourne. We discussed ideas about how we'd make the lifestyle work, and what we'd need to do to turn it into reality, but that, too, was now just another broken dream we'd never realise, at least not together.

It was only after I'd booked and paid for my flights and accommodation that these memories of Bali came flooding back to me, as did my awareness that the first place I'd travel to post-divorce was the first place we'd travelled to post-marriage.

It didn't bother me as much as I thought it would, as with or without her, Bali still ticked all my holiday destination boxes. It was still warm, still close to Australia, and half the price of similar destinations. I knew how to get around and already had my favourite places for breakfast and dinner. Most of all, I knew exactly how I wanted to spend each of my days; doing exactly what *I* wanted to do, when *I* wanted to do it.

I was going to walk the streets during the day and sit by

the beach by night. I would drink coffee in cafés, eat out at fancy restaurants, try yoga, get out of bed when I was awake, go to sleep when I was tired, lie by the pool, drink from coconuts, and be still. I was going to tune into my likes and dislikes, and I was going to spend more time pondering what made me happy.

A young man dressed in a batik shirt and black trousers had picked me up from the airport and had driven me to the villa. There were hundreds of men who looked just like him, all holding pieces of paper with guests' names on them. The arrivals hall felt like a zoo enclosure, with drivers intently watching travellers walking forwards and backwards along the dividing rail, searching for their name and reward of escape.

It had taken me about fifteen minutes to find mine, and another forty-five for us to drive the ten kilometres to the villa. As my minivan pulled up to the front reception area, I turned my head to get my bearings, abruptly stopping at the sight directly across the road from where I was about to stay. I knew exactly where I was, because the last time I was here, we'd stayed at the villa complex opposite.

Awesome.

I checked in and was shown around what was to be my home for the next four days and four nights by my driver. It wasn't as opulent as the accommodation across the road, but it was perfect for me. A timber door led the way through a three-metre-high wall, to a decked path across lush gardens, towards a ten-metre pool. To the left of the pool was an open pavilion with a kitchen, dining suite, L-shaped couch, coffee table and TV. The thatched roof had two ceiling fans, circulating the air, pushing a cooling breeze downwards. Behind the pool and separate from the living area were the bedroom and bathroom pavilions. The bed was a huge king-size four-poster, draped in mosquito netting, and had two towels on it, both folded into the shapes of swan-like creatures. Frosted-glass sliding doors provided access to an enormous bathroom with both indoor and outdoor showers, as well as a freestanding half-egg-shaped bath, peculiarly pre-filled with water and rose petals. The villa was described on the internet as being on three-hundred-square-metres of private gardens and they hadn't been generous in their estimation. The walls surrounding the villa on all four sides were my private fortress, a place where I would feel safe and comfortable.

I dropped my bag onto the bed and walked back towards the street, locking the doors behind me.

It was about 2:00pm and the outside air was warm like a bath. I raised my face upwards, absorbing the sun's rays like a solar panel, ready to energise and revitalise myself. Wispy white clouds danced across the sky, and an involuntary smile crept across my face from ear to ear.

This place already felt like home.

I turned left and walked towards Jalan Kayu Aya, the street in Seminyak I was most familiar with.

It was exactly how I remembered it, busy with pedestrians, motor scooters, and standstill traffic.

During our first time here, the sights and sounds had been overwhelming; the incessant beeping of taxi horns, the fumes from two-stroke engines and burning incense, the harassment from shop owners, the stray dogs, and the rubbish covering the streets. It had taken us our first few days to adjust and to block it all out, but here I was today, at the start of my fourth trip, embracing it all like an old friend I hadn't seen for over a year.

I wove my way through the crowds to Kayu Aya beach and took a seat on a rock wall facing the sea and horizon. The beach sand looked dark and dirty, but it didn't matter. It felt good to be here, and it was the first time I'd felt good in months.

My mind had stopped racing and had submerged itself into my body, making me feel whole again; allowing me to *feel* again. I was out of my head and in the here and now, and in this moment, it was as though the past and the future no longer mattered.

I sat with my eyes closed for long stretches at a time, failing to notice that hundreds of people had been swarming onto the beach in front of me. They were wearing traditional Balinese-looking clothing and were gathering in three distinct groups, most-likely based on the colour of their shirts.

They appeared to be celebrating some sort of religious ritual, but there was no discernible leader, and no consistency in the actions of the various groups of people. Some were praying, and others were socialising; some shared food and

169

drinks, whilst others walked to the ocean for a quick dip, fully clothed. Megaphones were passed around and words were said in Indonesian or Hindi. It was an interesting spectacle and I wished I knew more about what I was witnessing.

After about an hour, the ceremony was over, and the people dispersed as quickly as they had arrived. I watched them leave and as I returned my gaze to the beach where they'd been sitting, I was overcome with an unreasoning fury.

They'd left hundreds, if not thousands of pieces of plastic rubbish on the sand. Cups, plates, spoons, knives, forks, and wrappers were scattered across the beach and being caught in the sea breeze. I scanned the area for cleaners or anyone in uniform still here to clean up, but there was no one. The beach was empty except for a handful of tourists, kite sellers, and me.

What the fuck is wrong with people?

These holy people had used Kayu Aya beach as a rubbish tip, leaving their trash for the ocean to clean up.

Surely, it's not so hard to clean up after yourself, and to take your rubbish with you? How can people be so spiritual, and so irresponsible at the same time? They obviously understand the importance of the ocean as they used it for their ceremony, so why aren't they looking after it?

It was the type of behaviour which consolidated my long-held view of the hypocrisy of religion.

I was raised as a Roman Catholic and was forced by my dad to go to church every Sunday until I turned eighteen. As

I didn't want to be there, I spent the hour people-watching, and soon noticed the duplicity of the congregation and the system to which they adhered. I watched on as a rabble of sinners, all praying for forgiveness and making promises to 'love thy neighbour', shouted and swore at each other in frustration as they tried to leave the carpark. Their prayerfulness rarely lasted longer than five minutes, and I could only see the church for what it was; a place where sinners went for an hour a week to be forgiven for the other one-hundred and sixty-seven.

Fuckers.

I'd been in a great mood an hour ago and now I wasn't; changed by people I didn't know, by things I didn't understand, or couldn't appreciate.

I got up and dusted myself off and made my way back in the direction of my villa, knowing I'd pass my favourite café along the way. It was too late for a caffe latte, but the perfect time for a fresh coconut and some sort of fruit platter.

The café was in a converted garage, down a narrow blink-and-you'll-miss-it alley. She'd discovered this place for us on our first visit, but I'd appropriated it and it was now mine.

As I stepped through the old timber door and down the two steps into the sunken dining room, adrenalin shot from my core into my limbs. My mouth dried and my pulse became turbo charged.

What if she turned up here?

What if she was giving herself a break from Melbourne and had come here at the same time as I had? We used to be so connected; so alike; maybe we'd both thought of doing the same thing at the same time.

I looked around at all the tables with heightened senses, wishing to see no one who matched her description.

But what if she walks in later? What then?

My elation at being in this place took a sudden dive.

Bali was feeling like a bad idea and being in this café a worse one.

Stop being ridiculous and take a seat.

I inched towards the counter and to a bench seat I knew was positioned in an alcove behind the coffee machine. It would be the perfect place to hide if she showed up.

I got the attention of the barista with a wave.

"May I sit here?"

"Sure thing boss, if they don't mind."

Another shot of adrenalin fired out of me.

In my panic, I hadn't spotted a person sitting in the shadows at the other end of the bench seat. They had a big round beaming face and blonde dreadlocks, a giveaway that it wasn't her. I took a moment to catch my breath.

I stayed standing. "I'm so sorry, I didn't see you there. Do you mind?"

"Not at all, make yourself comfortable." The voice was friendly and had an American accent.

"Thank you."

"Are you looking for someone or waiting for someone?"

How had they noticed that? Were they watching me coming in?

"Um, no. I'm here on my own for a few days."

"Yeah, me too."

I wasn't interested in meeting new people, and was kicking myself for not noticing them, let alone sitting down next to them. I was here to get some downtime, and the last thing I wanted right now was to get into a conversation with a stranger; but even though I didn't know them, I didn't want to offend them by getting up to leave or sit somewhere else.

"Can I get you something boss, or would you like a menu?" A young hipster man with an upward pointing moustache had emerged from the darkness on the other side of the coffee machine. He was dressed head to foot in black, camouflaging him in the shadows.

"Can I get a fresh coconut please?" I mimed a sphere with both hands.

"Just the water, or a whole one?"

I didn't know there was an option, but I wanted the real deal. "A whole one please."

I sat back into the seat and closed my eyes to try and slow my pulse and reduce my blood pressure. My irrational fear that she might be here was like sticking a knife into an electrical socket and I needed time to recover.

"Have you heard of the *vesica pisces*?"

The American was asking someone a question.

I opened my left eye to see them staring at me.

"The *vesica pisces*, do you know what it is?" They were holding a book in their left hand, with their thumb bookmarking the page they were up to.

"Um, no, no I don't."

"It's a really interesting ancient symbol and idea." They shuffled closer and opened the book to the bookmarked page. "That's it there." They pointed to two overlapping circles of the same size.

"You see, these two circles share the same radius. The centre of each circle intersects the perimeter of the other, so that either can rotate around the other without ever completely covering the other. It's an ancient symbol and has been used throughout history, by different religions, in architecture, and has been used to represent everything from the divine trinity, to the Jesus fish, to a woman's vulva."

The American then used their fingernail to trace over the centre area of the two circles, showing me how it formed the fish shape.

I looked at them blankly.

Who are you and what are you on about?

"Here's your coconut, boss." The man in black had returned and placed a light green coconut onto the rectangular coffee table in front of us. Its top had been lopped but was still sitting askew in the opening, prevented from closing by a black straw and silver spoon protruding from within.

"Thank you, that's great."

He scampered away, failing to rescue me from this person and their *vesica pisces.*

I took a breath, not wanting to engage, but knowing I had to, to be polite.

"So, why are you reading about the *vesica pisces*?"

"I'm not. I'm reading about love and relationships." They returned to their page and continued reading, but my interest was now heightened.

"Love and relationships; alright, I'll bite. What has that symbol got to do with love and relationships?"

They put the book on their knee and looked into the space in front of them.

"What is your understanding of love; of marriage; of soul mates?"

I smiled and comically rolled my eyes. "Geez, could you ask a deeper question? I'm not the right person to ask because I'm just coming out of a relationship."

They smiled. "Me too. Well, here's a simpler question, tell me this, are you a *two become one* kind of relationship guy?"

"Absolutely. That's what a soulmate is, isn't it? When you find the other half of yourself and you become one?"

I leant down to take a long draw from the straw in my coconut.

"Well, that's not what this book says. What it says is that each person should remain whole, like the two complete circles, and that relationships between two people should be the shared radius, or the shared bit in the middle. It says that each person should be able to rotate around the other along that shared radius but that neither should eclipse the other because its geometrically impossible. The relationship bit between two people is the overlap, and the bigger part is the person outside of the relationship. This book says that healthy relationships are between two whole people who look after themselves and who come together with a small overlap."

I took another sip from the coconut.

"Interesting." I may have well as said 'bullshit' because that's what my tone implied. This person wasn't making any sense, and neither was their book. They were obviously still young, and had never truly been in love, or found the one. They didn't understand the nature of handing themself over or of the sacrifices required to make a relationship work. The *vesica pisces* was a cute symbol and a cute story, but I wasn't buying it.

I took another two quick sips and bid the American farewell, leaving my half-finished coconut on the table. I didn't want to talk about relationships, and I needed to get out of this place and away from their conversation.

I exited the café, and walked past the street my villa was on, and towards Jalan Raya Seminyak, one of the main drags through to Legian and Kuta. I'd done this walk at least once a day on each of my previous trips and it felt right to do it again.

At Jalan Camplung Tanduk I turned right as I always did and headed to the boardwalk at the end of it. The late afternoon was perfect for strolling; not too hot, not too humid, and without too much direct sunlight. I'd put the ceremony and the American out of my mind. and it felt good to be moving again.

After an hour or so, I arrived at the Kuta shopping centre, but wasn't yet ready to turn around and walk back. I'd not walked past this point on any of my previous three visits, and the idea of doing something new and different on this trip was overwhelmingly appealing.

After another hour, I reached the end of the path and what looked to be the outer perimeter of the airport. The sight of planes taking off and landing surprised me as much as the realisation I'd walked ten kilometres without really noticing I had.

Apart from the shopping centre, what had I seen along the way?

What had I noticed? What had I felt?

Nothing. Nothing, except the vision of two overlapping circles projected like a hologram into the middle distance in front of everywhere I looked.

With the path at its end, I spun around to walk back the way I came, but with a commitment to try and be more mindful and present as I did.

The sun was dropping in the sky to my left and would disappear over the horizon in about an hour and a half, not that it mattered. I had nowhere to be, and no one to get home to. I had nothing planned for tomorrow and could stay out the whole night if I wanted to. There were no rules, except those of the *vesica pisces*.

Why is this thing affecting me so much?

Two become one, or two sharing a radius, what does it matter?

How does it apply to real life?

I stopped at a concrete bench and sat, staring out over the Bali Sea to where the water met the sky.

The simple comparison of relationships to the *vesica pisces* was worming its way into my core. The idea that relationships didn't need to be all-consuming was scouring my insides, as was the premise that the best thing anyone could do for a relationship was to look after themselves and to keep their own circle whole.

Was this true?

I remembered back to when I was ten years old, and a school nurse had conducted my first eye test. She found I was short-sighted and prescribed me with glasses for the first time. The experience of wearing corrective lenses to see properly shook my world as I couldn't believe I'd spent my whole life seeing the world incorrectly. Until that day, I'd spent a decade trusting my eyes, only to find out they'd been lying to me. My new glasses didn't just change my eyesight; they changed the way I saw everything.

Once I'd put my new glasses on, I knew my sight had been bad. There was no need to question it, or validate it, and there was no turning back. Wear the glasses to see clearly, or don't wear them to see poorly; it was a simple and undeniable truth.

Thirty years later, the idea of the *vesica pisces* seemed to be doing the same thing, and in the same way. Apply the *vesica pisces* to my relationships to understand what went wrong, or don't and let it all happen again.

I had always seen relationships as two people coming together to create a new third entity, as two becoming one, but why? Where had I learnt my idea of relationships and why had I believed what I did until this moment? Where had I learnt the concept of two becoming one, and why had I blindly believed that all relationships were about the joining of two people?

Was it from my parents, from religion, or from romcoms?

My parents' and most of my uncles' and aunts' marriages operated as co-dependent single units and they were joined in everything they did. They didn't have their separate friends, rarely socialised without the other, and they didn't have their own lives outside of their marriage. Family was the most important thing to them.

I'd grown up wanting the opposite of those relationships, so I how did I end up with one so similar?

There was no doubt in my mind that I'd aimed for our marriage to be one united married unit, but I didn't want to own her, and I didn't want her to own me. I didn't want to colonise her, and I didn't want her to colonise me. I wanted her to be independent and to have her own friends and interests, and she'd wanted the same for me, so how did we fail to follow through?

The answer wasn't difficult to see.

We'd got into the habit of doing everything together, and not doing things if we were apart. I'd accompanied her to her fashion shows and cocktail parties, not because I'd wanted to, but because she hadn't wanted to go on her own. I'd not travelled without her, not because I didn't want to, but because she didn't want me to. We each strove to be independent, and for the other to be equally so, but we kept doing things to stop that from happening. By sheer accident, we'd become co-dependent, just like the relationships I'd never wanted.

If I'd ever had my own circle, I'd given it up in favour of the new relationship with her. I never kept my own circle intact, and I never thought my own circle needed looking after.

Looking after myself to look after my relationships was another simple and undeniable truth I couldn't believe I hadn't known until now.

I rose from the bench to continue my slow walk home. My head was full again and my thoughts were weighing me down like anchors. It was clearer to me why I couldn't answer the counsellor's question about what I liked, and what made me happy. It wasn't just that we were always doing the things she liked, it was because I'd given myself up to her and no longer existed in my own right. I had no circle; I didn't even have half a circle.

Her circle had contained me.

I was who she needed me to be, and now that she was gone, now that she had kicked me out of her circle, I had no idea who I was anymore.

Chapter 11

My counsellor shook my hand, greeting me in reception and commencing our second session as I followed him down the corridor to his office.

"What's news? What have you been up to, and how are you feeling about things?"

"Good, I think. I went to Bali a few weeks ago and I felt great being over there. It smoothed out my rollercoaster ride of negativity and for the most part I was able enjoy myself without needing to think about her."

"Seems you found something you like, and which makes you happy?" He was smiling, as if he knew it would happen before I did, and I'd just caught up.

"Yes, I worked it out after our last session and pulled the trigger without overthinking it. Oh, and I got a job! I figured that if I'm paying for your advice, I may as well take it. I put in a call to a mate who is also an ex-colleague, and he had a business requirement I could fill. It's a casual job, three days per week reviewing his training and development function. It's right up my alley and won't be arduous but will give me the structure you spoke about. It's for about three months."

"Nicely done."

He closed the door behind us, and we took our respective seats, but before he could ask me another question, I got in first.

"Have you heard of the *vesica pisces*?"

"No, I don't think so. I've heard of pisces like the star sign and the fish, but don't know what a vesica is. Why?"

"It was something I heard about in Bali and it may just explain why my relationships keeping ending in failure."

"Interesting segue, as my first question today is about your past relationships. Can you tell me about them?"

There was something about this guy's no-nonsense, no small-talk approach which I liked and disliked in equal measure, but I couldn't work out why. He seemed to have an agenda for today and didn't want to be distracted by the topics I may want to talk about.

I got comfortable and decided to put the *vesica pisces* out of my mind.

"I'm a bit of serial monogamist. Prior to my last relationship, I had three years off, and prior to that, my relationships lasted about three years each before fizzling out. There were a couple in there which lasted a year or less, but they were weird situations where both girlfriends returned to their ex-boyfriends before me."

I knew he'd asked the question to try and establish my

patterns, but I'd already asked myself the same question, and knew there were none. My past partners were all different ages, had different looks, diverse upbringings, education, and career paths. I didn't have a type, if that was what he was trying to ascertain.

Regardless of my thoughts on the subject, I answered his question in full and described each relationship in reverse chronological order. I kept my explanations brief but went through the circumstances of the relationship as a whole, and not just the person I shared it with.

My counsellor listened without interrupting, nodding along, taking notes.

"Tell me about your childhood."

"Do I have to? I don't particularly like psychoanalytical psychology. The idea that our behaviour is dictated by our subconscious thoughts, feelings, and desires from our childhood isn't one that resonates with me."

"Tell me, anyway."

It was clear who was in charge of these sessions, and he wasn't going to easily let me off the hook.

I could appreciate psychoanalysis for what it did for psychology, but I didn't like its fatalist approach to human development. I believed in free will and in our future being written by our choices, not influenced by the way in which we were raised. Talking about my relationship with my parents had no bearing on how I was going to get over my failed marriage, but I knew I had no choice but to do it anyway.

"Well, I don't remember a lot about my childhood. I can recall some of the things I did, but I can't remember when I did them. I don't think I can give you any detail about any particular moments or memories."

"Interesting; do you have any siblings?"

"Yes, a younger sister."

"Did you have a happy upbringing?"

I smiled, as there was nothing happy about my upbringing.

"No. I rarely think about it and there isn't much to think about."

"How do you mean?" He had the end of his pen in his mouth again and looked intrigued, like I was telling a good story.

"It's ancient history and has no bearing on today. I dealt with it in my early twenties and have moved on—"

"Moved on from what?"

I sighed. Bringing it up again was just going to divert attention and time from what I really wanted to talk about.

"Firstly, you should know that I have a good relationship with my parents now and I see them every week for a Sunday roast at their house, but as far as my childhood goes, I remember being terrified of my dad, as he had a strong temper. Looking back on it now, I think I spent most of my childhood in fear, which is probably why I don't remember much of it."

"Why? Was he violent? Did he ever hit you?"

"Yes but—"

He looked concerned. "Like, a smack on you bum?"

"No, a bit more than that."

"How much more?" He leant forward, his eyes locking onto mine like guided missiles. Clearly, he wasn't letting me get out of answering this one. I leant back reflexively.

"Just *more*." I continued: "Put it this way, my nose and jaw are both out of place."

"I'm really sorry to hear that. And was he violent towards your sister, and mother?"

"Yes, with my sister on occasion, but I'm not sure about Mum. I never saw it happen."

His head was down, and he was still scribbling on his pad of paper.

"Go on."

"To be honest with you, it's all a blur. Please don't get the wrong idea, it may have happened half a dozen times, or maybe more, I really can't recall. The only thing I can really remember was my desperation to become an adult so I could move out and be independent."

"What were your sister and mother doing when your father was coming after you?"

I fidgeted in my chair and wanted to pull my collar away from my neck to release some of the heat building up under my shirt. I'd tucked my hands under my thighs to avoid my body language betraying me, and could feel my fingers becoming numb. His eyes were still locked onto mine, increasing my discomfort with each passing second.

"I'm not sure about my sister, maybe she was hiding. As for Mum, I'm sure she would have been yelling for it to stop. She would have been upset and screaming as you would imagine, but she wasn't as strong as my dad, so I imagine she was a bit powerless to do anything."

"Did she ever stand in the way of your father, to protect you?"

"Not that I can remember. She may well have, but like I said, I don't have clear memories of that time. Whilst my parents are both the same height; she seems so much smaller than him.

"What are you thinking and where are you going with this?" As far as I was concerned, my childhood had nothing to do with my marriage, and nothing to do with learning the techniques I needed to get closure on my divorce.

"Did you ever stand in the way of your father, to protect your sister or mother? Do you think that by being hit by your father that you were protecting your sister or mother from being hit?"

What the fuck?

My eyes widened in shock at the absurdity of the idea.

"No, not at all. I don't think so. I usually got hit for something I did, or he thought I did, not for something they did; and I never had to stand in the way of him hitting Mum, because I never saw him do it."

He rested his pen on his pad and crossed his legs.

"You'd be surprised about what may have happened. Unfortunately, a lot of these situations are caused by marital issues and by work and life stresses that have nothing to do with the children; but the children wind up being used as scapegoats for redirected pain, anger, and frustration.

"The child is never to blame," he continued. "You may have had sixth sense about where your father's rage was going to be directed, even if you couldn't make any sense of it. You may have seen your sister or mum in distress and deliberately diverted attention away from them and to yourself."

"Ha, I doubt that very much."

"Again, you'd be surprised. The bonds between sons and their mothers, and brothers and their sisters, are still mostly unexplainable, unless of course, you subscribe to psychoanalytical theories." He smiled, to try and lighten the mood. "Do you think your parents were depressed?"

"I guess so, but we've never talked about it. They both had difficult upbringings and I think there are a lot of unresolved issues for both of them. They've never been diagnosed though. I can't see them ever going to a counsellor."

"And in your previous relationships, do you think your ex-partners may have been depressed? I mean, apart from your wife?"

He put the cap on his pen and sat back in his chair, as if he'd finished making his point, even though I was just getting started.

"I don't know, maybe."

"And do you think that through your relationships with them, that you helped save them?"

"Save them from what?"

Clearly, I wasn't keeping up. The all-business counsellor had formulated a theory, but I was still a million miles behind him.

We sat, staring at each other, each waiting for the other to say something to break the silence. His lips were closed tight, but mine were open even though I had no answers. I zipped through my previous relationships silently in my head, using the frame of depression and saving to see where it took me.

My ex-wife suffered from bipolar and depression, and had escaped her controlling mother, and was trying to escape her controlling ex-boyfriend.

The one before her had a verbally abusive ex-boyfriend and was looking to escape from the country to the city.

A third had a drug-dealing ex-boyfriend, whose behaviour she explained away because of his own drug use.

A fourth had emotionally and physically abusive mentally ill parents and was never going to be allowed to live her own life.

And the one before that, well she had a violent and abusive ex-boyfriend who was never going to let her go.

Fuck me.

Was there a pattern here all along, hiding in plain sight? Correlation wasn't the same thing as causation, but which word described my situation? Was I consistently involved with women who were escaping shitty situations; or was it all just a coincidence?

How have I not seen this before? I've always considered myself as a smart guy and I've always been great at seeing patterns. I have university degrees and have studied psychology and human behaviour. I see big pictures and I make connections. My ability to see all the moving parts of system, and to know which bits affect others has been one of my strengths. How could I not have made this connection before?

My counsellor was shining a torch into my psychological shadows and revealing what was hidden there. Was this why all my past relationships had moved so quickly? Was this the reason why my partners were so fast to latch on and move in with me? Were they all running or hiding from something? Making an escape?

I'd been keen to be with them, but it wasn't like we ever sat down as a couple and consciously decided that living together was the best thing for our relationship. It was just something we did, mostly because they needed to get out of their previous situation, and they didn't have anywhere to go. I hadn't thought at the time that I was saving them, but it was now clear they all needed an escape.

It was an unwelcome thought. *Is that all I was to them? An out? Had I just been in the right place at the right time, or perhaps the wrong place at the wrong time?*

Had they done it on purpose, or were they as oblivious as I was to the underlying motive? Was it deliberate? I wondered if it was something they'd uncovered in their own counselling sessions, if they'd had them.

I sat in my seat, stunned, and exhausted.

"Water?" he asked, getting up from his seat and opening the door to his office.

"Sure."

As he left the room, I retraced the circumstances of why each one of my past relationships had ended.

You've got to be fucking kidding me …

One, two, three, four, five. They all ended in a similar way, without warning or reason. When they didn't need me anymore, they upped and left. They used me until I'd outlived my usefulness, and then they simply disappeared. Sometimes back to ex-boyfriends, and sometimes to new ones, and in the case of my most recent, who knew?

Could it really be that women who needed help; women who were broken and who needed some sort of 'fixing' were the only ones attracted to me? Women who showed signs of depression and who needed to get out of their situations to get better, or to be better?

And how about my attraction to them? Why was I attracted to women in similar situations? What did I get out of it? How was that healthy? And her? She was the most broken of all, and yet she was the only one I'd wanted to marry.

"Here you go." The counsellor had returned to the office with two glasses of water and handed one to me.

"Thank you." My hand was shaking but I got the glass to my lips and drank its contents slowly in one long sip.

Fuck, fuck, fuck, fuck.

"Thinking back, how did your past relationships start? Did you do the chasing, or were you chased; or was it a mixture of both."

Finally, he was asking an easy question, one I could answer without thought. "I've never chased, but also have never really been chased. All of my relationships started as platonic friendships. I never expected anything more, but they all made the first move and turned our friendships into something they weren't.

"By the way, what has any of this got to do with my mother, and my parents?"

He smiled again. "Maybe something, and maybe nothing, but there is a chance you find comfort in certain situations, situations which feel like home, ones that feel normal. Your own childhood experience of fear may be causing you to empathise with other people in similar situations, and as you couldn't do anything about it then, you're doing something about it now. Seeing people in trouble might be a primordial trigger, compelling you to get involved and help."

"Comfort in uncomfortable situations? Rescuing myself by rescuing others? Fixing my past by fixing the present?"

"Exactly."

First the *vesica pisces*, now this.

I needed more time to process things. My life as I knew it was unravelling before my eyes, and with it, everything I thought I knew about myself.

If he was right, I didn't just have a type or a pattern; I had a repeated history of attraction to people who fitted in with my previous life experience. I'd most likely grown up with depressed parents, and depression was therefore my 'normal'. But I didn't like it, so why would I chase more of the same?

And what about my other friendships? Did they follow a pattern too?

I thought about my two best mates, both of whom had lived with me prior to my move to the UK. Both had moved in at separate times and at different junctures in their lives; one when his living situation with a housemate turned sour, and the other when his wife left him. Their moves were never a part of any grand plans; both seemed to have just happened.

They were tenuous connections to my pattern, compared with my more intimate relationships, but I was beginning to feel sick. My thoughts began to swirl.

What's the difference between being a nice guy and helping someone out, and a behaviour pattern that my counsellor is trying to bring to my attention? More to the point, if this is a part of my programming, and a part of who I am, how do I change it; and do I actually want to change it? Am I depressed; is that why I attract depression? What do I get out of fixing broken people? Is this an ego thing or something more? I've never wanted thanks or praise, or have I? It's not who I want to be, so why am I being this way?

The American in Bali had imprinted two circles into my mind, and my counsellor had stamped a circular pattern of behaviour into my psyche. These two theories were my new prescription lenses, and now I'd seen through them, it was going to be impossible to pretend I hadn't.

Chapter 12

I t had taken nine weeks, but today was the day when she was finally coming over to pick up her things and her half of ours. I hadn't seen her since the morning we arrived home from Greece and hadn't spoken to her by phone since she told me we were done. We used text and email to organise logistics and close out our relationship, a poetic bookend to a relationship we'd started in the same way.

The doorbell rang at 11:11am, shocking my heart into palpitations like a defibrillator. I had no idea what to expect, or how either of us was going to react to seeing the other.

During the past few weeks, it had repeatedly dawned on me that with the exception of the morning she'd walked out, the last time we'd been together had been a good time. We'd spent four days enjoying each other's company in Naxos, and there'd been no sign we were at the end of our life together.

I opened the door hesitantly; thankful she hadn't used her key to do it herself. I hadn't changed the locks as I didn't see the need, but as she came into view, I couldn't help but wonder how many times she'd been here during the past few months without my knowing.

She cut a lonely figure and looked thinner than I remembered. Her gaze was still expressionless, making it easier for me to reflect the same in mine.

"Hey."

"Hey."

I pulled the door wider to see if she had help, spying the same furniture removalist truck we'd used to move us here eighteen months ago. A team of three men decanted themselves from its cab, ready to help us get this part of our breakup over and done with.

I stepped backwards into the hall to give her some room to walk past me, but as I did, her brother stepped out of hiding and into view.

Why the fuck are you here?

"Hey."

"Hey."

I spun around and walked to the end of the hall; my heart racing faster than it was a second ago. What was he doing here; and why? Was he a part of the crew helping her move? She had three professionals, and surely didn't need a fourth amateur, so what was his purpose? Was he here for moral support, or was she expecting some sort of trouble? What had she told him to get him here? Did she lie to him by saying she felt unsafe and needed protection? Is that why he was here; to protect her?

I felt as if I'd been kicked in the stomach. I put my hand out to steady myself against the wall; at the same time, I felt two large hands steady me by my shoulders.

"You okay?" Her brother's booming voice was behind me.

"No. I just wish that none of this was happening."

He gave me a light friendly shake and a one-armed hug across my chest. "Yeah."

We'd moved to this house as a solution to a temporary problem. Prior to moving to Bristol, I'd lived here, but it was a house she'd never wanted to live in. She called it my *bachelor pad* even though it was no such thing and I'd only spent a year in it before being expatriated.

After we moved back from the UK, she was keen for us to find our own home, so that's what we did. She'd not owned property before, and didn't have the money to do so, so when we found a place she liked, I used my savings and equity to help us out and to pay for whatever needed to be paid.

We followed that system another three times after selling that first house; to buy a second, then an investment apartment, and a block of land.

Our asset accumulation was going well until she had her breakdown and had to quit work. She drew down on our mortgage to give herself a financial buffer, and to start a business to keep her occupied, but when the business failed and the money ran out, she told me we had no option but to sell what we owned so we could get out of our debt.

I nodded along, knowing it was the right thing to do, but was annoyed she'd thrown so much money away on a business she knew nothing about during a time when she was least able to manage it.

By the time we'd sold our joint assets, I had no interest in moving into my bachelor pad either. It had been a rental property for nine years and looked beat up and run down. She was turning a corner on her depression and I wasn't keen on us doing anything to put her back there. We needed to live in a place we liked.

We looked for rental options, but none suited, so I bit the bullet and completed a top-to-bottom renovation on the bachelor pad to remove all signs it had previously been lived in. I put in a new kitchen, new bathrooms, new flooring, and had the entire house repainted. Even though it was a temporary solution, I wanted her to be comfortable and to enjoy being there.

Staying in my bachelor pad was supposed to be a stopgap between her getting back on her feet and us being able to buy something else, but it was an ambition she'd lost interest in between then and now.

On the day of my first counselling session, following my internal rant and mind spiralling towards the depths of hell, I'd sprung off the couch with the expressed aim of doing something proactive to give me some semblance of control back over my own life.

I'd started the exercise by trying to move a vase I'd given

her as an engagement present out of sight and into a drawer; except, when I opened the drawer, I found it filled with her CDs and DVDs and other bits and pieces.

For the rest of that evening and into the early hours of the morning, I stripped anything and everything that reminded me of her out of our living spaces and into our spare room. Clothes, shoes, accessories, jewellery, appliances, soft furnishings, artworks, and everything else that wasn't mine was moved out of sight, and out of mind. It was a cathartic exercise and had temporarily made me feel better.

In the ensuing days, I asked her to decide on which pieces of furniture she'd like to keep, as well as what she wanted from our kitchen, living room, and bedroom. I sent her a spreadsheet detailing a register of the things we owned together so she could make her choices, assigning estimated values to each item so neither would end up financially worse off than the other. I'd pay her for half of the things that she didn't want, and she could do the same for me. I couldn't have cared less if she'd wanted everything, but I didn't want to be left with a huge bill to replace it all.

My predictions for what she'd tick on the spreadsheet couldn't have been more mistaken. She wanted the coffee table, but not the uncomfortable couch. She wanted our kitchen utensils, and saucepans, but not the dining table and chairs; and she wanted all the items both my parents and hers had bought us as wedding gifts.

She took all the nice things that were easy to carry, leaving me with the heavy stuff I didn't really want.

Deliberately or not, she also chose the items with a lesser value on the spreadsheet, so not only would she get all she wanted, she'd also get a sizeable cheque for the difference.

I had no energy to kick up a fuss, or negotiate, and remained my passive, restrained self to get the job done. After all, it was all replaceable, and none of it had sentimental value.

After she'd emailed me the completed spreadsheet, I spent another day packing her choices into the study. It had been a surprisingly effective detoxification exercise, but it had also been a favour to us both, as her move today was going to be made much simpler and easier. There were just two rooms her moving team had to visit today; all the heavy lifting had already been done.

With the removalists in tow, she brushed passed me in the hall and headed towards the stairs. With the flurry of bodies moving past me, it occurred to me that I hadn't yet told her what I'd done.

"All your stuff is in the spare room and study."

She didn't pause and kept climbing the stairs without turning around. "Thanks."

Her brother was last in line, and I followed him upstairs, to keep in contact and to supervise from a distance.

She didn't stop at the study or spare room and lead the team directly to the kitchen.

She opened and closed the cupboards and drawers, rifling through each with her hands and eyes, inspecting them for her things and the things she'd asked for.

Perhaps she didn't hear me.

"I moved all your stuff to the study and spare room; it's all in there."

"Yes, thanks."

Another kick to my stomach. Why was she being like this? What had I done to cause her to not trust me?

Ignoring me, she finished in the kitchen, and did the same thing in the living room, dining room, our bedroom, and bathroom.

Seemingly satisfied that nothing of *hers* was hidden away, she directed her moving team to the rooms her possessions were actually in.

"It's all in there; everything in those two rooms can go." She was using her deeper-than-normal business voice.

I slumped into a chair in the dining room, with my head in my hands, only to look up again as she came back into the kitchen.

"Is there something specific you're looking for?"

She didn't stop and didn't look at me. "No, just double checking."

"Where are you moving to?"

"To an apartment."

"Yep, but where?"

"I'd rather not say."

"What? Why? I'll need your address to forward your mail."

"I've organised redirection, but if anything arrives here, you can forward it to my work."

What the hell is going on?!

In our nine years together, she'd never been so cold, and her iciness today was catching me off guard. We were yet to argue, and yet to fight, but she was treating me like we were in the midst of a war; as an enemy even though I still saw myself as an ally.

I rubbed my forehead, as if to force my brain into under-standing what was going on.

Why didn't she want me to know where she was moving to? Was she worried about me turning up announced? I thought I'd been clear that once we were over, we'd be over and that she wouldn't hear from me again. Why couldn't she understand that?

I held my face and swallowed away some of my anguish.

"I think I have an idea as to why all of this is happening. I think I know why you're leaving." I wanted to talk to her about the *vesica pisces*, and how I now understood that we may have both ended up somewhere we didn't want to be.

She stopped what she was doing and glared at me from behind a cupboard door.

"You don't know anything. I'm not going to tell you why I'm going. I have my reasons but I'm not going to tell you. There are things about me you will never know."

She closed the cupboard and rushed down the stairs.

I let my head drop onto the dining table.

What the fuck was that about?!

I slouched deeper into my seat, wanting to dissolve onto the floor.

the opposite of a psychopath

What had happened during the past few weeks? Who was this person in my house? She'd become unrecognisable; not the wife I knew. How could she say such things? Why was she goading me like this? What had I done to deserve it?

I'd been playing nice, I'm sure I had. Our emails had been civilised and I hadn't been unreasonable. I'd not made a big deal that she'd used my house as storage for the past nine weeks, and I'd not made an issue out of what she wanted to take and what she didn't.

I'd wanted her stuff gone as soon as she'd left, but I kept that to myself, patiently waiting for her move. I'd wanted to keep the cutlery set my parents bought us, but I didn't argue the point. All I'd ever asked from her, was to know the reason she was leaving, so I could try to protect my own sanity and find my own closure.

I'd never been unkind to her and I wasn't going to start now. Whilst we'd split our stuff, we still needed to finalise our divorce settlement and the split of our remaining assets and finances, and I'd been made painfully aware by my *friends* that I had more to lose than she did.

I'd helped her build her wealth to the detriment of my own. I'd come into our relationship with assets, but she'd come into it in debt. We'd turned that around, but for the past five years, I'd been selling my assets to prop us up. She hadn't contributed to any of it, and I hadn't wanted her to, as my property before I met her was my source of income, and my way of keeping myself afloat without having to work in an office.

During our relationship, we didn't pool our money and didn't have a joint bank account. We kept our incomes separate and used a joint credit card to split our living expenses. It was a part of our mission to ensure we weren't financially co-dependent, and it was something we both agreed to. I didn't want to have a say in what she did with her money, and I didn't want her to have a say in what I did with mine; so long as we could both meet our mortgage payments and joint expenses, it wouldn't matter anyway. Except when her depression was diagnosed, it threw all of that out of the window.

With the sale of our house, land, and apartment, she had cleared her debt and put cash into her account, and was in the best financial position she'd ever been in. I, on the other hand, still had assets and debts I'd accumulated before her, and had remained worried since her phone call to end our marriage that she'd want some those assets too. She'd assured me during our emails that said she'd only want was hers, but her lack of empathy during the past few minutes was putting me on edge.

My biggest fear beyond losing her, was losing everything I'd spent my life working towards. Investing in property was something I'd started doing when I was nineteen years old, and I'd sacrificed my twenties and thirties to get to where I was.

I'd made good financial decisions, and bad, and had used my financial position to help her achieve hers. The thought that she could ask for half of everything I worked for before I even knew her was one I couldn't stomach.

Not long after she called to end things, I'd hired a family lawyer to guide me through the process of doing what needed to be done to split our assets and liabilities fairly. He told me I needed to prepare consent orders for the family court, a contract similar to a prenuptial agreement but made after the fact.

My lawyer had asked me to document our relationship from start to end, through the simple lens of transactions; in other words, dollars and cents. He wanted to know how we started our relationship; what each of us brought to it; what we'd earned during the time we were together; what we'd bought and sold together and separately, and what our financial situation looked like on the day it ended. It was a forensic and mathematical exercise, and it was emotionally exhausting and terrifying. Reducing our relationship to a bunch of transactions forced me to see things I'd never seen; things which I'd been happier not knowing. By using me to bankroll her wants and desires, her wealth had grown exponentially whereas mine had slipped backwards. I still had more than her, but much less than when we'd first started out. I wondered if she knew and couldn't shake the feeling that it was all a part of her plan, a part of her grift and long game.

Vesica or not, my insides were churning with resentment for what I'd learnt and how she'd gone about it and drafting the consent orders did nothing to settle them.

The consent orders were currently sitting with her and her lawyer and as they hadn't been signed yet, I'd be stupid to do something in reaction to her provocation today and give her cause not to.

Apart from the items in the spreadsheet and our consent orders, there was just one set of possessions which remained in contention and which hadn't yet been resolved: our rings.

I asked for us to re-swap rings, just as we did on our wedding day. I wanted to return my wedding ring to her, and I wanted her to return her engagement and wedding rings to me, a symbolic ending to what we'd started. Whilst her jewellery was ten times more valuable that mine, it was of no consequence, and I didn't want it back for that reason. I wanted her rings back because they symbolised our promises and our vows; and because she'd broken both, I thought it was only right that she return them.

I peeled myself off my seat and descended the stairs to see where she was and to check on the progress of the removalists. The three men were working briskly and had cleared two-thirds of the rooms' combined contents. She was on the street near the front door, watching them load her things into their truck.

I joined her on the street, clearing my throat to let her know I was there.

"What do you want to do with the dog? She's still technically yours and is still registered in your name."

She didn't acknowledge my presence or look my way.

"You keep her, she's yours now."

"Are you absolutely sure?"

"Yes, I don't want her."

I don't want her. It was a four-word key to another locked door in my memory vault. How had I forgotten?

From the start of our relationship, she'd wanted a pet dog; however, with our lifestyle of travel and late nights, I didn't think a pet was a responsible thing to take on. In our early days, we were rarely home, and I knew we wouldn't be able to properly care for a pet, especially whilst it was still young.

I'd never had a pet of my own and hadn't ever wanted one, and I'd already felt I was looking after two lives and didn't need the responsibility of a third. She understood the logic, but she didn't care.

Two years after her breakdown, and as her depression was intensifying, she announced at dinner one night that she'd bought a two-month-old rescue puppy. She told me I wouldn't need to do anything for it, and as I didn't want it, that she would care for it on her own.

I'd read that animals were supposed to be good for people with depression by giving them a sense of purpose above themselves, so I backed off on trying to convince her otherwise. I clearly had no say in the matter, anyway.

Within days, she drove to Gippsland with a friend and picked up her very own first pet. It was her new love and became an integral part of her life, until it wasn't.

It was about two years ago, when I'd dropped in on her in the study to give the dog a pat and to see how they were both doing.

She didn't look up. "Do you think your parents may want her? I don't want her anymore."

I thought I'd missed something and didn't know if she was talking to me or herself. "I'm sorry, what are we talking about?"

"Pup. I don't want her anymore, she's too needy and I don't like it. I don't want her relying on me." Hey eyes were glued to her monitor.

I wasn't sure if she was joking as her question and statements were delivered with her usual deadpan humour. She'd had her dog for less than two years and hadn't previously hinted at what she was now saying.

She'd been true to her word and had done most of the looking after of the puppy, only asking me to fill in when it was absolutely necessary. I never minded being called on and was happy to do more and more, as the tiny pup had weaselled its way into my heart and I couldn't imagine not having her around.

I couldn't hide my confusion and bewilderment.

"Are you serious?"

"Deadly."

"We can't do that! We rescued her! She's our responsibility!"

"But I don't want her anymore; I'll just take her to the pound if your parents don't want her."

The shock of what she was saying and how she was saying it was all-encompassing. How had she turned so spiteful and heartless? How could she want to throw our dog away like a used toy? How could she turn her back on the rescue animal that had helped rescue her? How could she want to get rid of one of our family without a discussion and without any thought?

"No, we can't get rid of her. You saved her and you need to look after her. She's your responsibility."

"But I don't want her anymore. She's too needy and I'm starting to hate her for it."

"We can't get rid of her. If you don't want to look after her anymore, then I will."

She didn't hesitate and relented in an instant.

"Are you sure?"

"What do you mean, am I sure? If that's my only option for us to keep her, then that's what I'll do."

"Are you sure your parents wouldn't want her?"

There was something about what I was saying that wasn't getting through. I repeated my earlier words:

"It's not the point. She's our responsibility, and I'm not going to ask them."

At the time, I'd explained her callousness away as a low point in her depression, another emotional ebb we needed to ride out. My aim was to buy some time, so she didn't do something she'd later regret. I told myself I'd take care of the pup for the next few weeks until everything went back to normal, except it never did.

It was easier to blame her behaviour on her mental health, as I always did, than to accept that she could be capable of such callousness. No sane person could want to dump a helpless animal at the pound just because they felt it was *too needy*.

I'd locked that memory away and hadn't remembered it until now, along with the memory of the exact thing I thought a few seconds later. *I bet I'm next.*

Had I known two years ago that this day was coming?

I winced, pushing the memory away, and brought myself back to the current question:

"Have you decided on what you want to do with our rings?"

She swung her head around to glare at me again, wide-eyed, and blush faced.

"I've already told you on email; I don't know. I don't think I'm in the right frame of mind right now to decide on something that important. I need more time to think about it."

She switched her gaze back to her possessions being loaded into the back of the truck.

My familiar golf ball-sized lump rose into my throat, again corking everything that was trying to erupt out. I spun on my heel and re-entered the house, sprinting down the hall, up the stairs, and into the living room.

I sat down, shaking.

Why was she acting like such an arsehole?

Here she was, more than capable of making a decision to destroy my life, but when it came to a rock on a piece of metal, she needed more time. If this didn't prove that her head wasn't right, then nothing would.

She was using her words and actions today as weapons to inflict as much damage on me as possible. She knew me, so she would know she was deliberately torturing me by the things she was saying and doing.

She'd brought her brother here for no reason that I could see, questioned my integrity by searching through my cupboards and drawers, and was now deliberately being provocative with her hurtful words.

She was showing no emotion and no remorse for what she'd done to me and no empathy for how I may be feeling.

She'd chucked the dog, and she was now chucking me.

If she ever had the capacity for love, she was no longer showing it, and if she had a conscience, it had gone AWOL.

It was difficult to believe, but I could only think my wife was turning into a fucking psychopath.

Chapter 13

I 'd scheduled my third counselling session for the week after her move, as I'd predicted I'd need some help and support with the fallout of whatever arose that day. Based on what had happened, I was glad I did as I was still recovering from the harrowing experience. She'd been like a small tornado, twisting through my space, sucking the light and happiness out of every room; and in the process, causing maximum destruction to my ego and sense of self. The debris she left behind in her words and the sentiments she voiced were the wreckage I'd be picking through and cleaning up for weeks or months to come.

So here I was again, seated in my chair looking across at him. His appearance was the same as in my previous sessions, even down to the same suit and tie. Not that it had any bearing on what we were here to do. Just that I noticed.

"How was it?" He asked.

"Worse than I imagined."

"Why?"

I didn't want to go through the details again as I'd been reliving the past nine days over and over in my head, but I knew I needed to. He sat and listened but didn't take any notes.

"Do you think you might have known more about what was going on than you're admitting here? Two years is a long time since the dog incident; there must have been other signs."

"Of course, I'm sure there were, but I blamed them on her depression. I blamed everything on her depression, and I'm still not sure that it's not the case."

"Nice double negative."

"Huh?"

He was smiling. "Never mind. Apart from her wanting to get rid of your dog, have you had any other lightning bolt memories from the past year or two?"

"Actually, yes, quite a few."

He sat back in his chair and gestured with his hand for me to continue.

"I'm not sure how I forgot the conversation, but it popped back into my mind yesterday. It was roughly at the same time that she wanted to dump the dog, so about two years ago, when she told me that she thought she was turning into a psychopath. She actually used that word!

"That's a bizarre thing to say. Intriguing. But it does show she was capable of some introspection."

"Or maybe she was just trying to shock me. I remember she'd got home from work and barged into the study in a huff to tell me what she told me.

"I looked up from whatever I was working on and remember smiling and asked her, 'what do you mean *turning*'?

"She hit me on my arm and told me she was serious, so I turned to face her and to provide her with my undivided attention and asked her what she meant.

"She leant against the wall near the doorway and told me she felt different; that she didn't feel like she was herself anymore, and that she thought she was fundamentally changing.

"She told me that she started enjoying heavy metal music. We'd always hated it because of the screeching. She felt she was losing her general sense of empathy, too. People were giving her the shits, she said, and she just didn't *care* about things like she used to.

"At the time, I'd thought it was a nonsensical conversation, so I dismissed it. I told her I thought she was fine and that changing tastes in music didn't make her a psychopath. That there was nothing to worry about and it didn't mean anything. I told her not to stress about it. I thought it would comfort her to know she was still normal.

"At that stage we'd been together for about seven years, and she seemed to be recovering from her depression and appeared to be more normal than she'd been for quite some time. I had learnt during our marriage not to fuel her random thoughts, especially if they were self-critical; it led to a calmer existence all round.

"At no time, did I consider that her changing tastes might one day also include me."

He put his hand up to stop me.

"So, she told you she was changing." He'd opened his notepad and was writing something as he asked the question.

"Yep, it seemed so, and I could see it, but into a *psychopath*?"

"Who knows? I can't diagnose her from here but based on what you've told me during our first two sessions, there are definite signs she may have had APD or even NPD."

"APD; NPD?"

"Antisocial personality disorder; narcissistic personality disorder. Again, it's not my job to diagnose her, nor is it fair for me to, as I only have your side of the story, but NPD is characterised by a feeling of exaggerated self-importance, excessive need to call the shots, and a lack of empathy. People with it value themselves over others and show disregard for the feelings of anyone else."

"But don't you get those same symptoms in depression?"

"No, not really. People with depression don't usually have heightened sense of self-importance, or worthiness in themselves. NPD is quite the opposite of depression, but it's a personality disorder, and not a mental illness, so it's possible to have both NPD and depression.

"NPD is far more commonly aligned with mania and bipolar. The saddest fact about NPD is people with the disorder are rarely diagnosed, as they view their doctors as inferior and as not knowing what they're talking about."

I sat back in my chair. I knew the Greek myth of Narcissus but couldn't recall studying NPD during my degree.

Could she have been a narcissist?

She'd always been self-centred – and self-absorbed. It was something I'd been attracted to in her from the very start, as I'd interpreted it as strength and independence, but as our relationship progressed, it was something I struggled with as she never gave me equal billing. I never felt as if I was her equal, in her eyes.

I wanted to be important to her and be given priority, but she couldn't quite get her head around the idea. I'd naively hoped things would change when we got engaged, and when they didn't, I'd thought the situation would surely change when we got married. It never did.

I'd once made her cry by sitting her down and explaining to her that I was on her team and that she would never need to face anything alone ever again. I thought I'd broken through, but it seemed she shed her tears, not because she was happy or sad, but because the concept of being equals was so foreign, that she couldn't get her head around it.

She acted as though she was alone in her world and was the only one she could trust to look out for her best interests. I thought it was a result of her mental issues but was learning that maybe it was more.

Could it be the reason that she never told me she was thinking about leaving was because telling me just didn't register with her? And maybe that's why she said what she'd said to me in Naxos, about expecting to me stick around as her friend. She was conducting her life as if she were conducting an orchestra, and she had the baton.

"What else? You mentioned you had more than one lightning bolt memory."

The counsellor's question brought me back into reality.

"Um yes."

I ran my hand through my hair, still not quite believing these memories had been locked away for the past two years. "You know how I told you that she made me promise that we'd always travel together, and never apart?"

"Yep, it was one of the three promises."

"Well, she actually reneged on that."

"How do you mean?" He took a sip of water, providing me an opportunity to do the same.

"She was quite upset one day and was standing in the middle of our spare room crying. I asked her what was wrong, and she told me that she wanted me do to the things I wanted to do, even if that included travelling on my own."

"When was this and what brought it on, do you think?"

"I'm not completely sure, but I reckon it was also about two years ago. It was at the same time she'd just started her new dream job and had found her new tribe. Her new employer hired mostly young tech professionals in their early twenties. They had few cares, and even fewer responsibilities, and hedonism seemed to be the focus of their lives. They were mostly single people, and they did whatever it was that young single people did. She was ten years older than them, and was the odd one out, but she didn't see it that way."

"How so?" His face was contorted into an expression I hadn't seen before, as if he was going to sneeze.

215

"Within a year, she'd changed the way she dressed, the way she did her hair and makeup, and the way she spoke and acted. Her whole attitude and demeanour changed, like she wanted to turn into someone else, a younger version of herself, and would keep regressing until she was actually there. She wanted to work hard, play hard, drink hard, and she wanted to do it all whenever she wanted, without regard for me or anything else. She stopped her depression meds and replaced them with alcohol, and I suspect drugs, as well as an escalating obliviousness towards me and our marriage."

"And how is this connected to her reneging on the travel promise?"

"Oh yeah; well at the time her lying was becoming worse and her mood swings were wilder and deeper—"

"Lying?"

"Yes, I'm fairly sure she lied throughout our relationship but for me, it was just a hunch; not anything I knew for certain. It felt like a powerplay, like she was proving to herself that she was smarter than me, and that she could make me believe anything. I played along, and I never confronted her as I didn't have any proof and didn't want the conflict; but yes, at the time, my perception was that her lying was getting worse."

I stood up to stretch out my back.

"Sorry, just needed to get that out. So, at that time I was at a loss on how to support her through whatever it as she was going through. So I just stopped trying. She was running her own race, and I couldn't make any sense of what was going on, so I stayed behind her, in her wake. I told myself that it was just another phase, and like the many before it, would eventually be replaced with something else. Anyway, it was at that time that she told me I should do the things I wanted to do."

"And why didn't you?"

"Well, I thought I already was. I was supporting her and that was what I wanted to do. I didn't want to travel without her, and I wanted us to be a team. Besides, at the time, I didn't think she was actually talking about *me*. What she should have said was, 'I want to do the things I want to do', as that's what she really meant, as it was already what she was doing."

"Tell me, why did you put up with all this?"

"To be honest, I don't really know. It felt right at the time, but as I hear myself say the words, and recount our history, I really can't explain it."

"Interesting. So, all this happened at roughly the same time, say two years ago? She wanted to get rid of her dog"— he tapped the back of his pen on his pad—"she told you she felt like she was turning into a psychopath"—he tapped again—"she got a new job, and regressed to a twenty-year-old, and she cancelled one of the promises she made you make." He tapped his pen twice with the last two points.

"Yep, sounds about right."

"And when did you sell all the assets you owned together?"

"About eighteen months ..."

I cleared my throat, my thoughts screeching to a halt.

I'd not made the connections between her wanting to shed her adult responsibilities and her actually *doing* so, but here it was laid out clearly in front of me. I couldn't recall what had happened first and in what order they occurred, but I wasn't sure it mattered. The signs had been there all along, and I hadn't been paying attention, or perhaps I ignored them and blamed them on her mental illnesses and just did my best to just stay out of her way and let her do whatever it was she wanted to do, like I always did.

I'm such an idiot!

"I want to ask you something." He had his pen in his mouth and looked uncharacteristically nervous.

I smiled supportively. "Go on, that's your job."

"Why do you think it was depression she was suffering with during the past few years?"

"How do you mean? It wasn't my diagnosis; it was what the doctors diagnosed her with."

"Yes, but based on your timelines, their diagnosis was six years ago, and wasn't revisited after she'd decided she was better."

"Yep, sounds about right, but that was because she wouldn't go back to see them."

"And her bipolar diagnosis was nine years ago, or even more; is that right?

I tucked my hands under my legs, unsure of where he was going with this. "Yep, that's also correct."

"Based on your descriptions, and your account of the things that have happened, and based on her previous diagnosis with bipolar, why is it you think her behaviour during the past two or three years was symptomatic of depression? You've made it sound like she was living her best life; she was happy at work, full of energy, partying hard, and shedding all her adult responsibilities.

"Doesn't that sound more like mania to you?"

He may have well stood up and punched me in the face with all his strength. *Why hadn't I seen her behaviour as mania?*

"I guess I never saw it that way. We had a diagnosis and I'd pinned everything to that."

"There's a recurring problem here, as I'm sure you're becoming aware. You seem to be stuck in the past and fail to notice that things are changing around you, but we'll come back to that.

"Do you know the difference between bipolar-one and bipolar-two?"

"I do. Two has something to do with the manic episodes not being as severe as bipolar-one, with mania also being split by a major depressive episode, whereas in one, there may be no depression."

"And she was diagnosed with which?"

Fuck me.

"Two."

I brought my hands to my face and rubbed my eyes with my palms.

"Are you okay?"

"Yes, but I feel a headache or migraine coming on."

"Let me know if you need anything."

"Thanks, but I'm sure I'll be okay."

"Interestingly, mania and NPD look very similar too."

I grasped the underside of my seat as the room felt like it was tilting, like a carnival ride ready to throw me off.

"I think there may be even more to it than that!" I stammered.

He looked genuinely curious. "How do you mean?"

I squirmed in my seat, mortified. "How have I not seen this before?"

"It's difficult to see when you're in it—"

"No, not that. Based on what you've just told me, not only was she mostly likely manic during the past few years, but she was probably manic when I met her. Her depression may have been a trough between two peaks, but I hadn't noticed her first manic episode because it was the only state I'd ever seen her in.

"I thought she was healthy when we first got together, but everything you're saying now, makes better sense. Our first three years together were really happy, and really energetic, and I remember thinking how amazing it was, but also how completely unsustainable it was going to be. And now I look at it with fresh eyes, she was most likely not in a normal state, but in a manic state back then as well."

Nine years ago, she sent me a flirty text, broke up with her long-term boyfriend, left her home, couch-surfed, got herself a new job, started a long-distance relationship with me, found a new apartment in Brisbane, got another new job, moved to

Melbourne, found another new apartment, got another new job, and moved to Bristol, and she'd done all of it in the space of eleven months. It had all felt normal to me at the time, as we were on a rollercoaster of love and doing whatever it took to be together.

"Dammit!" I let go of the seat and rubbed my eyes again.

"What? What else have you remembered?"

"She was completely open and honest with me at the time and had even told me she'd stopped taking her lithium when we got together! Lithium levels out mania, doesn't it? Unbelievable! She'd been manic that whole time, and I'd interpreted it as her being in love. How's that for ego?"

"Are you okay?" He looked concerned.

"Yep, I'm fine. This all makes so much more sense, but there are just too many pennies dropping for me at the moment. I feel like a slot machine."

He sat back in his seat to let me catch my breath.

"I have another penny for you."

I sat back in my own seat, exhausted. The kaleidoscope I'd been using to view our relationship was becoming clearer, so whatever he said next was going to be easier, and not as shocking as what had already happened.

"We need to change this discussion from her to you, because you can't do anything about her, but you can do something about you. Do you know the Ancient Greek aphorism, 'know thyself'?

"Yes, I do, but what is becoming abundantly clear is that I don't."

221

"Don't be too hard on yourself. It's why we're here. To learn and discover. There is an another old saying that 'it is impossible to control someone else's behaviour; and that all we can ever do is control our reaction to it'.

"Do you know what your Myers–Briggs Type Indicator is?"

Aphorisms, sayings, MBTI; can you just pick a topic and stick to it please?

"Yep, I've done it a few times, at university and for various job interviews over the years. I think my MBTI personality type is I-N-something-something."

"You're not the first person to have that misconception, as most people forget that the *I* in MBTI stands for indicator. It's not a personality type, but an indication of your preferences or traits; things you like, how you process information, and how you make decisions. It sometimes gets a bad rap, but I think it can be really helpful in understanding yourself within the broader world, and to better understand why you do the things you do and think the way you think."

He got up and walked to the laptop on his desk and typed something into a browser. He unplugged it and handed to me. "Go on, you can retake the test now; answer it quickly and don't think about it too much. The results are most accurate if your responses are based on instinct."

For the next ten minutes, we sat in silence as I answered the questions.

"I-N-F-J." I handed the laptop back to him.

"As I thought. Your preference set is quite rare, and I don't think I've met someone with I-N-F-J traits before. Only one percent of the population has your type-indicator, and it's only zero-point-five percent for males."

I looked at him blankly.

Who the fuck cares?

"I'll send you this report, but here's a quick summary. Your ninety-percent introverted trait means you value time alone, and can be easily drained by social situations, and over-stimulation. You prefer to process information on your own, and don't like to talk to people about the things you're thinking about. Most importantly, you need to recharge your batteries by yourself, and you should do it regularly.

"Your eighty-six percent intuitive trait means you're open minded and imaginative, but it also means you're always thinking 'what if?' You need to try and get out of your head every now and then, and just do something practical.

"Your seventy-five percent feeling trait means you're more empathic than most, but because of this, you can easily burn out by caring for other people—"

He looked up. "Are you hearing this?"

"Yep, sounds like me."

"It also means that you need to tap into what your feelings are telling you, rather than rationalising everything with your head.

"Lastly, your eighty percent judging trait means you value structure, clarity, and closure"—he looked up at me again, as we both knew closure was the reason I was here. "It also means that your view of things could be too rigid, and that you're probably too stubborn with your rules for how things should be.

"So, what do you think? Any of that resonate with you?"

I hadn't heard much of what he'd said as I was still drowning in our conversation about her bipolar and her mania, but I didn't want to let on.

"Yes, all of it."

He closed his laptop and left it on his lap.

"I haven't given you much homework until now, but I want you to do something. I want you to tune in to what you like, to your preferences, and traits, to your gut, and what feels good. Don't try and understand it, and don't try to rationalise it, just feel it, and let it be. Think with your gut, not with your head."

He just told me I lived in my head, so how exactly was I supposed to stop? A simple *just do it* wasn't enough for me. I needed the tools and the knowhow.

I was battered and bruised like I'd been through twelve rounds with my arms up, receiving blow after blow, and it was no longer just the room around me tilting, it was my whole life.

Had our relationship started on false pretences? Had I thought she was someone she wasn't? Had I thought she was happy because of me and because we were together? Did our relationship have *anything* to do with me or could I have been anyone?

"I'll give it a go, but no promises. Forty years is a long time of programming to unwind."

"I know it is. Go easy on yourself.

"If you're interested, I'd like you to see a colleague of mine. She specialises in this area and I think she'd be good for you if only for a session or two. If you'll allow me, I'll share my notes with her, so you don't need to cover old ground."

I couldn't think about another session right now, not with him, and not with anyone else. There was too much in this one to process and I needed time.

"Sure, I'm happy for the referral and happy for you to share everything."

He handed me her business card and shook my hand. "Good luck."

Chapter 14

I t had been a month since my last counselling session cracked me open, and a month and a week since she'd ransacked my house to take all her stuff.

A letter addressed to me had just arrived in the post, its envelope printed with the details of my lawyer.

I took a massive breath and ripped it open.

It was notification from the Family Court that they had approved our consent orders.

My sigh of relief could have blown the walls of the room out.

Until now, I hadn't realised how stressed I'd been, waiting for this letter, waiting to read those words. Whilst we'd agreed to the terms of our split, and had both signed our parts weeks ago, there was still a chance the court could challenge any clause they deemed unfair or not in the best interests of each party. Thankfully, they didn't.

My lawyer had been a typical lawyer and had prepared me for both the best and worst. He'd straddled the fine line between optimism and realism, and I'd been holding my breath ever since.

I made a beeline for my laptop to email her to her know I'd received the stamped orders, and with nothing to lose, I asked her one last time for her rings, and for the reason she'd ended our marriage. I also asked her to diarise the date she walked out of the house, so she could use the same date in a year's time to file for our divorce. *A month's notice to get married, and a year's notice to get divorced, only in Australia.*

After clicking send, I walked around the house, taking deliberate notice of every surface, and everything within it. It was all mine again, and none of it was under threat. The worst was over, and there was just one step to go before I could close this sordid chapter of my life for good.

I was still swimming against the tide on the lessons I'd learnt during the past few months; it was as though I was in the Middle Ages, discovering the earth revolved around the sun and not the other way around. *Vesica*, patterns, psychopath, mania, and INFJ were ideas still percolating; all pieces to a puzzle I couldn't yet put together.

I'd read the Myers–Briggs report a few times but apart from taking its advice to spend more time on my own; something I was already doing; I wasn't sure how else to apply it. I didn't know how to get out of my head as it was where I lived, and how I made sense out of the world. I didn't know how not to care for people in need, but most of all, I didn't know how to go without closure in my life.

What I did know was that the idea of travel still made me happy and with my financial position now secure, I could pull the trigger on a plan to embark on an around-the-world divorce holiday to celebrate and commiserate the event. Even better, I'd accumulated enough frequent flyer points during the past twenty years to pay for the flights and would only need to stump up the cash for accommodation and spending.

I wanted this trip to be somehow *different* to my previous ones but wasn't sure what that meant or how'd I go about it. I didn't want to be frivolous, but I also didn't want it to be more of the same. If I kept doing the same things, I wasn't going to grow. I needed to do what I'd done in Kyoto and challenge myself to be my opposite. It worked for me there, albeit temporarily, but it had worked.

I rushed back to my laptop and searched for reward flights I could board as soon as possible.

It had taken me all night, but I'd found a flight to New York City, returning via Paris and Hong Kong. First class there, and business class back; I blew all my frequent flyer points with a series of clicks of the mouse. My inner voice had pleaded with me to stretch the points in economy so I could do the trip again next year, but I didn't pay it attention. I'd always given in to that voice, and I'd always travelled in the discomfort of economy.

I wasn't going to slum it in my accommodation either, especially for my fourteen nights in New York. I'd got the flights for free, so was going to pay a bit more per night to enjoy the places I slept, rather than feeling the familiar need to escape each morning.

I remembered the first time I'd been to NYC and smiled to myself at the horror of my accommodation. I'd arranged to holiday with two friends, so we could spend New Year's Eve in Times Square. I'd booked a hotel in the theatre district based on price alone and when I arrived to check in, I was confronted with a fistfight in the foyer and staff protected by bullet-proof glass. It was the scariest place I'd stayed, and I'd been careful to read customer reviews ever since.

The two-month wait to board my flight felt neither too long nor short, but the first-class experience to fly to the USA was worth every minute of the lead up and every point I'd spent on it. It was the epitome of unnecessary luxury and kicked off my holiday before I'd departed.

It was my fourth time in New York City, although the second time didn't really count as it was for work. Besides the dodgy hotel in Times Square, I'd previously stayed near Grand Central Station, and the Upper West Side, but for this trip I wanted to be somewhere different; somewhere more pedestrian, and away from the main tourist hotspots. I wanted to be closer to what I imagined NYC real life to be, so I could blend in and pretend to live like a local for the next two weeks.

I used the same website she'd used to find our accommodation in Tokyo and Greece and found myself a boutique art deco hotel at the intersection of West Village, Greenwich Village, East Village, and SoHo. It was opposite

New York University and looked like the perfect place to call home.

I only had one rule for myself on this holiday, and that was there were no rules. This trip was going to be like Kyoto every single day. I'd do the things I wanted to do, how I wanted to do them. I'd stroll the streets and see what I saw. I'd be mindful in the moments and I'd enjoy my time, even if I was doing nothing. I would go to sleep early and wake up late and I would never feel like I was wasting time.

During breakfast in the hotel's bistro on my ninth day, a waiter I'd seen every other morning stopped by my table. Apart from taking my order and my tip, he'd never said anything to me beyond 'hi', and 'bye'. He was plumpish and had greasy long black hair tied into a ponytail. He stayed in the shadows and watched the guests, ready to pounce whenever he was required.

"Where you from?" He had a Latino accent.

"Australia; Melbourne, Australia."

"How long you here for?"

"Just another five nights unfortunately."

"Oh, that's a shame. I'll miss you when you're gone."

I stared at him, unsure of what he meant as it was the first time we'd spoken, and I wasn't sure if it was a pick-up line. His eyes were friendly, and he had a wry smile curving the corners of his mouth.

"You're always so still when you're here. I feel peace when you're around. I don't know how, and I can't explain it, but it's really cool, and I wanted to say thank you."

It was the most unusual thing anyone had ever said to me. I was no buddha sitting under a tree, and after the turmoil of the past eight months, I thought I was still a complete mess. That someone could get peace out of my presence felt contradictory and as if I was a sham. *Why couldn't I get peace out of my own presence?*

"Are you finished?" He was gesturing to the table.

I was but was no longer ready to leave the comfort of my chair. "No, not yet, but thank you for saying what you just said, that's very kind."

His smile grew wider, and he walked off.

What did he see that I couldn't? Was I doing better than I thought?

I'd spent my time in New York living without structure and rules. I'd eaten granola and yoghurt for breakfast each morning even though I'd thought I hated both. I strolled when the mood took me and caught the subway when it didn't. I walked from Washington Heights to Wall Street, and I lay on the grass in parks to watch the clouds pass overhead. I saw the ballet, Philharmonic, and the opera, and I swayed along with jazz musicians in Washington Square Park. I snoozed on Roosevelt Island and I did shots of Tequila with two Canadian brothers I met at a jazz bar. I visited museums and galleries, and I explored almost every street in West Village and SoHo. I shared a bagel with a homeless lady on a park bench on Houston Street, and I sunbathed on the Highline every few days. I'd never done so much, and so little at the same time, and maybe I was feeling all the better for it.

I was tuning into my gut, to what I liked, and to what felt good. I wasn't trying to understand it, and I wasn't trying to rationalise it, at least not as much as I would normally have.

I hadn't thought about her much either, and if I did, it was with a mild curiosity rather than judgment. My anger still lingered, but it felt less severe, more like a memory or a shadow, as if I was the one holding on to it when it was trying to escape.

Perhaps I was finally getting out of my head.

Perhaps I was reaching peace.

During my many daily walks along 8th Street, I'd spotted what looked like a subterranean meditation studio. It was diagonally opposite the hotel and it shone like a beacon each time I exited the foyer. I'd not yet been inside as I hadn't felt ready but buoyed by my interaction with the waiter this morning, today was going to be the day.

I left my table and walked past reception to the revolving timber door leading to the street, high-fiving the doorman on my way out, a custom we'd started on my third day.

8th Street appeared extra vibrant today; the sky seemed bluer, and the creams and beiges of the buildings weren't as dull. The air was warm and still, and the lights and sounds of the city seemed sharper, and more vivid.

I crossed the road but was stopped at the stairway entrance by a rush of panic blowing through me. What was I doing? Was this how I really wanted to spend today?

I'd not done a meditation class before, and my anxiety was rising with the realisation that I had no experience of it, but then I asked myself: wasn't that all the more reason to step into the studio?

I took a breath and descended the stairs.

Beyond the front door was a rectangular room, bright and white, with pale oak floorboards. To my right were two benches in a similar-coloured timber, and above them were square cubby holes holding shoes and bags, as well as coat hooks holding nothing. At the back of the room were slouchy grey fabric couches and cushions, and an all-white kitchenette. In front of me was a tiny reception desk and a bookshelf stacked with books, socks, t-shirts, and hoodies, and in front of it was the most beautiful woman I'd seen in ten years.

My heart had skipped a beat as she came into focus. Tall, brunette, and with flawless skin. Her voice was deeper than I expected and oozed joy and happiness. She wore bronze-coloured leggings and a white sweatshirt and was shoeless.

"Welcome! I hope you don't me asking, but can you please take your shoes off, and can you also put your phone on silent? Thank you so much!"

I couldn't take my eyes off her but knew I should.

I wonder what's wrong with you?

Broken, depressed, in a bad relationship, need an escape?

"Are you here for one of our classes?"

"I am; I'm here from Melbourne but haven't done one of these before."

"Based on your accent, I take you don't mean Melbourne, Florida." Her hands were clasped, and she was still smiling at me like I was the only person in the world.

"Ha, no; Melbourne, Australia." I couldn't restrain a matching smile.

"What brings you here?"

I sat down to unlace my shoes. "Just holidaying. I'm here for two weeks, but only have five days to go."

"Great, let me show you around. You have nothing to worry about. We have lots of first-timers joining us."

She explained the studio's purpose and how it specialised in twenty-minute mindful breath meditation sessions, with each class focussing on a specific theme. She told me I could come in to relax on the couches whenever I wanted, and that I was free to enjoy their complimentary herbal tea and books on the bookshelf. She pointed out the meditation rooms, and a space at the back of the building where guests could meditate in their own time. She also told me that there were just three rules, no shoes, no phones, and no loud voices.

I nodded, taking it all in, and absorbing her aura and the serenity of the studio.

"Our next class is in ten-minutes; would you like to join?"

I didn't have anywhere else to be except right here. She'd made me feel comfortable and whatever panic I'd experienced earlier had evaporated. "I'd love to."

"Great, we've only just opened this month and we have

some special pricing. It's fifteen dollars per session, and you can book your cushion online or in person, or it's fifty dollars for a pass for unlimited sessions for a month."

Even though I hadn't yet done my first session, I already knew I'd want to come back, even if it was for a cup of tea and sit down. "I'll take the pass please."

She took my money and registered my details in their system. She asked me to wait on the couch, until the teacher called us forward.

I'd been so awestruck by her and my orientation that I hadn't noticed the studio had been filling with participants for the next class. They were all beautiful people, sculpted to perfection in yoga and gym gear. They looked like models and I'm sure one of them was an actor I'd seen on TV. I seemed to be the only male in the room, and was the only one wearing jeans, and a collared shirt.

My panic was back.

I didn't belong here. This was a place to be and be seen. I was reminded of the cocktail parties we used to go to, vacuous and vain.

I sat cross-legged on the couch and closed my eyes to shut them out. It didn't matter if this was the place to be, and the place to be seen. There still might be some value in the session, and if there wasn't, I'd only have used up half an hour of my day and wasted fifty bucks.

"Those of you here for the mindful heart session, please follow me."

I opened my eyes to see a short man with a big belly; his

untucked shirt draping off his front like an apron. He had what looked like dyed black hair and authentic joy in his face.

He led a group of about fifteen of us through a hidden sliding door and into a room I hadn't noticed earlier. Four rows of six round cushions lay on the floor, equidistant front to back, and side to side, and our teacher asked us to sit wherever we liked, taking his position at the front of the room to face us.

I'd never sat on a cushion before, so I moved it aside and sat on the floor.

"Seems someone is getting low, and properly grounding themselves for our time together."

He was looking at me and smiling; and if he'd just made a meditation joke, I didn't get it.

When everyone was seated, he asked us to straighten up, as if a fishing line was pulling us up from the base of our spines, through the crowns of our heads, and asked us to breathe slowly, in through our noses and out through our mouths.

"Use your breath as an anchor, an anchor to keep you present in the here and now."

An anchor? Was this why I shut my eyes and inhaled deeply every time I felt overwhelmed? Was I anchoring?

I hadn't chosen this heart class because it was the one which appealed to me the most, it was because it was the only one on at this time. I wondered afresh if I should be here. And then he spoke again:

"Let your hands rest comfortably on your thighs. As you close your eyes and become conscious of your breath; in, and out; in, and out; I want you to notice each time a thought pops into your head.

"Each time a thought arises; and they will, I want you to say the words, 'just thinking' in your mind, and then return to your breath."

"In, and out; in, and out. Just thinking."

The sounds of Manhattan disappeared and were replaced with a high-pitched ringing in my ears, much like tinnitus. There was nothing causing the sound, and the room of people around me had fallen into a deep silence. I could feel my skin warming against the airconditioned air, but not in a painful way, and a blur of reds and purples had started morphing across the insides of my closed eyelids, like the gentle blobbing of a lava lamp.

The quiet between the teacher's words was amplifying my other senses, and I found myself reciting the words, 'just thinking' more than I was breathing.

I felt a rising sensation of panic. Quite the opposite to how I thought I should be feeling. I wanted to open my eyes, get up and shake myself off, but I didn't think the others in the room would appreciate it.

I remembered the words of the beautiful brunette. That meditation was only ever practised, and not merely *done*. She'd told me that the aim of meditation wasn't to get good at it, but to just do it. "The art of meditation is in the practice," she'd told me.

I couldn't make sense of what she was saying, but now that I was struggling to be here, the meaning behind her words was becoming clear. I wasn't sitting here to meditate; I was meditating by sitting here; and I was finding it challenging.

Just thinking.

"I want you to imagine you're on a raft. Imagine you're floating down a narrow canal, or a stream. On either side there are reeds, and every now and then, your raft brushes through the reeds.

"Your raft keeps going though. The reeds scrape your raft, but you keep moving, floating towards a clearer part of the stream, where there are no reeds.

"These reeds are your thoughts, and your raft is your meditation practice. Your thoughts will always be there, on the sides of the stream, and they will brush your raft every now and then, but the practice is to let your raft keep floating through.

"You don't need to do anything with your thoughts. Just let them be, let them pass. Just let them brush your raft and keep moving."

Don't do anything with my thoughts? What the hell is this man talking about?

I opened my eyes.

The teacher's eyes were still closed, as were everyone else's around me.

I shut my eyes quickly, not wanting to get busted doing the wrong thing.

"Imagine your thoughts and even your feelings as sitting next to you on a park bench. Like a friend you're so comfortable with, that you don't need to speak. You can just sit together, knowing that the other is there, and not having to interact. Let there be comfort and knowing in the silence.

"In the same way as before, you don't need to interact with your thoughts or feelings. You can just sit next to them and just let them be."

I opened my eyes again.

Sit next to my thoughts and feelings without doing anything with them? Not interacting, not understanding, and not solving? What planet is this guy on?

At the end of the session, I made a cup of tea and sat on the couch. Two or three others did the same, but apart from polite smiles, we didn't say anything to each other.

The past twenty minutes were as revolutionary as they were simple.

Until now, I thought I'd meditated in one form or another for my whole life, using it as quiet space to solve problems, rationalise my thoughts, calm myself down, and to suppress or eliminate my feelings. I could now recognise that my version of meditation wasn't meditation at all.

I'd been stuck in my head because I believed that my thoughts and feelings had to be mulled over, processed, and resolved. For my whole life, I'd never allowed them to just sit there and be left alone.

I thought about Tokyo, and the weeks after; Greece, and the weeks after; my counselling sessions, and the weeks after. During all that time I'd been forcing myself to process, and problem solve what was happening, and I'd not allowed anything to just *be*. I was always *doing* something with the information; assimilating it, or accommodating it, but I would never just leave it alone.

To get out of my head, I was going to need to keep my raft moving through the reeds and I needed to accept that I would most likely never find the reasons why my marriage ended.

Closure for me had always been about gaining *understanding*. Now, I had to accept I wasn't going to understand what had happened, regardless of how much I thought about it. Closure for me now, needed to be letting go, letting the past pass, and letting my raft move through.

And in the end, getting closure on my breakup wasn't going to change the fact that we had broken up. I'd come some way since and was now ninety-nine percent sure I didn't want that outcome changed, anyway.

Chapter 15

My psychological chrysalis was starting to fracture, but I wasn't sure who I'd be when I emerged from it. I was questioning everything and was no longer fearful about what I'd learn about my own behaviour. I remembered back in Tokyo when I'd been shut down by what she was saying to me, not wanting to ask her questions for fear of her answers. If it were happening to me now, I think I'd react differently, but I really couldn't know for sure.

Knowing what to look out for was my primary challenge as I didn't have someone else there to point out my flaws and help me with my quest. I'd glimpsed new perceptions and knew my current reality was better than my old one, and that my future one would be better still. I needed to try and let go of the structure and rigidity of my life and continue to be hyper-alert for signs of my old stubbornness and hypocrisy.

My time in New York City had been so much more than a holiday, even though that hadn't been its purpose. It had been an education, and a spiritual retreat. I'd attended fourteen meditation sessions in my last five days, and I'd learnt something new in every one of them. I was sad to leave my Greenwich Village home, but was grateful for the experience, and even more grateful for not needing to head back to Melbourne just yet.

I arrived in Paris at nine o'clock at night, perfect timing for a walk along the Seine towards the hourly light show projected from the Eiffel Tower. As was my habit when I'd travelled here from Bristol, I stayed near Gare du Nord for the convenience of both the airport connections, and the easy stroll to Montmartre.

I was here for four days and was keen to continue my new practice of doing what I wanted when I wanted, without an itinerary, or guilty feelings of obligation.

I woke early for my first full day in Paris, and for ease, started with breakfast in the hotel's dining room. Pink grapefruit, fruit salad, and croissants with butter and jam were my fuel for the day, or until such time as the sugar-hit wore off.

I was keen to start this trip by visiting somewhere I hadn't been before, so I checked my map and headed east to Parc des Buttes-Chaumont to explore its grassed hills and rooftop views of Paris. I found a quiet spot near a huge conifer tree and lay down, crossing my ankles, and resting my hands on my ribcage.

My mood had quietened since last night, and I hadn't yet

worked out whether it was jetlag from the seven-hour flight back through time, or because of something else more unsettling. My lesson from New York was to sit with it, or lie with it, as I was now, and to not force a rationale that might not be there.

I'd been graphing my mood for a few months after my counsellor suggested I track how I was feeling on a daily basis and so I could see that things were getting better over time. I used a scale of minus ten for when my mood couldn't be worse, to plus ten for when it couldn't be better. Zero, for me, was a perfectly acceptable mood; it meant neither elation nor its opposite. And I was content with that.

I'd been tracking in negative numbers right up until my trip to Bali, at which time my self-rating jumped into the sevens and eights. It dipped below zero again after I'd returned to Melbourne but had climbed again and stayed above five for the past two weeks.

I rated myself each night based on my average feeling across the day, and yesterday's score had been a five; but ever since I'd woken up, my mood had been bouncing around as if on a pogo stick.

If I were to put a number against my mood right now, whilst laying in this lush green park, in the warmth of the sun, and with all Paris to look forward to, it would be a minus five. It wasn't making sense, and the more I tried *not* to make sense of it, the more uneasy it made me feel.

Just sit with it.

I was learning more about me and as difficult as it was, I

knew that in time, everything would feel normal again. I wanted to keep alert, remaining vigilant to my programming and habitual mistakes, so I could make changes where I needed to. I wanted to let my thoughts pass more often, without interference. I needed to sit with my feelings and just let them be.

I'd learnt that my view of relationships was skewed, and that I should question everything I thought I knew. I could no longer take anything for granted, not my thoughts, not my likes and dislikes, not my assumptions, and especially not my judgements.

I was involved in everything that had happened to me, and if I was present when something happened, then I was partially, if not entirely responsible for it happening.

It felt like I knew more than I was consciously remembering. Something else had happened two years before Tokyo, something more than her getting a new job, and wanting to get rid of the dog. What was it? What part had I played in setting the wheels in motion? Once, I had blamed everything on her depression; but now I felt there was more to the story; a repressed memory battling to get out.

I was doing horribly at lying there with this feeling, and I wanted to shut it down.

I started up at the inky greens of the tree's billions of needle leaves, trying to focus on them, and to not care about the thing that was bugging me.

Care; caring; carer; that was it! That's where I fucked it all up …

We were in our kitchen, and I was cooking us dinner. She was sitting on the kitchen bench, surrounded by her usual aura of negativity, whinging and complaining about something, or everything.

I remember looking at her and of the visceral sensation of the last drop of energy leaving my body. I leant on the bench and felt an emptiness I didn't recognise, as if I had nothing left in my tank. I felt like an empty shell, fragile on the outside, and with nothing to support me from inside, I thought I was going to crumble. I'd given her everything and she'd taken it all, not once supporting me in return, or giving anything back.

It was the first time I'd realised I needed help, and that I couldn't continue to be there to support her without some support of my own. After dinner, I did web searches and called agencies and eventually found an organisation willing to assist.

I made an appointment, and during the subsequent consultation, the person I was speaking to kept using the word, 'carer' to describe me. I kept correcting them, calling myself a husband or partner, but they kept calling me her carer.

They told me I'd been expending most of my energy caring for her and her mental health, that I'd been neglecting myself. They told me that I wasn't giving myself any respite, and that I couldn't continue to 'pour from an empty jug'.

I'd left the appointment bemused, but I did take their point that I needed to try and do things to top myself up. At the time, I didn't see myself as a carer, but I did see myself as caring.

When I got home, I'd told her about the meeting, word for word, telling her I wouldn't be going back as I didn't agree with their assessment. She'd got upset with me as she thought I was lying. She thought I was using coded messages and that I was using their words for my own feelings. She'd only ever heard the word 'carer' and nothing else. She didn't want to be a person who needed care, and it was entirely possible that from that day on, she did everything she could to prove she didn't.

It was around that time, she stopped leaning on me for support and stopped telling me what she was thinking and how she was feeling. She withdrew from me and threw herself into others.

I'd not reacted to her changes in behaviour, because at the time, I thought my wife was trying to get better. She'd had enough of her depression, and I had too, and her actions were those of a person getting back on to their feet. I hadn't realised until now, that in order to for her to be able to prove to herself she could do it without me, she needed to *show* me she could, pushing me away until she was ready to do so.

The branches above me swayed as if to celebrate my discovery, even though I was feeling oddly queasy, as if there was nothing about this to celebrate.

Could one word have started this all? Could I have changed what happened by keeping my mouth shut as I'd done in the past?

I sat up to stretch my shoulders and to look at the manicured landscaping in front of me. My depressed mood from earlier felt like it had dissipated, but it was now replaced with something more intense. It seemed that the rolling hills of Parc des Buttes-Chaumont were providing me with unexpected insight, and I was seeing things I'd previously suspected, but had deliberately ignored.

This situation wasn't just about caring, it was about her lying.

I'd suspected she'd been a compulsive liar for our entire relationship, but if she had indeed been manic at the start and end of our relationship, then I could now be confident she actually was.

I remembered her lies during my internal rant after my first counselling session, and during my third, but my gut was now telling me it was more than that, and I'd probably accepted being lied to all along.

Her lies had started during our very first texts and she continued to lie to me on a daily basis through to the end – and even beyond. I'd disrespected myself by allowing her to lie to me, making it easier for her to disrespect me by doing so.

My memory of our nine years together was disintegrating, only to reassemble itself in a more logical and understandable way. I'd made up so many storylines on her behalf, to explain the things I didn't want to know about, to tell myself the story in the way I wanted it told.

My intuition had told me that she was still with her ex-boyfriend when she'd started up with me, even though she told me she wasn't. I'd not made a fuss when she travelled to

Perth with him two months after we got together, because she told me she had to. She told me she hadn't told her parents that they'd broken up, and she didn't want to ruin their Christmas by telling them beforehand.

I'd felt it in my bones that she was having an affair with her housemate in Brisbane whilst we were living in different countries and doing the long-distance relationship thing. I'd asked her about it after he'd pledged his love to her in front of me on one of my visits, but I'd accepted her explanation of one-sidedness as I didn't want to believe it could be true.

My gut told me she was having affairs when she thought she was over her depression, with colleagues, friends, and anyone who could give her a thrill. I knew promiscuity was a major symptom of mania in bipolar, but until recently I'd thought she was depressed, rather than manic, so it had been easier to square things away.

She'd lied about her business trips, and about how much time she needed to spend in Canberra and Sydney. She lied about where she was going and who she was spending time with, but I'd convinced myself she wasn't.

She never knew my suspicions because I never let on. Knowing the truth seemed worse than not knowing, but my gut wasn't fooled, no matter what I told myself.

What was bothering me again, was that she had no idea I suspected her. She thought, and probably still thinks that she'd pulled the wool over my eyes,

Ego, it's just ego.

Let it go.

I'd blamed everything on her mental state, but why? I hadn't wanted to make her suffer any more than she already was, but why? Why did I treat myself as having lesser needs than her? Why did I consider myself less important than her? Why did I make myself less worthy than her? Why didn't I want to face the truth?

They were good questions, and ones which would have enraged me just two or three months ago, but which were now having minimal effect on my affect.

Recognising what I already knew was a step forward; and confronting it could be next.

I was going to *sit* with all of this without actively doing anything with it, and I was going to trust that the answers would present themselves at the right time, whenever that may be. I was confident that all this would eventually make sense, and thankfully for me, Paris had many park benches to sit on to help me on my way.

As the heat from the sun increased its intensity, I picked myself up and walked south towards the Pyrénées Metro station. My next stop was going to be Promenade Plantée, the original park-on-a-disused-elevated-rail-line, built long before New York's Highline.

The five-kilometre-long park was used in a scene in one of my favourite movies, the second part of a trilogy about a long-term relationship between two star crossed lovers. The three movies were set nine years apart and offered a vignette of the couple's trials and tribulations at ages twenty-three, thirty-two, and forty-one. I was roughly the same age as the protagonists throughout the movies and they felt like friends I'd grown up with in real life.

I arrived at the entrance to the French Highline via Rue de Lyon and climbed the stairs as fast as my legs would take me. I was excited to be here, my mood ratings rising into the positives.

The first of the three movies had a profound impact on me, and after watching it two or three times, I made a wish to the universe for my own love story to mirror theirs; I wanted a chance meeting with a beautiful girl, a journey through conversation and connection, and a passion and love based on nothing vaguely rational or logical.

As I followed in their footsteps along the narrow, grey-speckled path, through the lush greenery of bushes, vines, and trees, a sudden dizziness stopped me in my tracks.

I reached out towards a metal bench seat and stumbled towards it, flopping down on to it and leaning back.

Are you fucking serious?!

The universe had given me exactly what I'd asked for.

My failed relationship had mirrored theirs.

We'd lived in different countries and then together, just like they did; their relationship was intense at the start and mechanical at the end just as ours was; they lasted nine years just like we had; and it all ended in Greece, just like ours did.

Wow!

My head was spinning like a top, but I was smiling to myself like a crazy person.

It had to be sheer coincidence, but what a fantastic coincidence!

My smile spread across my face and converted into laughing out loud; everything about this discovery was hilarious. I raised my eyes to the sky and pointed to the clouds, not caring who was watching or what they'd think.

"Careful what you wish for, eh? Thanks for the lesson, universe!"

I'd hated the ending of the third movie. We'd watched it together at its premier night at the cinema, and I'd squirmed my way through its second half, knowing where it was going whilst wishing it wasn't. The characters' dispassionate, almost heartless argument in the hotel was all too real, the topics they were sparring over the same ones we were being silent on. It was a heart-wrenching portrayal of an imploding relationship, but it also felt too close for comfort.

When did that movie come out? I pulled my phone out of my pocket, to find the answer.

Oh, you fucker.

It was exactly two years before we went to Tokyo; and roughly the same time she'd got her dream job, wanted to ditch the dog, called herself a psychopath, and started regressing to the careless and carefree person she'd become.

My life had imitated their art, and I'd seen what was going to happen to me and to us, two full years before it did.

Why had I ignored all the signs?

Chapter 16

My four days in Paris had been *magnifique* but I'd been looking forward to my five days in Hong Kong since I'd booked the holiday eleven weeks ago. I knew and loved Paris and New York, but I also craved something new, a place I hadn't been and somewhere which could push me out of my comfort zone.

During my time in Paris, I'd become conscious that the first three locations I'd travelled to after our separation, were places I'd previously been with her; Seminyak, New York City, and Paris. At the same time, I remembered reading an article about memory, and the theory that a person's memory of a place, or a time, or an event, was only ever a memory of the last time they remembered it, superseding all previous memories. The hypothesis was that memories were simply memories of memories of memories, and not a direct memory of the actual time or place.

I'd found the article intriguing at the time I'd read it, but now that I was returning to places I'd already been, and already had memories of, I wondered whether I was subconsciously travelling to these cities to overwrite my past with her, and to create a new one which just contained me. It was an interesting train of thought, but one I didn't spend too much time processing. I loved New York and Paris long before I knew her, and the things I loved about them were still there, whether she was or not.

The weather in Hong Kong was warmer and more humid than I'd anticipated, but nowhere near as much as Tokyo had been last year.

I spent the first day exploring the Wan Chai and Central districts by foot before realising there was nothing about walking through Hong Kong that was enjoyable. I was doing it under sufferance, out of habit, because I'd always done new places on foot. The massive traffic-filled roads, the concrete skyscrapers, and endless urban development did nothing for me, except tell me that my old patterns were dying hard, and that I needed to be more conscious of what I felt I *could* be doing, rather than what I thought I *should* be doing.

On my second morning, I bought a weekly MTR pass, and a new feeling of freedom to explore places I wouldn't have been able to get to by walking. I used a chain of dim sum restaurants as hubs for my expeditions across Hong Kong Island and Kowloon, and for tasty sustenance to keep me going.

On my third day, I took myself out for a special degustation lunch at one of Hong Kong's finest restaurants. The maître d' seated me at a large round table, big enough for six people, and faced me towards the spectacular view of Victoria Harbour. I had three wait staff looking after me, and their attention to detail made me feel like royalty. As they continued to check that everything was to my liking, I wondered whether they assumed I was a journalist or international food critic, even though I had no notebook or experience as either.

At the end of the meal, I summoned the maître d' with a smile and a beckoning wave of my hand.

"Is everything okay sir?" His intonation exhibited neither question nor statement, a skill I found fascinating.

"Perfect, thank you. The meal, the service, your restaurant, all perfect."

"I'm incredibly pleased to hear. Is there anything else I can organise for you; more tea perhaps?" He pulled a silver gadget out of his inside jacket pocket and scraped an area of crumbs to my right.

"Would it be possible for me to have a copy of my menu today please?"

It was customary practice for Melbourne's best restaurants to present a printed version of what you'd eaten, especially when served with a verbal menu, and I thought it would be a wonderful souvenir of the afternoon.

The maître d' looked taken aback. "Certainly, sir, I will find you a copy." He quickstepped away and disappeared through a hidden door in the back corner of the restaurant.

You idiot! You've offended him. You don't know the customs here and you've probably just done the worst thing you could have possibly done! I wondered how I could pay my bill and escape before I did any more damage. I'd had a spectacular lunch and didn't want to ruin it by my own ignorance.

I scanned the room to plot my exit, but the hidden door again swung open with the maître d' and another man in a chef's uniform and toque, walking through. The maître d' was holding a piece of cardboard, and the chef was holding a glossy ox-blood-red box. They approached the table and set their items on it.

As if by reflex, I stood up.

The maître d' gestured to the chef. "This is the chef of your meal today."

They both bowed slightly, so I reciprocated.

"Thank you for a wonderful meal and experience today. It was really breathtaking."

The chef responded in broken English. "Thank you for coming here. I pleased you enjoy."

I bowed again.

The maître d' opened the folder and withdrew a thick piece of A4 sized card. "This is your menu from today." It was beautifully presented and looked specifically printed for me. It had my name on it, as well as today's date. Elegant calligraphy detailed each dish and smaller text described the ingredients that went into them.

"Would you like to chop?" He punched his right fist into his open left hand.

I had no idea what he was talking about and he could tell I didn't. He opened the red box and pulled out a heavy-looking brass rectangular cube and set it aside. He then took out a red rectangular stick, smaller than the metal one, and more plastic in appearance. From his pocket, he removed a gas lighter and clicked it on. He held the lighter to the base of the red cube, melting it to drip onto the bottom of the menu. It was wax, but I still wasn't following what was going on.

With the splotch of wax about four centimetres in diameter, he turned the lighter off and held the wax cube upside down to cool. The chef picked up the brass object and held it in its middle.

"Put your hand there." The maître d' was pointing to the top of the brass. I did what I was told, and with both the chef and I holding the metal object, he directed it downward into the wax, rocking it backwards and forwards, before lifting it to reveal two embossed logographic characters.

"This is our chop, our seal."

Both men looked moved by the ritual and the chef had what looked like tears in his eyes, but in the haste of the moment, I couldn't be sure. Emotions of happiness and pride were emanating from both of them, igniting corresponding emotions within me. It was as if we'd switched bodies, and I was now them, being as moved as they were by a ceremony of overarching significance. I had no idea what was happening, but I felt like I was participating in something special, the current of emotion stronger than I'd felt at any other time during the past six months. I couldn't understand why.

Just sit with it.

I spent my last few days checking out The Mid-Levels, The Peak, The Ladies Market, and being a part of the crowd each night on either side of Victoria Harbour watching the 8:00pm light shows dance across the skyscrapers.

I'd wanted to visit the Temple Street Night Markets since I'd been here but was usually too tired to be bothered, at least until now, my last night.

I caught the MTR to Yau Ma Tei Station, figuring I'd walk through the markets from north to south, rather than the other way around.

The northern part of the market district was not what I expected with pop-up marquees filled with psychics, palm readers, clairvoyants, astrologists, and crystal balls. I kept my head down and walked quickly to avoid eye-contact, not wanting to instigate an encounter I didn't want to have. I'd never been interested in knowing the future, not since being scared as a child by the mythology of Pandora's box.

I'd first heard the story when I was eight or nine and my vague recollection of the ending was that of all the evils let out of the box, the only one left trapped inside was knowledge. When the story was explained to me, knowledge was defined as foresight and the ability to know everything about the past, present and the future. The Pandora story that

I remembered described this type of knowledge as the greatest evil in the world because people couldn't live their lives freely if they knew how or when they were going to die. I'd since researched and re-read the story from multiple sources and couldn't find any reference to knowledge being the trapped evil in any of them. I may have been told the story incorrectly or I may have made up my own version of it, but it didn't matter: the idea still resonated with me. I still didn't want the evil of knowing the future.

Beyond the future-tellers were the *normal* markets, with stall after stall selling everything from handbags to watch batteries. They were exactly what I'd imagined Hong Kong markets to be like; brightly lit, noisy, overcrowded, and full of stuff no one needed. I liked that I felt tall amongst the throngs of shoppers and thus able to see over their heads to scope out what was ahead.

As I approached the middle section of the market, I felt something change. It was as though dark clouds were gathering overhead and a violent downpour was imminent, except they weren't, and the sky was still starry and clear.

I felt dread and despair and like it was the end of something, but of what, I wasn't sure. My holidays? Could it be a subconscious reaction to this wonderful trip coming to an end?

The base of my sternum was tightening, and I felt queasy, but without needing to be sick. I stopped in the middle of a crossroad in the market and breathed deeply to anchor myself and to make the feelings go away, but it wasn't working.

Sit with it.

The meditation teacher's words were again echoing through my ears.

I took some elongated blinks, not wanting to completely close my eyes in a place as busy as here, remembering more of his words. 'Try to meditate with your eyes open; it's how you live your life, so you should try to meditate the same way'. A novel approach to a practice most people did with their eyes shut.

I breathed in the feelings of dread and despair and leant into it.

What are you?

I wasn't supposed to be thinking about it, but I was, flicking through thoughts to test the feeling. End of holidays? *Maybe, but I'm grateful to have had it and am looking forward to heading home.* Divorce? *No, I'm good with that, or at least I better understand my part in it all.* Something I ate? *But I hadn't eaten for a few hours and it would have hit me earlier.* Agoraphobia? *No, I didn't mind these crowds, and I'd only been here a short time.* Were these feelings even mine?

Huh, if not mine, then whose?

I released my 'brakes' and moved forward into the next section of the market.

Walking felt better than standing still, so I resolved to keep moving towards the exit.

The next section was what looked like the pet supply aisles. Stacked cages held puppies, kittens, rabbits, hamsters, birds, and reptiles. Fish of assorted colours and sizes hung in plastic bags with just enough water to keep them immersed. There were walls and walls of small plastic bags, suspended by hooks on temporary stall walls.

The noise in the animal aisles matched the visual intensity of the scene. People were shouting at each other to negotiate prices, and dogs and cats wailed for new owners as they were passed from hand to hand. Birds crammed into tiny cages flapped their wings and screeched for their freedom, not knowing they were never going to be bought for that purpose. I wanted to cover my ears and shield my eyes, but of course I couldn't do both. I needed to get out of here, and out of the anguish and desperation permeating the air.

Beyond the pets were the fresh food stalls and a sense of quiet, at least comparatively so. I breathed a sigh of relief and kept moving down the aisles, keen to finish off this experience and head back to the hotel to pack for tomorrow's flight home.

To aide my escape, I turned right to move to the market's perimeter, hoping I'd be able to move more quickly and freely, but it proved to be an unwise choice.

I'd arrived in the fresh seafood section, which also seemed to double as the market's food court. Hundreds of buckets crammed with live fish and crustaceans lined the path with consumers pointing and choosing which ones they wanted to eat for dinner. Sieves were used to scoop out the chosen meals, and sea life was carried straight to pots of boiling water, or sizzling woks, to be thrown in or tossed around. I didn't recognise half of the species I saw, but I wasn't interested in sticking around to ask any questions or to learn more.

Now more than ever, I needed to get out.

I picked up my pace and almost rushed through the trestle tables packed with patrons and their freshly killed seafood, bumping into several of them along the way. It felt as the though the people were multiplying, and their voices amplifying the further I went. The sounds of shouting, laughing, and chomping felt suffocating, and the sight of them using chopsticks as shovels, and their mouths overflowing stirred up feelings of anger and disgust which had been lying dormant.

This market was cruel, excessive, and unnecessarily barbaric.

Surely, we're better than this.

Chapter 17

I'd been home for a week and was doing my best to keep some of my holiday euphoria alive by meditating on my travel experiences. The feeling of contentment I remembered having on the train returning from Kyoto, and whilst lying on the grass in Parque de El Retiro in Madrid ten years ago was coming back, and I felt like I wanted for nothing more, except perhaps, for more travel.

My marriage was becoming a distant memory, and so too was the bitterness and resentment which had consumed me for so long. I felt I was making progress, but towards what, I didn't know and wasn't really concerned. I still had no closure on why things happened the way they did, but it no longer mattered; as with or without it, I'd still be here, exactly where I was. My circle was filling in, and I was becoming whole for the first time, or at least, I thought I was.

It had been four months since my last counselling session, but I'd not forgotten about the counsellor's referral to see one of his colleagues. The business card he'd handed me was still exactly where I'd left it, slotted into my computer keyboard above the 3 4 5 keys.

My three sessions with him had cracked me open faster than I could manage at the time, and I'd needed a break and some respite to let it settle and help it make sense. I hadn't yet accepted my counsellor's theories as *fact*, but I did have some new meditation practices to help me decipher reality from fantasy.

During my fifth week post-holiday, my motivation to make an appointment to start counselling again had aligned itself with my demotivation to do anything else. I'd fallen into a lull where my mood was flatlining at zero and where each day seemed a carbon copy of the previous. I'd lost my sense of time, and with ten months passed since Tokyo, and the impending anniversary of all that happened last year, it was something I thought I better get to grips with.

In my current apathetic state, it came down to the toss of a coin to decide whether I'd go back to see my previous counsellor or see the new one. Heads for old, tails for new. The coin landed head-side up, but I felt a slight jab of disappointment that it wasn't tails, so I ignored the coin toss, and called the new counsellor he'd referred me to.

She answered the phone and told me she knew who I was and had been wondering if I'd ever get in touch. I apologised, but she said cut me off to say she understood, even though I provided no reasons. Her accent was Dutch – or maybe Danish – and her voice soft and comfortable. We scheduled an appointment, and she gave me her address, telling me she looked forward to meeting me.

The details she provided were for a home in an affluent suburb of Melbourne. The house was a beautifully restored double-fronted federation-style building, solid brick, and with all the period features. Beyond the iron gate, a hedged path led to a tiled entrance and a green double width front door. To its right, a large bay window with five leadlight panels jutted out like the bow of a ship, its red and green glass glowing from the lighting within.

She greeted me at the door. "Welcome, it is nice to meet you."

I wondered idly how difficult English was to learn as a second language, and if it was the reason so many non-native English speakers had trouble with contractions.

"Thank you, it is good to be here."

Why did I say, 'it is' rather than, 'it's'?

Why was I reflecting her?

My new counsellor was in her forties or fifties and was shorter than I'd imagined, not helped by the fact she was wearing no shoes. She shuffled to her right and led me into the room with the bay window. "Please take a seat anywhere."

A three-seat black leather couch sat at the base of the leadlight windows, facing inwards. I'd sat with my back to windows during all my previous counselling sessions, so it felt instinctive to do so here too. I sat on the middle cushion and sank into it, my thighs engulfed like I was on a beanbag. There were two armchairs in the opposite corners of the room, and she took her position on the one to my left.

"How are you feeling today?" Her question was whisper quiet, but it was her accent which forced me to lean forward to better understand what she'd just said.

"I think I'm feeling—"

"Sorry to interrupt, but I'd like to know how you're feeling, not what you're thinking. Thinking is with your head, and feeling is with your heart."

Huh? Was this some sort of neurolinguistic programming session?

"I think; um, sorry; I'm feeling fairly good. My relationship breakup is almost a year old, and I *feel* like I'm in a better place; much better than I've been in for a long time. I did some travelling recently and have realised it's something I need to do more of. It makes me happy."

"This is good to hear."

I noticed she had no notepad and no pen and that she was rubbing her index and middle fingers against her thumbs in circular motions, something I also did when I was sitting or thinking.

"Do you know why you are referred to me?"

I'd not thought about it, but now she'd brought it to my attention, I didn't. I had no idea at all.

"No actually, I don't."

"I am a psychologist, like your previous counsellor, but I

also specialise in holistic therapy for the mind, body, and spirit, but especially spirit. I have read your previous counsellor's notes, and he believes you may benefit from learning some new ways to process problems and information."

"I think I know what you mean—"

"There is that *think* word again." She was smiling.

I straightened up in my seat. "I know what you mean. I did some guided mediation classes recently and learnt some new tools about sitting with my emotions, and letting my thoughts pass without trying to do anything with them. I think; um; I mean, it appears to be something that is working for me."

"Why do you think your wife left you?"

Wow let's not beat around the bush!

"I think; oh yes, I'm allowed to use that word now; I think I'm still subconsciously processing it and that I will make sense of it one day; however, I think she left because she was feeling trapped."

"How so?" She'd stopped smiling but wasn't frowning either.

"I'm not sure, as you'd really need to ask her, but with renewed hindsight, I think we'd become victims of our circumstances. She was ill and I was her carer. I didn't want to be he carer and she didn't want to need one, but that's just the way it was. She had her own problems, and I think she was a pathological liar from the start, but I gave her permission to be that way as I let her get away with it, and maybe the web of lies, and our relationship dynamic looked irreversible, irretrievable. I also think I was stubborn in my approach to how I thought our relationship *should* be, rather than how it *could* be, or actually *was*.

"In our third couples counselling session together, she called me controlling. It was the worst thing she could have possibly said to me because I'd spent all my time in relationships trying to be the opposite. She later apologised, but the more I think about it, the more I think she was right. I tried so hard not to control her, but all I did was divert my energy into trying to control myself and the situation around us; and as she was a part of the situation, my behaviour had the inverse result to what I was aiming for, so yes, I think she was right."

"You have been doing some work. I was not expecting this answer based on your file." She was smiling again.

I have a file? Of course, I had a file.

"Tell me about your holiday."

I ran her through my highlights from the three cities, telling her what I did, and what I didn't do in equal measure.

"Did you have any experiences that you could not understand, or which did not make sense to you?"

How could she possibly know?

"I did!"

I gave her a detailed rundown of my experiences in the Hong Kong restaurant, and at Temple Street Night Markets, and how my mood had abruptly changed at the latter, causing me to want to flee.

"Interesting." Her hand played with a gold necklace, slung around her neck.

"I want to ask you some 'yes/no' questions, if that is okay?"

"Sure!"

She got up from her chair and walked out of the room and returned a few seconds later with an opened book. Before she sat back down, she started.

"Do you often feel overwhelmed in crowds of people?"

"Yes."

"Do people, even strangers, come to you when they have a problem?"

"Yes."

"Does conflict, especially arguments between people, make you anxious?"

"Yes."

"I think I already know the answer to this one. Do you find your emotions confusing and difficult to understand?"

"Yes."

"Do you pick up when someone says something but means something else?"

"Yes, absolutely. I've always had this weird feeling that I can see and hear intentions more than words, but I try to ignore it."

"Do you prefer your alone time, or time with other people?"

"Well, that depends—" she shot me a look to let me know I was breaking the rules "—, okay, yes."

"Do you feel like you have intuition beyond your understanding?"

"Yes."

"Do you feel drained after being around negative people?"

"Oh, yes, absolutely."

"Do you suffer from fatigue?"

"Yes. I was actually diagnosed with chronic fatigue syndrome in my early twenties, but at the time I didn't believe there was such a thing."

"Do you focus on the needs of others, more than your own?"

"Yes, I do, but I've only just realised it, and will try to balance it better from now on."

"Do you feel as though you take on other people's stress or emotions as your own?"

"Yes."

"Are you overwhelmed by loud noises, strong smells, bright lights, feelings on your skin, or intense tastes?"

"Um, yes, yes, yes, yes, and yes!"

"Does watching violence, pain, injury or cruelty affect you?"

"Yes, but only when its real, not when it's fake, like in action movies. I can't explain it, but I can feel other's physical pain through my lower abdomen and groin."

"Do you have dramatic mood swings, or changes to your emotions that you cannot explain; and does that sometimes lead you to feeling numb and unable to express them?"

"Yes, that's what happened to me in Hong Kong; and as for the numbness, it happens to me all the time."

"Do you feel like you fit in to society, to this world?"

"No, no I don't."

She turned to the next page and ran her finger over it, mouthing words without any voice. When she'd finished, she closed the book and put it on a glass table to her right. I looked at her, anticipating a response. When none was immediately forthcoming, I asked:

"So, did I pass? What were those questions a test of? Doesn't everybody answer 'yes' to all of them, except, maybe the last one, and the one about crowds?"

"No, they do not, but we will come back to that soon."

I leant back into the softness of the couch and relaxed the muscles which had become tense during her interrogation.

"I understand you have a dog."

"Yes, a rescue pet I never wanted, but which I could now not live without. I think she has actually rescued me."

"And she was your wife's, before she did not want her anymore."

"That's right!" I was surprised by how thorough my counsellor's notes had been, especially as that story was only mentioned in passing.

"I have a made-up situation for you. Let us say you were out walking your dog, and you were attacked or mugged, and were injured on the ground. Your dog is okay, but is near you, barking. What thoughts would be running through your mind, and what would you be feeling?"

"Apart from pain?"

She smiled. "Yes, apart from pain."

"Well, I'd be worried about my dog, and what she'd be experiencing seeing me getting attacked. I'd be worried for her and what would happen to her if something were to happen to me, especially if I died. I'd be distraught on her behalf, as I wouldn't want her to deal with that. I actually feel sick thinking about it."

"How about calling for help, or an ambulance, or the police?"

"Yes of course, I'd do those things too."

"I have something I'd like you to watch." She got up from her seat again and left the room, but I wasn't sure if I was supposed to follow her. The session seemed to be jumping all over the place and I wasn't keeping up.

As I got to my feet, she re-entered holding a laptop.

Not another test!

She opened it and took the seat next to me, causing me to move away from her in an instinctive effort to give us personal space.

"I would like you to watch these two videos. They are short, about two minutes each, but I would like to get your thoughts on them."

She pressed play and handed me the computer.

The first video was filmed from a child's perspective in a shopping centre. Their mother was close by and was talking to another adult, possibly a friend they'd bumped into along the way. The filming was done from the child's perspective, as if through their eyes, and showed what they were seeing, and hearing. It was a strangely riveting scene, authentic in its child-focus, complete with the screen blacking out every few seconds to mimic blinking, and showed the child looking around, left to right, and up and down.

The second video was similar, again filmed from a child's perspective, except this time the child was holding their parent's hand walking down a street. Like the first, the film was done through the child's eyes, and showed what they were experiencing along the way.

When they'd finished, I felt like I'd failed whatever test she'd just administered. The videos showed everyday life and there was nothing out of the ordinary about either of them. I didn't see any hidden images or words and didn't notice anything that wasn't supposed to be there. I wanted to watch them again, just to ensure I hadn't missed anything important, like an invisible gorilla dancing across the screen.

"So, how did you feel watching these videos?"

Feel? I thought she wanted my thoughts on them.

"I'm not sure if I missed something. I didn't really feel anything; maybe a little anxious about seeing those scenes through the eyes of a child again. I didn't like being that low down looking up. They both seemed completely normal to me."

She got up and returned to her seat, putting the laptop on top of the book she'd used for the questions earlier.

"I am not here to diagnose you with anything as that is not my place, but those videos were simulations of what it is like for children to have autism, you know, ASD, autism spectrum disorder. A non-autistic person seeing this would find the lights, sounds, and noises amplified to an unreasonable level. The idea is to show them what the world is like through the eyes and ears of a child with autism. The fact that you saw them as normal does not mean you are on the spectrum, although you could be, but what it does mean is that you have extremely sensitive senses, over and above those of a normal person. Did you know this?"

I scowled at the Dutch woman.

Her questions, her scenario, and her videos were disconnected, disjointed, and were not making any sense. What were they proving, and what did they mean? I knew I had overly sensitive hearing. I could hear sounds my ex-wife couldn't, noises which would drive me crazy. Like the sound of someone dragging their feet a hundred metres away; the sound of people around me breathing. I couldn't understand why people needed to converse so loudly all the time. I hated that plastic wrappers were allowed in theatres, and the sound of people chewing made me murderous on occasion.

I could see the supposedly imperceptible flashing of LED lights, and strobing effects made me nauseous. I couldn't see a footpath for the chewing gum stuck to it and couldn't avoid seeing every single cigarette butt, piece of litter, or any object that shouldn't have been where it was. I noticed everything, everywhere, and all the time, but didn't all people?

I sat deeper into the couch and fell into silence.

She leant forwards with a look of motherly concern. "Are you okay?"

"Yep. It's just a lot to take in. I knew I had overly sensitive hearing, as ordinary sounds sometimes drive me crazy, but I'm not sure what to do with this new information."

"You do not need to do anything with it. My job is to increase your awareness and to show you new things so you can consider them as they apply to you. There is no good or bad, or right or wrong. There just is what is."

I raised my eyes from the floor to her smiling face.

'Just is what is', is a little too philosophical for me right now.

Sitting in this room was like being ten years old all over again, learning that my senses had been misleading me and that my perception of the world was still all wrong. How could I continue to trust my views and opinions if I couldn't trust the way I was receiving information? How could I know what was real and what wasn't?

She sat forward in her armchair and uncrossed her legs. "Have you heard the Taoist story of the farmer and his horse?"

Another tangent! Her scattergun approach to this session was disconcerting to say the least.

"No, I haven't, and I don't know what a Taoist is."

She recrossed her legs, clasped her hands, and leant back in her chair, consciously or subconsciously adopting a classic story-telling pose.

"When an old farmer's horse wins a prize at a show, his neighbour comes to his house to congratulate him and to say how good it is, but the old farmer says, 'Who knows what is good and what is bad'?

"The next day someone steals his award-winning horse.

His neighbour comes to commiserate with him and to say how bad it is, but the old man replies, 'Who knows what is good and what is bad'?

"A few days later the horse escapes from the thieves and leads a herd of wild horses back to the farm. The neighbour calls in to share the farmer's joy and to say how good it is, but the farmer says, 'Who knows what is good and what is bad'?

"The next day, while trying to break in one of the horses, the farmer's son is kicked, breaking his leg. The neighbour calls to share the farmer's sorrow and to say how bad it is, but the farmer says, 'Who knows what is good and what is bad'?

"The following week the army passes by to sign up soldiers for the war, but they do not take the farmer's son because of his broken leg. The neighbour now thinks to himself, who knows what is good and what is bad?"

She stared at me for feedback. "Do you know what it means, this story?"

"If you had have told me that story a few months ago, I wouldn't have. I was so two-dimensional—"

She cut me off mid-sentence. "Three-dimensional."

I screwed my face at her again, not understanding how it wasn't two-dimensional. "Okay, I was so *three-dimensional* in my view that my ex-wife had wronged me, that I considered her bad. I now understand that circumstances and perception are far more important, and that there are reasons for everything, whether we know them or not. There is no pure good and bad, or right and wrong."

She clapped her hands. "And that is the start of four-dimensional thinking."

I could feel my eyes about to roll. "I don't know what that is. I thought the fourth dimension was time."

She moved forward to the edge of her chair, planting her white-socked feet onto the ground. "Okay, so this is where I will drift slightly from pure psychology. Is that okay with you?"

"Sure, whatever helps."

During the next twenty minutes, she talked me through the concepts of third, fourth, and fifth dimensional consciousness, explaining that whilst people experienced the same reality, the *way* they experienced reality might be different.

She told me that the 3D reality was rooted in ego, individuality, judgement, dichotomies, competition with others, the pursuit of material belongings, as well as conforming to a perceived social standard. She went on to say that people experiencing 3D reality lived their lives in fear, were self-righteous, and that their love was conditional. She said 3D was what most religious and political systems were based on, as the primary focus of each was on rules and control.

She described 4D as a doorway to the fifth dimension, where people started asking questions about their own previously held beliefs, and where former realities began to crumble. It was a time of awakening, and purging, and out of body experiences. She told me that the pursuit of self-knowledge and self-understanding underpinned the fourth dimension, as did the deconstruction of self-identity and ego.

Fifth dimension reality was egoless, and was hallmarked by flow, unconditional love, acceptance and self-work. She described it as a recognition that everyone and everything is connected and that the best we can hope to do is change ourselves to change the world. She told me that in 5D, judgement falls away and is replaced with idea that perception conquers all; that there is no good or bad, or right or wrong, just the way we *think* about it.

"I think the best comparison is with prescription glasses," she said, and I nodded in understanding. She said that once a person has 5D sight, they wouldn't be able to lose it; but that they may apply different realities to different parts of their lives based on where they're at and what they need. She said that all three realities could coexist simultaneously, but that people couldn't be forced, or trained, or taught to go from three to four, or from four to five, and she stressed, and stressed again that higher numbers were not necessarily better than lower ones.

"It is just something that happens when people are ready, and some will never be ready. The realities are not a place or a destination, and one is not essentially *better* than the other. 5D is not an aspiration for someone who perceives in three or four; they will not understand it. They will just not get it."

She sat back in her seat again and put her hands on her knees, rubbing them in clockwise direction. "How do you perceive the reality of your world?"

I'd never heard of what she'd just told me, so it was difficult to answer on the spot. "I think I'm firmly across all three, but with my current life falling apart, I'm probably mostly in four."

She sat forward again. "Good. You are keeping up."

Chapter 18

I left her house less clear about who she was and what she did, than I had been when I'd arrived. Throughout the session she'd come across as reassuringly wise and knowing, but her anecdotes and questions were fragmented and a little too all over the place for my orderly thinking. No matter. I was keen to see her again and booked my next session for a week's time.

"Do you like reality TV shows?" We were in her front room again, but this time we both sat in the armchairs opposite each other. She'd asked me to join her in a pot of chamomile tea and I'd accepted. She looked younger today than last week; a trick most likely played on me by my residual memory of her as a wise old woman.

I wasn't sure what to make of her first question, as there had been a distinct dearth of small talk at our last meeting.

"No, I can't stand them."

"I do not like them either, but why is it you do not like them?"

"They're always so angsty, and they all seem to be about people's personalities or personality disorders. They glorify conflict and exploit people's insecurities and suffering. It's a modern-day blood sport like the colosseum two thousand years ago and I don't see the point."

"How about normal sport?"

"Do you mean, do I like to watch normal sport?"

"Yes."

"I can watch it, and I enjoy it every now and then, but I don't like the close games, and I don't like seeing injuries. Both turn my stomach."

"And nature documentaries?"

"Again, I don't mind them, but won't go out of my way to watch them. I also won't watch anything where animals are hunting other animals. I don't want the zebra to get eaten, but I also don't want the lion to go hungry."

"So, what do you like to watch on TV?"

"I like most arthouse films, and foreign films, where you have to do some thinking to work out what's going on. I like to be misdirected and shocked by an ending I didn't see coming, but I don't like anything suspenseful or stupid."

"Can you tell me more about your ex-wife?"

Well, that chitchat was short lived.

"Aren't there notes in my file?"

"Yes, there are, but I want to hear the story from you."

I gave her a ten-minute rundown, spending about a

minute on each of our years together, but this time inserting the memories I'd recently remembered into their rightful place on my timeline.

"Sounds a little like narcissistic personality disorder to me."

I bit my lip. "I wish I could tell the story differently, so it didn't come across that way. I don't know if that was what she had, and it honestly doesn't matter anymore. Funny story though, especially in light of those videos you showed me last time, I heard from a friend that she's been going around telling people she's got Asperger's. I really think she needs to stop looking for mental illnesses and disorders to blame her behaviour on and just put some effort into not being an arsehole—" I put my hand to my mouth—"Oops, I'm sorry about my language."

She smiled at me. "Do not worry about it. She does sound like an arsehole."

She shuffled forward and poured the tea into two cups on a table between us.

"And your father, do you think he is a Narcissist too?"

I smiled. "Are you saying I married my father?"

She smiled back and shrugged one shoulder, as if to say, 'you tell me'.

"Maybe. He's always been the centre of the family and his universe, so yes maybe, but I haven't really thought about it and don't think I can judge."

"He hit you, yes?"

Are you deliberately blunt, or is it just your accent making you seem that way?

"Yes, it happened, but a long, long time ago."

"And you grew up in fear?"

"Yes, that's how I remember it."

"Do you know that children who grow up with trauma or in violent households, develop skills that most other people do not have?"

"No, I didn't. Like what?"

"They learn different skills to survive and to keep out of danger. They learn how to read situations, and environments, and people, so they can diffuse the situation or get out of the way. Do you know what a micro-expression is?"

"I think so, there used to be a TV show about a human lie detector."

"Ah yes, I know the one. Well, that is based on real science. People can learn to read other people's micro-expressions in a millisecond, and can know what it means, even if the person who has made the expression does not. Children who feel unsafe and afraid are the best at it, but they do not know they are doing it. When they grow up, they continue to subconsciously develop these skills without their knowledge. Some call it intuition. At our last meeting, you called it 'seeing and hearing people's intentions'."

She sipped her tea, but I knew mine would still be too hot for me. As she set her cup down on its saucer, she cleared her throat. "What did you and your family do for fun when you were a child?"

Ha! Fun, what fun?

"I don't remember us doing anything for fun. I played

cricket with friends, and I used to ride my bike, and play with toy cars."

"Did your parents play with you?"

"Not that I can remember, no."

"And now? What do you do for fun?"

I put my hand out to touch the side of my teacup, but it was still too hot to hold.

"I'm still working that out. I like live theatre, and the ballet, and symphony, and I do like travelling, but that's about it."

"Are those things fun?"

"Well, now you're asking the question, I don't know. I enjoy those things, so I guess so. Why do you ask?"

"I ask this because you always look so serious, and your answers are so serious. You need to try and loosen up. You need to go with the flow."

It wasn't new information, and her question about fun was something I needed to think more about. The last time I remembered having real fun was when I was eighteen years old, and I'd just got my license and legal entry to nightclubs. Life at that time was one big party and full of laughs, but they'd all dried up, and been replaced with something not as enjoyable: real life.

Geez, when was the last time I laughed?

"What do you believe in?"

I smiled. Being in this room was like being double bounced on a trampoline. As soon as I got into a rhythm of thought, she'd randomly change topics!

"Sorry, how do you mean, believe? Like religion?"

"Yes, religion, faith, spirituality, call it whatever you want."

"I don't believe in a lot really. I was brought up Catholic but never really subscribed to any of it. I like the idea of Buddhism, as being kind, and gentle, and aiming for enlightenment is my kind of belief system, but I've never done anything to pursue it. I don't like that most religions are masculinist in their nature, and that they are fundamentally responsible for power, and control, and inequality between the sexes.

"I think I believe in a higher power, and after my recent trip to Paris, I think I'm starting to believe in the power of the universe." As I finished my sentence, the memory of what I'd written on my *ema* in Meiji Jingu leapt into my mind. 'Please, get us out of this, thank-you'. "Actually, now I think about it, the universe seems to have been delivering on my wishes for quite some time.

"The truth is, I just don't know what I believe in. I think my brain is too small and my processing power too weak to ever be able to understand the things that science can't explain. I believe in everything and I believe in nothing. I'm open to everything but closed to anything that involves rituals, rules, and worship. I don't believe in any human being better or more worthy than another. That's the one idea I can't get my head around.

"I believe in being considerate and respectful towards others, and really believe that everything else stems from that.

"Sorry, I just realised I'm rambling. Does any of that make sense?"

"Yes, it does. You do not have children, is that correct?"

Double bounce.

"No, I don't."

"Why not?"

"It's something I've never wanted; it's just not in me, like I was born without the gene for procreation; and my ex-wife was the same."

"That is not a reason. What is your real reason?"

Shit. I'd been doing so well.

"To be honest with you, this is a conversation I don't like having as it is just my view of the world. I think it's deeply personal, and it's an area where I don't fit into normal society."

"Tell me anyway; I am interested in hearing your reason, not somebody else's."

"I think my view is seen as extreme – sometimes *I* see it as extreme! So I don't want to convince others of my view. I'm not anti-natalist, it's just the way I feel."

"So, tell me."

There was no way out. I took the deepest breath possible, as this would be the first time I shared this information with anyone, apart from my ex-wife.

"Usually, when people ask me about why I don't have children, they ask because they think I'm selfish. They say that I only care about myself and that I won't know true love until I bring a child into the world. That's the bit I can't understand. To me, it is the most selfish action to bring in a child into the world just so you can feel true love. Creating a whole life to fulfill yours is something I can't comprehend. I think some people have children to play god, to do-over their own lives, to re-live their childhoods in a better way, to bolster their egos, and leave a legacy. Like I said earlier, it's deeply personal to each individual, but I just don't get it."

"Or maybe you do not want to have children because your own childhood was bad, and you are worried you will do a bad job."

"Quite possibly, but I think your summary is a little *3D*."

She smiled wryly as if she was testing to see whether I'd been paying attention.

"What do you know about empaths?"

Double bounce.

"I've not heard the word before, but I'm guessing it's someone with empathy."

She shook her head disapprovingly. "Actually no. Empaths may have or may not have any empathy in the traditional sense, but the traditional sense is actually wrong—"

I interjected to show her again I'd been listening. "I thought there was no right and wrong?"

She didn't look amused at my attempted levity. "Anyway, it is the textbook belief that sympathy is feeling your feelings about someone else's situation, and that empathy is imagining your feelings if you were in the same situation as the person you are empathising with."

"Yep, sounds like my understanding also."

"Well, to be an empath is to feel someone else's feelings as your own."

Huh? I squinted my eyes to try and understand.

"Isn't that the same thing? Didn't you just describe empathy and empaths the same way?"

She picked up her cup again and drank its contents whilst looking me in the eye. "No, empathy is imagining, whereas empaths *experience* other's feelings as their own. So, Empaths believe that what they are feeling is theirs; and unknowing empaths have no idea that it is not."

I was struggling to understand what she was saying. "Are you saying that there are people out there who genuinely feel the *exact* feelings of other people, and not their own versions of it?"

"Yes. They absorb the feelings and emotions of others and experience them as if they were their own. Think of it as an energy transfer, as an almost *physical* thing.

"Imagine if I heard some bad news before you arrived today, and when you came into the house, you started to have a bad feeling in you. You would think the feeling is yours even if you cannot explain it and would not know that it is not yours, but mine."

"Sounds like science fiction to me."

"Have you ever had feelings that you could not explain, feelings that did not feel like yours and that you could not make sense of?"

"I'm sure I have; actually, I told you about that last time in Hong Kong."

"Yes, you did. "Do you think your ill feelings in the Hong Kong market had anything to do with the pets in cages and live seafood in buckets?"

I ran my fingers through my hair. "No, because I'd had the feeling prior to entering the section with the pets and before I'd entered the eatery bit. If it had been after, then yes, maybe, absolutely."

"Needing to be in that section is irrelevant. Remember those fifteen questions I asked you at our last session?"

Thank goodness she brought that up, as she hadn't got back to it at our last session, and the lack of explanation about what it was for had been quietly bugging me ever since.

"I do, and I wanted to ask you about it."

"I have another question, and I am sorry to ask, but I must—" her mood turned serious, "—did you love your ex-wife?"

Her question wasn't one she needed to be sorry about as it was something I'd been pondering since Tokyo, and maybe even before that. I'd been sitting with the question since I'd learnt I should, and it had taken up residency in a small part of my brain through my days in Paris, Hong Kong, and now at home.

"It's a really good question and I'm not sure I have an answer anymore. Once, I thought I did, but I'm not sure if recent history has changed my memories. What I keep coming back to, is that I loved that *she* loved *me*. I was committed to her and I was obliged to her, but I'm not sure that's the same thing as loving her. I was infatuated with her at the start, but that waned after the first year. She was my world, because when she left, I had no sense of myself, but I'm not sure that's love either. I've since worked out that even though I wanted her, I didn't actually need her; but for her, it was different. She needed me; at least until she didn't anymore, but hadn't necessarily *wanted* me. Is any of this making sense?"

She picked up her empty cup, and lifted it to her lips, forgetting there was nothing in it. "I will make another one. You still have not touched yours. Is it okay? And yes, it does make sense, especially the first part."

She walked out of the room but kept talking. "You loved her for loving you. What do you think this means?"

You tell me, lady!

"Well, maybe it was reciprocation. Maybe I loved that she'd chosen me and wanted to spend time with me, and that was enough for me to want to do the same."

I could hear the kettle boiling again and the clinking of teaspoons and containers, and within a few minutes, she was back in the room with a replenished teapot.

She sat down and looked at me with a combination of seriousness and kindness. "Do you think you absorbed her feelings and emotions and experienced them as your own, thinking they were yours towards her?"

So, this is where you're going with this!

I sat back and folded my arms and crossed my legs. "It's an interesting question, but I don't think I'll ever know. What I do know is that I always imagined how she would feel, in any given circumstance; actually, I tend to do that to anybody,

289

I find. I can't help but put myself in their shoes. I guess it's why I don't like participating in conversations or arguments because I can always see both sides."

Her gaze dropped to my arms, causing me to unfold them. "What if it is not your imagination, but a real feeling?"

"Either way, it is a real feeling for me. If someone is frustrated at me, I can imagine their frustration, and I can feel it, and I shut down, as I don't see the point in continuing the conversation. I also don't talk about things if I feel that the other person is not going to be receptive."

"So, you do not put your view across? You do not participate in conversations if you feel a person is not understanding, or will not understand?"

"I can't explain it, but I feel like I can predict how most conversations are going to go, and without wanting to sound arrogant, I am usually ten or twenty steps ahead in the conversation. If I predict the conversation is going to get a bad reaction, or if it isn't going to go anywhere, or if it is going to cause angst, I put the brakes on."

This time it was her scowling at me.

"But how do you *know* where it is going to go? Are you not being a bit premature?"

"I don't. It's just a feeling."

Her scowl intensified, and she leaned forward in her chair to pour herself another cup of tea.

"You need to stop doing that. You need to be an active participant in conversations. People can learn from you. You need to stop being disrespectful to other people and learn to participate in the conversation as well. It is like our conversation about children earlier. So what if people do not agree with you? Tell them anyway!"

It was a verbal slapping I hadn't seen coming.

I thought I was being respectful by being kind and not aggravating them, but this lady was telling me the opposite was true; by not responding, I was denying them the chance to learn and debate …

"Okay, I will give it some thought."

"Not thought; *action!*"

And then she changed tack in the disconcerting way I was coming to expect.

"Back to our previous conversation about feeling love. How about your other partners; do you think it was the same with them?"

I reached for my cold tea and finished it in a single sip. I could feel a fatigue setting into my limbs. Her questions were becoming iron weights, pressing me down into my seat.

"Yes, probably. I've never chased anyone I liked. I've always reciprocated what they sent my way. It's like I have very low self-esteem, and that if someone likes me enough to want to be with me, then I should grab the opportunity with both hands, regardless of whether or not I think it's a good idea.

"My previous counselling sessions showed up a pattern I didn't know I had. It seems I'm attracted to needy women, broken birds who need an escape so they can fly freely again. I also recently learnt about the *vesica pisces* and how its

291

geometry relates to relationships, and I learnt that I've got all that wrong too."

"Ah yes, the *vesica pisces*. It is a good model and should apply to everything you have a relationship with. Your job, your friends, your house, your family, your possessions. None of them should cover you and you should not cover them. You should share the radius but that is it. You should always remain whole."

"I know that now, but I'm still not sure how to apply it."

"You will, in time it will make more sense. As for your self-esteem, most children who are abused do not grow up hating their abusers, they grow up hating themselves; and maybe this is true also for you. Maybe you do not feel worthy, because you were made not to feel worthy, so now you respond to anyone who shows interest in you.

"You told your previous counsellor that you have dealt with your abuse in your twenties, but I am sorry to tell you that I would be very surprised if you have. Your emotional numbness is a result of you being full of things you have not dealt with, and still do not know how to face. You need to work out how to let go and to release this stress."

I'm beginning to think you're right.

"One more question, did you get any love from your parents and do you feel love for your parents?"

I could feel myself becoming overwhelmed, and desperate for some clarity of direction. Suddenly, I was driven by the need to take control over the aimless session and get us back on track. My voice was matter-of-fact. *Let's get to the point!*

"I was looked after and cared for and I never went hungry or without anything I needed, so I guess that is how they showed me love, and I guess I show them love in the same way. We share a meal once a week and it is our time together."

Now, for the question I wanted the answer to.

"So, back to our earlier conversation, it seems obvious that you think I may be an empath?"

"It does not matter what I think. Empath is just a label and labels do not matter in the fifth-dimension reality. However, your answers to the fifteen questions I asked you last time you were here are indicators that you experience the world as an empath. Your experience in Hong Kong suggests the same, as does the way you experience feelings and emotions. The way you experience relationships suggests you do not have boundaries and that you absorb and project others' emotions as your own. Empaths make up about one percent of the population and typically align with the INFJ traits, and you are INFJ. Empaths also usually have highly sensitive senses and intuition levels beyond what is considered a normal range."

"I wouldn't have thought I was empathic at all. I get angry at stupidity and have a low tolerance for people, especially when they don't own their decisions, and try to blame their actions on others."

"Remember, empathy and empaths are different. Have you ever wondered why you cannot watch reality TV shows, or people being injured, or animals dying?"

"Not really, I just don't like them."

"Or it is possible they create feelings and emotions in you that you do not understand, because they are not *your* feelings or emotions. The feeling of fear or anxiety about being attacked, or the feeling of pain and loss from a sporting injury, or the feeling of panic of an animal which is in danger or is hungry. To me, you appear as an emotional sponge who absorbs it all, and until now you did not know it."

It was a nice hypothesis, but that's all it was. I needed a road map.

"So, what am I supposed to *do* with all this information?"

"That is also for you to decide. Knowing is usually better than not knowing, and it will be up to you to tune into it or not. Test yourself. When you have a feeling you cannot explain, notice it, and have a look around at what is going on around you. Is there a crying child? A homeless person who needs help. A couple arguing or fighting? Look around and see if it relates to anything else.

"It is quite sad really. The majority of empaths never know they are empaths, but due to their inner tumult, they usually turn to alcohol or drugs or are diagnosed with chronic fatigue or depression."

"Chronic fatigue? That was my diagnosis in my early twenties when my doctors tested me for everything and couldn't find anything wrong with me."

"Do you do drugs, or drink a lot, or have any other vices?"

"No, I'm quite the opposite. Drugs scare me, and I rarely drink. I used to smoke, but that was many years ago."

"Good, it is best to keep it that way, and your chronic fatigue, well that may have been better explained by you not understanding the cause of your fatigue. Some people are like energy vampires, draining others around them."

"I know what you mean. I have had the experience where I have felt my energy being sucked out of me."

"Also, being an empath is not always a bad thing. You will absorb positive emotions too, like when you are in the crowd for the ballet or symphony; you may feel huge euphoria, with your hair on your arms and neck standing on end."

"Ah, yes, I know that feeling too. My strongest emotions happen when I hear people at a concert singing together. I can't explain it, but it feels like ecstasy beyond words.

"Is this empath thing a scientific diagnosis, or a bit made-up?"

"You are still looking for the black and white. Maybe it is and maybe it is not, but again. it is not for me or you to say. There are many books on the things I mentioned earlier; about trauma and children learning subconscious skills to survive, and apart from learning to read micro-expressions, there is lots of evidence to show that these children are also able to sense things beyond words.

"They can hear what is in silence, as well as the most subtle changes in tone, volume, and speed of voice; and can notice micro-gestures as well. A subtle twitch of a finger, or a change in breathing pattern will tell these children all they need to know.

"I have been watching you watch my every move. Last time, you saw me rubbing my fingers together, and when I was playing with my necklace, and when I was rubbing my knees. Just now, you knew my tea was finished when I tried to drink from an empty cup; you took a breath to tell me, but you did not say anything. I can see you noticing everything I do, and I can see you reading into it, and reacting to it.

"Maybe this is what intuition is; reading between the lines, or maybe it is more, something that cannot be fully explained by science."

It suddenly occurred to me that this may be the reason my first counsellor had referred me here. "Are *you* an empath?"

"I am not anything, but I identify as an empath."

She now had my unfettered curiosity. "So, what does it mean for you?"

"It means that I am always learning and that I cannot trust my own feelings at face value. I need to sit with things to understand if they belong to me or someone else. It means I need to meditate and be on my own so that I am away from other people's energy. Only then, can I know if my feelings are my own; but also, I must be careful that I am not picking up energy from animals, or from the environment, as this can happen too."

Energy from people, animals, and the environment? It still sounded like gibberish, and possibly a bridge too far for my belief systems; but if I could believe in the universe, then surely, I could believe in this? Especially if it could help me better understand myself and why I felt and acted the way I did.

Even if it wasn't real, what would be the harm in investigating it further and paying extra attention to me? I was already an introvert so further introspection should be easy. All I'd need to do is introduce one new question to my battery of tests, 'is this feeling mine?'.

"Thank you for this information, it's all really interesting."

"You are welcome." She reached for her cup with a smirk on her face. "Do you know what a psychopath is?"

I laughed. "Of course I do, I lived with one for nine years!"

"But to use your words, do you know the scientific definition?"

"I know bits and pieces, but no, not really."

"Psychopathy is an antisocial personality disorder, much like NPD, except psychopaths do not have a conscience. They have no little voice keeping them in check. They are egotistical and display irresponsible behaviour, and they lie and manipulate to further their own ends. They do what they do with complete disregard for others. Most of all, they are the opposite of considerate; of sympathetic; of compassionate.

"Do you know anyone like this?"

"I think I know a lot of people like that. My ex-wife definitely, many of my ex-girlfriends too, some of my ex-friends, ex-colleagues, and maybe even some family members I no longer talk to."

She finished her tea, put her cup and saucer on the side table, and eyeballed me with an intensity I couldn't escape.

"You know the saying, opposites attract?"

"Yes, yes, I do."

"Do you know what is … the opposite of a psychopath?"

Part II
The Opposite of an Empath

MMXXII

About the Author

Charles Tyler is an author from Melbourne, Australia. Since the age of five, he's been investigating his own sensory perception and his constructs of ego and subjective reality. He is fascinated by the debate on nature/nurture and enjoys experimenting with ideas, perspectives, and possibilities to imagine implications and outcomes. Charles is less interested in the questions 'who', 'what', 'when', 'where', and 'how', and is far more interested in discovering the reasons 'why'. He is intrigued by the way his mind works, and continually questions himself as to why he thinks and acts the way he does. He is equally interested in understanding why others think and act the way they do, regardless of who they are, or what they've done. Charles' personal philosophy revolves around peeling back the layers of people and situations until he can find a core truth or universal meaning.

The Opposite of a Psychopath is part one of a trilogy and the realisation of a twenty-five-year writing project.

charlestyler.com.au

Lightning Source UK Ltd.
Milton Keynes UK
UKHW040744100822
407113UK00002B/704